BLACKBERRY FOX

BLACKBERRY FOX

KATHRIN TORDASI

TRANSLATED BY CATHRIN WIRTZ

Simon & Schuster Books for Young Readers

NEW YORK   LONDON   TORONTO   SYDNEY   NEW DELHI

SIMON & SCHUSTER BOOKS FOR YOUNG READERS
An imprint of Simon & Schuster Children's Publishing Division
1230 Avenue of the Americas, New York, New York 10020

Originally published in Germany in 2020 by Fischer Sauerländer
as *Brombeerfuchs: Das Geheimnis von Weltende*
First US edition June 2024
Jacket illustration © 2023 by Violet Tobacco
Jacket design by Sarah Creech

Simon & Schuster: Celebrating 100 Years of Publishing in 2024
For information about special discounts for bulk purchases, please contact
Simon & Schuster Special Sales at 1-866-506-1949 or
business@simonandschuster.com.
The Simon & Schuster Speakers Bureau can bring authors to your live event.
For more information or to book an event, contact the Simon & Schuster Speakers
Bureau at 1-866-248-3049 or visit our website at www.simonspeakers.com.
The text for this book was set in Berling Nova Text Pro.
Manufactured in the United States of America
0424 BVG
2 4 6 8 10 9 7 5 3 1
Library of Congress Cataloging-in-Publication Data
Names: Tordasi, Kathrin, author. | Wirtz, Cathrin, translator.
Title: Blackberry fox / Kathrin Tordasi ; translated by Cathrin Wirtz.
Other titles: Brombeer fuchs. English
Description: First edition. | New York : Simon & Schuster Books for Young
Readers, 2024. | Audience: Ages 10 up. | Audience: Grades 4–6. |
Summary: During a summer holiday in Wales, Portia and Ben discover a
mysterious door in a forest, unaware that it is a portal to a perilous
Otherworld, and they unwittingly open the door, unleashing a powerful evil
that endangers both the human and fairy realms, forcing them
to confront the consequences of their actions.
Identifiers: LCCN 2023028552 (print) | LCCN 2023028553 (ebook) |
ISBN 9781665910194 (hardcover) | ISBN 9781665910200 (paperback) |
ISBN 9781665910217 (ebook)
Subjects: CYAC: Friendship—Fiction. | Space and time—Fiction. |
Shapeshifting—Fiction. | Magic—Fiction. | Fantasy. |
LCGFT: Fantasy fiction. | Novels. Classification: LCC PZ7.1.T6266 Bl 2024 (print) |
LCC PZ7.1.T6266 (ebook) | DDC [Fic]—dc23
LC record available at https://lccn.loc.gov/2023028552
LC ebook record available at https://lccn.loc.gov/2023028553

For Erika Grams
& Wolfgang Gramps

Contents

Characters   ix

PROLOGUE   1

A Vacation in Wales   3
A Thief in the Night   8
Pendragon Books   22
Peculiar Events   30

INTERLUDE   38

The Human Door   40
Between Worlds   50
The Faerie Door   61
The Gray Riders   69
Dead End   79
Ridik's Final Journey   89

INTERLUDE   102

Gwil Glumheart   103
The Hollow Hill   109
The Audience   115
Shape-shifters   128
The Salamanders of Bryngolau   134
Merron Pathfinder   145
Departure   151

INTERLUDE   157

Titania 158

The Library 168

INTERLUDE 175

The Fairy Curse 176

Rune Magic 181

Shards 190

The *Book of Return* 197

A Fateful Sandwich 205

Farewell to World's End 214

INTERLUDE 218

Traces of Fog 220

Metamorphoses 229

The Pale Tower 234

The Dogs of Annwn 245

Mistwalkers 256

A Glimmer of Hope 263

Rosethorn and Brambleblossom 270

The New Hunting Master 276

The Gray King's Huntress 279

Companions in Arms 285

The Door of the Dead 295

A World of Fog 301

Where the Wild Things Are 307

A Wolf's Heart 312

The Gray King 317

Farewell to Faerie 329

London 338

Welsh Words and Phrases 341

Characters

HUMANS

Benjamin Rees	*Boy from Trefriw, Wales*
Portia Beale	*Girl from London, Viola's grandniece*
Olivia Stephen, *Bramble*	*Author, Viola's partner*
Viola Evans, *Rose*	*Editor, Portia's mum's aunt*
Gwendolyn Beale	*Portia's mum*

FAIRIES

Titania	*The Fairy Queen*
Oberon	*The Fairy King*
Peaseblossom, Cobweb	*Fairies from Titania's royal household*
Pricklethorn	*Titania's Lord Chamberlain*

SHAPE-SHIFTERS

Robin Goodfellow *Oberon's troublemaker*

BIRDS
(Welsh: *Adar*)

Ridik ap Mwyalchod *Scout*
Preet, Tatap *Scouts*

SALAMANDERS
(Welsh: *Salamandrau*)

Gwil Glumheart *Scribe and illuminator*
Meralyn Quickly *Head seamstress*
Tegid Grayfinger *Librarian*

THE PALE TOWER'S INHABITANTS

Arawn *The Gray King*
Hermia *Arawn's Huntress*

Prologue

*L*ong, long ago, humans and fairies could pass back and forth between their worlds effortlessly. The kingdoms of mortals and immortals were as close to each other as the banks of a river, with nothing but an empty stretch of land in between. No one ever gave the Borderlands a thought. But someone sensed every person who passed. And one night he who had been sleeping for a hundred years stirred.

Red autumn leaves fell from the trees as the Gray King rose from his lair. He roamed the in-between world, shrouded in swirling fog. Anyone caught in that fog either vanished without a trace or became a Mistwalker, a creature existing without a single memory of its former self. All at once, those traveling between the worlds had to fear for their lives.

And there was more. The Gray King sent his army into the Human and Fairy Worlds. Pale riders brought the fog with them, making lakes, fields, and villages disappear and dissolve into a gray ocean. Eventually humans and fairies joined forces, and together they pushed the king and his army back into the Borderlands. The fairies put him into a deep sleep—but they could not say how long their enchantment would last.

Exhausted from the battle, humans and fairies made a grave decision. They would seal up the border between their worlds, in the hope that the Gray King would never be able to leave his

Borderlands ever again. And that was what came to pass. The human folk turned to their druids. Those wise women and men used rune magic to close all the doorways to the Fairy World, or Faerie, as some call it. From that day onward, they were locked, and only a handful of chosen ones possessed a key. Those Key Bearers were bound by one rule: if they opened a door leading to the other realm, they had to close it as soon as they had crossed over. However, centuries went by, and the memory of the story of the Gray King began to fade into oblivion.

When we came into possession of one of those keys, no one remembered about the rule, or the Gray King for that matter. Unknowingly we crossed over to Faerie, and for a while, we lived in blissful ignorance.

We left the door open behind us, since no one had told us why it must be closed. When the Gray King returned, no one saw the signs, no one raised an alarm. That morning, when the fog surged from the woods like a storm flood, it was already too late.

OLIVIA STEPHEN
Stories from the Otherworld (1965)

A Vacation in Wales

The town of Conwy nestled against the coast like a blob of jam inside the curve of a croissant. The houses of the old section stood on a hillside, overlooking the blue bay. Its narrow alleyways lay in the shadow of a castle with the Welsh flag fluttering from its turrets: a red dragon on a green-and-white base.

At the foot of the castle, a short distance from the ramparts, was the train station. It had two sets of tracks, and a platform so narrow that two adults were barely able to walk down it side by side. Behind the station was a parking lot, which was as empty as the station itself—except for a brown seagull rooting through the rubbish bins in the hope of finding some lunch.

Portia Beale stood at the entrance to the parking lot, occasionally glancing down at the note in her hand. Her mother had written down her aunts' address and phone number on a piece of paper. "Just in case," she had said. "They'll come and pick you up, so you won't need the number; at least not for now."

Well, Mum, you thought wrong.

She pulled her phone from her pocket, trying to ignore

the lump in her throat. No reason to panic. She had taken the train from London to Wales all by herself, so why would she be scared of making a simple phone call? After all, her mother had warned her that the aunts were a tad scatterbrained—perhaps they had simply forgotten that their guest was arriving today.

Portia had already typed in the first three digits when a Nissan car came barreling noisily into the parking lot, brakes screeching and exhaust popping, and halted in front of her. The door flew open, and a stocky woman with a short gray braid heaved herself out. Portia's thumb was still hovering over the screen when the woman came stomping toward her, in clumpy green rain boots.

"Damn and blast it!" she said by way of a greeting. "I really thought I was going to make it in time."

That was Portia's first impression of Aunt Bramble.

Initially Portia and her mother had been planning to spend their summer vacation in Andalusia—but a week before their scheduled departure, her mum had canceled the trip. Portia had been disappointed, but not particularly surprised. Her mother had been feeling unwell all month. Signs that the vacation wouldn't happen had gathered like storm clouds on the horizon.

Gwendolyn Beale had broken the news to her daughter three days ago. Andalusia was off. Instead, she said, Portia would be spending a fortnight with some relatives in north Wales. Rose was Gwendolyn's aunt, and Bramble was Rose's partner. They lived in a cottage in the countryside, but had been traveling on and off for years, so Portia hadn't seen them since she was very little. Still, they were really looking forward to her visit. At least that's what Portia's mum had said. Now that Bramble was right in front of her, as large as life, Portia wasn't so sure.

"Where on earth is my blasted watch?" said Bramble in a voice as thorny as her namesake, rummaging through her trouser and coat pockets.

Portia had no idea how to greet the older woman, so in the end she simply stuck out a hand. "Hello, I'm Portia."

She felt foolish as soon as the words left her mouth, but Bramble paused for the first time since she had jumped out of the car. She looked Portia up and down with a smile on her face, before taking her hand in a firm grip. "I know who you are, girl. Even though I've got to say, you've grown an awful lot since I last saw you."

She produced a battered wristwatch from the depths of a pocket. "Shall we?"

Without waiting for a response, Bramble grabbed Portia's bag and headed back toward her dented gray Nissan. Portia followed, adjusting the straps on her backpack.

"That train's always, always late," Bramble grumbled. "And then today of all days it's on time. Have you been waiting long?"

"No, not really," said Portia, but Bramble didn't seem to be listening anyway. She opened the trunk, swore again, and pushed aside a big bag of bark mulch to make space for Portia's suitcase.

"Go ahead and get in! Rose is waiting with the tea, and if I don't deliver you on time, she'll do her eyebrow thingy."

"Her what thingy?" Portia asked as she opened the passenger door.

Bramble snorted. "Oh, you'll see, you'll see."

The trunk closed with a bang, and before Portia knew it, they were on their way.

The Nissan rattled and clattered so much during the ride that Portia was worried the old rust bucket would fall apart at any moment. Bramble on the other hand didn't seem to be bothered at all. She sped along the narrow streets at a speed that must surely have been over the limit. Portia clasped the backpack on her lap with both hands and nervously watched the stone houses swoosh by outside.

She would have liked to ask Bramble to slow down but didn't dare. In her half-moon glasses, she reminded Portia of the headmistress at her school, even though the tousled gray braid didn't quite fit the image of a strict teacher. Her clothes were what you might charitably call practical: a flowery blouse, a washed-out green cardigan, and a faded pair of jeans tucked into her rain boots. Portia wondered what Bramble had been up to before she had left the house to pick her up at the train station.

"When we last saw you, you were three years old," Bramble said, hurtling through a roundabout without even touching the brakes. A little gnome dangling from the rearview mirror bounced frantically up and down. "You probably don't remember, do you?"

"No, I don't, actually," Portia replied. *That gnome must be sick to his stomach*, she thought.

"Well, it would be quite unusual if you did, actually." Bramble rattled over a speed bump. "But I remember you used to love hiding things." She laughed. "Once, you put Rose's shoes in the oven. It must have taken her an hour to find them."

"Um. I'm sorry, I suppose?" Portia stuttered, thrown off guard.

"Not at all!" said Bramble. "I discovered your little hiding place after about ten minutes, but it was simply too much fun to watch Rose searching high and low. We could do it again, but I reckon you're too old for such shenanigans by now, aren't you?"

Portia couldn't help but smile. "I suppose I am."

"What a shame," Bramble sighed. "Music?"

Without waiting for Portia's reply, she turned the radio on. ABBA's "Waterloo" blared from the speakers, and Bramble immediately began humming along. Portia glanced over and noticed that her glasses had slid down to the tip of her nose. In fact, she didn't look like a teacher at all, Portia decided. She was more like an archaeologist who dug up buried treasures or explored pyramids.

The only thing missing is an old leather hat, Portia thought. As if she had read Portia's mind, Bramble glanced over at her and winked—perhaps she wasn't as thorny as Portia had feared after all.

A Thief in the Night

Driving inland from Conwy, the road took them along the edge of the Snowdonia National Park, home to Wales's highest mountains, most beautiful lakes, and most of its sheep, too. At least that's what Portia's mother had told her. The River Conwy meandered across green meadows like a blue ribbon, and it was true: there was barely a patch of grass not occupied by a grazing sheep. Twenty minutes later, Bramble had steered the old car to a place called Trefriw. Portia tried several times to pronounce the name, but couldn't manage it.

"Trair-vruew," Bramble corrected her. "And if you're having trouble with that, you just wait until we take you to Llanfairpwllgwyngyllgogerychwyrndrobwllllantysiliogogogoch."

"Come again?" Portia spluttered.

Bramble repeated the name.

"It's actually one of the longest place-names in the world," she explained. "It roughly translates to 'Mary's church resting in a hollow of white hazels near a fierce whirlpool and the church of Tysilio by the red cave.' The Welsh are quite particular when it comes to their names."

"Aren't you from Wales?" Portia asked.

Bramble shook her head. "Migrated here from Shropshire. But don't tell anyone." She honked the horn vigorously and waved at a man walking along the side of the road.

"We're almost there now," she promised, before glancing at her watch and stepping on the accelerator even harder. The Nissan roared out of Trefriw, over a stone bridge, and past a lush green meadow before entering a little wood of gnarled oaks that pressed up against the road from either side. Then they emerged from the trees, and Portia caught her breath.

The view was stunning—to their right, a beautiful little valley, with a stream running along its bottom, bordered by dark-hued willows; ahead, forest-clad foothills rising to distant, craggy mountaintops.

"Wow," Portia gasped.

Bramble grinned. "Beautiful, but remote," she said. "Don't worry, though. If you take my bike, you'll be in town in no time at all. And Llanrwst isn't far, either."

"Hlun . . . ?" Portia gave it a try.

"*Hlan-roost*," Bramble repeated. "They've got a little cinema and a bookshop and what have you. So you won't have to be cooped up in the house with us two old bags all the time. Aha, speak of the devil."

Portia peered ahead through the windshield. An apple orchard appeared at the end of the road, and beyond that, a gray stone house.

"Home sweet home," Bramble proclaimed as she parked under an apple tree. With another glance at her watch, she climbed out of the car. Portia did the same, all the while staring at her aunts' house. She hadn't expected anything as beautiful as this! There was even a conservatory, and a hammock tied between two trees. The aunts must have plenty of green fingers between them, she thought. Flowers flourished all over the garden and along the windowsills. A dog rose climbed up the front wall of the house, and the purple flowers of a clematis cascaded from the porch like a waterfall. Portia wouldn't have been surprised to see Peter Rabbit himself hopping around the garden.

"Are you afraid of dogs?" Bramble asked as she hoisted Portia's luggage from the trunk.

"No. . . . Why?" She had barely uttered her question when a black-and-white bullet came shooting toward them.

"Marlowe!" Bramble yelled sharply, but the dog was already jumping around Portia, panting excitedly. He trod on her feet with his paws, pressed his flank against her knees, and wagged his tail as if they were the dearest of best friends.

Portia squatted down to scratch Marlowe between his ears. Judging by the way he rested his head on her thighs, he liked that.

Bramble shook her head in mock disapproval. "Quite the fierce guard dog, aren't you?"

"Love at first sight, I see."

Portia turned around and looked up to see a woman of about Bramble's age walking toward them with a broad smile on her face, drying her hands on a tea towel. This had to be Rose. She wore glasses too, but unlike Bramble, Rose had short, curly hair, and was quite smartly turned out, in a red blouse and a poppy-patterned skirt. Portia wiped her hands on her jeans, anticipating a handshake. But Rose didn't waste any time with that. Still smiling, she placed both of her hands on Portia's shoulders.

"Portia, my dear," she said. "Just look at you. And look at how much you've grown! We haven't seen each other in far too long. How old were you when we came to visit the last time? Maybe two?"

"Three," Bramble cut in. "And yes, girls usually do a fair bit of growing up over nine years."

"You're late," Rose shot back in reply.

"You should have seen the traffic," Bramble retorted.

"The traffic?" Rose's right eyebrow arched in obvious disbelief. Bramble flashed Portia a meaningful glance.

Ah, Portia thought. *The eyebrow thingy!*

"Terrible traffic," Bramble confirmed without even batting an eye. "All because of those new traffic lights in Tal-y-Cafn. Why they built those things in the first place is beyond me, really." She carried Portia's suitcase toward the garden gate as Marlowe dashed past her and into the house. "On top of which, I had to drive sensibly. After all," she added, "one should never speed when traveling with young passengers, you know."

By now, Portia's red face could have given a ripe tomato a run for its money. She'd never heard anyone lie so smoothly.

"No less than I would expect from a driver as conscientious as you are," Rose said drily. She threw the tea towel over her shoulder and stretched out her hand. To her surprise, Portia glimpsed a tattoo on her wrist: a row of zigzag lines—like the traces of little birds' tracks.

"Come along, dear," said Rose. "You can help me set the table."

⌇

The house's name was written on a slate above the door-bell: *Afallon*. Portia stepped in through the open door and stopped dead.

The entrance hall was crammed full of stuff: a coatrack, a basket filled with umbrellas, and a knee-high elephant made of bronze. A vase filled with lilies and hydrangeas stood on an old telephone table with a gold-framed mirror hanging on the wall above it.

Portia had never seen that much stuff in one place—other than in a museum. Except that it didn't smell like freshly baked cakes in a museum. She sniffed the sweet air. *Vanilla*, she thought. *And lemon*. She walked slowly into the house and saw the open doors on each side of the hallway.

Perhaps this was the kind of house with secret passages? Great big oil paintings that swung open to reveal hidden doors? Portia's heart was racing. She would have loved to begin exploring all the rooms right away. She stared about her, taking in the walls, ceiling, and the dark-brown wooden staircase with ornate banisters that climbed up toward the second floor.

"So, what do you think?" Rose was leaning against the doorframe with folded arms. "Can you bear to spend a few weeks with us?"

"Definitely!" Portia blurted out. "Thank you so much for having me."

"Ah, nonsense, we've been looking forward to your visit.

In fact," she continued in a raised voice, "that tea has been looking forward to meeting you for more than an hour."

"You just can't help yourself, can you?" Bramble harrumphed as she edged past Rose and set off up the stairs with Portia's suitcase.

"Your room is upstairs," Rose explained. "But let's have some tea and cake first, shall we?"

"Cake sounds lovely," Portia said immediately.

Rose laughed. "I thought it would!" She pointed to a door to her right. "The living room is through there. Why don't you go ahead while I fetch us some tea from the kitchen?"

Portia shrugged off her backpack, feeling a pleasant tingle under her skin as the weight was lifted, and pushed open the living-room door.

"Amazing," she whispered.

The room was like a magical hollow dug beneath the roots of a tree. The low ceiling was held up by oak rafters, and the walls were painted a pastel green. A crimson Persian rug lay on the wooden floorboards between three wing-backed chairs facing a fireplace. But the best part was the books. Shelves crammed full of them stood against every wall. An open glass door led out to the conservatory. Even out there, Portia could see books piled up on a chaise longue, surrounded by buckets overflowing with greenery, and beautiful plants trailing from hanging baskets above.

Portia was so impressed by all the books that she was unable to take in anything else for a moment. Only on reaching the middle of the room did she realize that she was not alone.

13

A fox was sitting in the doorway between the living room and the conservatory. The animal looked straight at her, its fur gleaming like copper in the afternoon sun. Portia held her breath, but the fox stayed where it was, watching her with pricked ears and golden, inquisitive eyes. Fascinated, she held its gaze, until she heard a whimpering behind her. She turned around to find Marlowe crouching in the living-room doorway, his head tucked between his paws.

He clearly wasn't a hunting dog, judging by how frightened he looked. The fox, on the other hand, didn't seem to be scared at all. Quite the contrary—it was calmly sizing Marlowe up. Portia even thought she saw it give a cheeky smirk, although of course that wasn't possible.

"Marlowe, old chap," Bramble called from the hallway. "Are you begging for treats again?" A second later she came through the doorway and spotted the fox. "You!" she thundered, the sound of her voice making the fox flinch. "I can't believe it! Get out of here!"

The fox cowered, hesitated, and finally dashed back into the conservatory and out into the garden.

"Don't let me catch you in here again, or I'll make gloves out of you!" Bramble yelled from the open doorway. "Honestly, it's enough to drive a person mad," she said, turning back toward Portia.

"A fox!" Portia said, still in shock, as Bramble came back into the living room.

"Yes. Well, more or less," said Bramble evasively. Her gaze wandered to a closed door next to one of the bookshelves. Marlowe trotted over to her, and she scratched him between his ears, still shaking her head in disbelief. "You got a bit of a fright there, didn't you, boy?"

"What's going on in here?" Rose asked as she came into the living room, carrying a teapot and cups on a tray.

"A fox!" Portia cried. "Right here! In the living room!" It was unbelievable. She had never seen a fox so close up before. "Does that happen often?"

The aunts' house was becoming more exciting by the minute, but Rose didn't seem pleased by the fox's visit either. She flashed Bramble a worried look, but her partner merely tightened her mouth into a thin line in response.

"Welcome to the countryside," Bramble said curtly, pushing Marlowe to one side and taking the tray from Rose's hands.

By the evening, Portia could no longer say which part of the house she loved most. For a while, it was a neck-and-neck race between the kitchen, the conservatory, and the living room. In the end, however, she decided it had to be her own room. "We're just down the hall, in case you need anything," said Rose when it was time to go to bed. She gave Portia a hug. "We're so happy you're here."

"So am I," said Portia. The aunts had welcomed her so kindly—now she understood why her mum had always loved spending her summers here in Afallon.

"Sweet dreams," said Rose, turning to go.

"Don't let the dog in!" thundered Bramble from the other end of the hall.

Rose rolled her eyes, yet couldn't help but smile. "Goodnight," she said, and Portia wished her the same. When Rose closed the door, Portia finally got to take a good look at her new room.

The guest bedroom wasn't big. In fact it was rather cozy. A reading lamp shaped like a bellflower sat on a table beside her bed, and there was a white wooden chest of drawers for her to put her clothes in. The room was at the rear of the house, and Portia was certain that she'd be able to see the river from her window in the morning.

She turned on the lamp and opened her suitcase. Her pajamas were right on top. She picked them up, and then stopped short—underneath them lay her mum's favorite poncho. Staring at the carefully folded material, Portia suddenly felt a bit of a lump in her throat. She remembered the last time her mum had worn it.

It was the morning she canceled their vacation. Portia had been tiptoeing around the flat for the past fortnight, bringing her mum breakfast in the morning and tea in the evening. This routine was nothing new to her. Most of the time Gwen was a cheerful, positive person, but every now and then she would be hit by a wave of sadness. If they were lucky, the emotional storm would pass after a few days, but often it would loom overhead for weeks—and that's how it was this time around.

When Portia had walked into the living room that Monday before they were supposed to leave for their trip, Gwen was sitting on the windowsill. She was wearing the poncho, a big purple woolen one. Portia sat down and snuggled up against her mum, who put an arm around her daughter's shoulder. The poncho felt warm and soft against Portia's cheek.

"Andalusia isn't happening, I'm afraid," her mother had said quietly.

Disappointment had burned in Portia's throat, but she wouldn't let it show. "Never mind," she had replied. "We'll just go next year."

Her mum had pulled her into a hug and kissed the top of her head. "My brave Lion-Girl."

Portia had been sure she'd managed to hide her disappointment from her mum. But now it seemed as if Gwen must have felt it and packed the poncho for her as consolation.

Oh, Mum, thought Portia. She slipped into her pajamas and wrapped the poncho around her shoulders. The wool smelled faintly of Gwen's perfume. Portia pressed it to her nose and took a deep breath, trying to imagine what her mother was doing right at that moment. Portia hoped she was feeling better. That she was remembering to make herself breakfast, and perhaps to leave the house every now and then to get some fresh air.

Not for the first time that day, she wondered whether she should've stayed in London. But her mother had insisted that she should have a fun summer vacation. Portia ran her hand over the poncho and trusted that her mum wouldn't miss it too much.

She sighed, turned off the main light, and climbed into bed. Kneeling on the duvet, she looked out the window. Outside, it was already getting dark—too dark to make out anything in the back garden. The stars were hiding behind clouds, and the willows were no more than vague shapes lining the river. But there was something strange, too.

Portia squinted. A shadowy shape was moving across the grass down below. She leaned forward. The fox flitted through the beam of light falling from her window, and then disappeared into the shrubbery. Portia frowned. It really was persistent! Could its den be nearby?

Anyway, her feet were getting cold. Portia huddled under the duvet, and fished out of her backpack the book she had started reading on the train. The down crackled softly as she nestled against her pillow, the poncho still wrapped around her shoulders.

Portia had no idea what had woken her up. All she knew was that she was suddenly sitting bolt upright in her bed. It was still pitch black outside. She frowned. So strange! Had she had a nightmare?

She rubbed her eyes. Now that she was awake, she might just as well go to the bathroom. She had probably overdone it with the third cup of tea, but it had been so satisfying pouring milk into the china cups. Barefoot, she stepped out of her room onto the dark landing and groped blindly along the wall next to the door, but couldn't find the light switch. She was drowsily making her way down the landing when she heard a noise downstairs. She froze. There it was again—the low creaking of a door.

Her eyes had adjusted to the dark by now, and she could make out the outline of the banister. She crept over to the top of the stairs and stood, listening intently. But the house was still. She had just decided that the noise must have been old Marlowe bounding about, when a shadow flitted past the bottom of the stairs. The fox!

All at once, Portia was wide awake. For a second she considered waking her aunts, but her curiosity won out. She tiptoed down the steps. When she got to the bottom, she could hear noises coming from the living room: a scratching sound at first, followed by the thud of a book hitting the floor. What on earth was that fox up to in there?

Sneaking to the open living-room door, she peeked inside. Bluish moonlight was filtering in through the windows at the other end of the room, but even so Portia could barely make out a thing. All she could see were the dark shapes of the armchairs. The noises were coming from the next room now—the one she hadn't been into yet. She padded across the thick carpet and gave the door next to the bookshelf a gentle push.

She heard the sound of rustling paper. Something was moving in the shadows, rooting around on the top of a wooden table—something with a bushy tail.

Portia was still peering into the darkness when she heard paws scrabbling on the floorboards behind her. Then Marlowe bolted past her into the room, barking. The next thing she knew, someone had reached over her shoulder and switched on the lights. Portia's heart skipped a beat—but that was nothing in comparison to the fox's reaction: the instant the lights clicked on, the animal froze, its tail bristling like a bottlebrush. It was standing in the middle of a desk, surrounded by a mess of crumpled paper and open drawers.

"Oh no, you don't," growled Bramble, who seemed to have appeared from nowhere. She barged past Portia and charged into the study like a warhorse. The fox crouched down, flattened his ears, and hissed, but Bramble wasn't fazed. She lunged forward and almost managed to grab the intruder, but the fox was quick. At the very last second it ducked under her arm and shot out of the study as if the devil himself was after it.

Bramble swore. Then they heard a scream coming from the hall. The lights in the living room came on to reveal Rose, her hand on the switch.

"For heaven's sake, what is going on here?" she asked, tying the belt of her dressing gown.

The fox, Portia was about to say, but Bramble beat her to it. "*Crwydriadgoch*," she blustered in Welsh.

It didn't mean anything to Portia, but Rose looked shocked and did her eyebrow thingy.

"What in the world did he want?" she wondered aloud, clearly astonished.

"To steal something, as usual," snorted Bramble. "That scoundrel will give me a heart attack one day."

"Bramble," Rose said soothingly, but Bramble wouldn't calm down.

"I've had it. The next time he dares to show his face here, I'll get the shotgun from the attic. You know what, actually, give me the phone."

"Who do you want to call at this hour?"

"Pest control? A hunter? How should I know?" roared Bramble.

Marlowe nuzzled his angry mistress's leg, and Rose rubbed her back, making shushing noises until Bramble closed her eyes and took a slow, deep breath.

"I'm too old for this nonsense," she muttered, before starting to clear up the chaos on the desk.

Rose checked her watch. "I'll make some tea. The sun will be up in half an hour, and I'd say we won't be getting any more sleep tonight anyway."

"How did the fox get in, by the way?" asked Portia.

"Oh, I must have forgotten to lock the kitchen door," Rose said breezily. Portia frowned. She distinctly remembered Rose locking the door. And now that she thought about it, she felt certain that the door to the study had been closed as well. Could foxes turn door handles?

Rose went out into the hall, but Portia hung back. Something was going on here, and she needed to ask Bramble about it. But as she came to the study doorway again, she stopped short. Unaware she was being watched, Bramble was bent over the desk, feeling carefully along its edge with her fingertips. What was she up to? Then Portia saw the edge of the desk come away in Bramble's hand. A secret drawer slid out from its hiding place. Bramble took something out, and for a moment Portia saw a silvery object twinkling between her fingers, before she sighed with relief and put the shiny object back in its place.

Curious. Very curious, Portia thought. She tiptoed away before Bramble slid the drawer back into place, but she had memorized the exact spot she needed to push to open it.

Pendragon Books

Ben Rees stood on a ladder, arranging cookbooks on the top shelf of a rather crowded bookcase. The ladder was a bit wobbly, but he was used to it. Steadying himself against the bookcase, he pushed a book into a narrow gap with his free hand.

A few years earlier, his parents had taken over Pendragon Books from his grandfather, painted the shop front blue, and hung a string of lights in the window.

Like his mother, Megan, before him, Ben had grown up in that bookshop. He had learned to read in the armchair in the back corner. Megan loved to talk about how he had spent hours sitting there, poring over picture books. At first, his legs had been so short, they dangled over the seat of the chair.

Ben had been helping in the shop since he was six years old, sorting donated books and dusting shelves. He also drew pictures for the signs on the shelves: little pots for cookbook corner, bloody knives for the crime section, hearts for romance novels, and dragons for the fantasy collection.

He didn't exactly *have* to help, but he loved that bookshop, and he could hardly wait to get there after school. The smell of paper, the cracked book spines, and the sea of printed words made him feel at home.

The shop wasn't very busy today—no customers apart from the red-haired man, who stopped by from time to time, standing flicking through a novel. Ben was just stepping off the ladder when the bell above the door jingled and his mother called out "*Croeso!*" which means "Welcome!" in Welsh.

Ben went over to a pile of boxes filled with books to fetch a few more to add to the shelves. When he came back to cookbook corner, he noticed a girl he'd never seen before in the crime section. Kids didn't wander into the shop all that often. Most of them got their books from the school library, if they read at all. This girl didn't look like she was planning on returning home empty-handed, though. She was about Ben's age, in sneakers, jeans, and a blue T-shirt with a pink flamingo on the front. Her black hair danced around her freckly face in wild curls.

Ben carried on shelving books, watching the new girl out of the corner of his eye. *What sort of books is she interested in?* he wondered. He got his answer when she pulled a Miss Marple mystery from the shelf. Not his thing. Just then, she glanced over and saw him looking at her. She lowered the book and raised an eyebrow.

Ben spun around as fast as lightning and knelt over one of the boxes. His heart was racing, and he felt angry with himself. *Serves you right*, he thought. *You shouldn't have been staring like that.* He fished a tattered copy of *All My Chickens* from the box but stayed crouched down in his corner, rummaging through the books, hoping that the girl would forget all about him. He was relieved when a few minutes had passed without anyone speaking to him. But then he heard his mum's voice.

"Ben? Come over here, would you?"

Ben turned around, and his heart sank into his sneakers. His mother was behind the counter, and the curly-haired girl was waiting in front of it.

Great. Ben knew exactly what would happen next. He went over to the counter, hoping his nervousness didn't show on his face.

"This is my son, Ben," said Megan, beaming from ear to ear. "Ben, this is Portia. She's spending her summer vacation at Afallon."

The girl smiled at him. He could feel his face turning red, his cheeks burning. He hated these moments.

Megan was constantly trying to set him up with other children. She meant well, of course—she was just worried that Ben spent too much time by himself. He didn't play soccer or go to birthday parties. It wasn't even that the other kids were deliberately excluding him—they just never even thought of him when making plans. And as far as Ben was concerned, that was fine by him.

At school, he kept a low profile. During class, he never spoke if he didn't have to, and at break, he would sneak off to the library, where he would sit and read, write, or draw.

"Is there really no one at school you might want to be friends with?" his mother often prodded. "They can't all be that bad, can they? Why don't you just give it a shot?"

Ben promised her every time to do just that. What he didn't tell his mother was that he had a hard time looking the kids at school in the face—he always felt they were expecting something from him, waiting for him to say some secret code word that he didn't know. Or perhaps they were just waiting for him to say something odd and make a fool of himself.

Books were easier—when he was reading, he had loads of amazing friends. He journeyed to Mount Doom with Frodo and Sam, discovered Hogwarts's secret passageways with Harry Potter, and rode to Bolvangar on an armored polar bear's back. His life wasn't boring at all, but somehow it was impossible to convince his mum of that. She might have given up pestering him to join the soccer team, but she still never missed an opportunity to set him up with a potential friend. Which was mortifying for Ben, and must also have been awkward for . . . what was her name again? Portia. She surely had better things to do than make a conversation with a perfect stranger. But apparently she was too polite to let on.

"Hi," said Portia.

Ben managed to mumble a quiet "Hello." Brilliant. Now her smile did look a little forced. If only he could go back to his box of books.

Megan seemed completely unaware of the awkwardness of the situation. "How long will you be staying in Afallon?" she asked.

Portia turned toward her. "Two weeks."

"Ah, how lovely," Megan said. "Then you've got enough time to explore the area. Have you already made plans?"

"We're going to Conwy today, actually."

"Ah! To the pier?"

"To the castle."

Megan was still holding Portia's book in her hands, and Ben was hoping that she'd finally ring it up and wrap it—but no such luck.

"That should be exciting," she said, continuing to chat. "Are you interested in Welsh history?"

"I don't know much about it yet. But my mum says some of the oldest places in all of Britain are here in Wales," Portia replied.

"That's true," said Megan. "Did you know that there's a stone circle nearby? It's even older than Conwy Castle, isn't it, Ben?"

Ben cast his mum a pleading look. It was painfully obvious what she had in mind: trying to get him and this girl to go off somewhere together. And if that didn't work, she'd send him to Afallon on some made-up pretext. He would go along with it, for her sake, but his heart sank as he realized that his visits to the cottage weren't going to be much fun for a while.

Ben really liked the Afallon women. He had read all of Bramble's books, and he had even shown her some of his drawings. Bramble had asked to keep one of them—a Nazgûl dragon from Middle-earth—and Ben had taken that as huge praise. In return, she had gifted him a book filled with pictures of dragons, knights, and castles for his birthday.

"A stone circle?" Portia asked.

"Oh, yes, up by the lake. Why don't you head out there with Ben sometime—he knows the area quite well."

Bingo, thought Ben.

Portia hesitated for a split second, and then she smiled at him. "Sounds good. If you're up for it?"

Megan nodded encouragingly.

"Okay," he said, resigned to his fate. He would spend a morning taking Portia up the lake. They'd chat a load of nonsense on the way. Ben would show her the five knee-high stones his mum had so generously called a "stone circle." She would be disappointed, having expected something like Stonehenge. And then Ben would finally have his peace and quiet again.

Unless, of course, Portia found a last-minute excuse to not hang out with him—arguably the ideal scenario.

"If you're interested in the real Wales, you really must see that stone circle," Megan said as she punched the book's price into the cash register. "That castle is really a foreign imposition, built by the English to keep us Welsh in check."

Ben bent down to pick up a box of books next to the counter, and as he straightened up, he noticed something peculiar: the red-haired man, half-hidden by the shelves, was watching the counter closely. No, wait, that wasn't quite right. He was watching Portia.

"Hey, Ben?" his mum called. Ben winced. The red-haired man dropped his gaze and disappeared between the shelves. "Why don't you two make a plan right away?"

All right, Mum, Ben thought. Best to jump in at the deep

end. "Are you busy tomorrow morning?" he asked Portia.

"No, that's cool, tomorrow morning is great." Portia raised an eyebrow. "Eleven o'clock okay?"

Ben nodded.

"Fabulous," Megan exclaimed, clearly satisfied. "Ben can come pick you up from Afallon." She handed Portia the wrapped book. "Have lots of fun in Conwy, then. And tell Rose and Bramble I said hi, okay?"

"Will do." Portia turned to Ben one last time. "See you tomorrow, then?"

"Okay," he said, feeling incredibly foolish. Portia waved goodbye before stepping outside. The bell rang, the door swung shut, and she was gone. Ben sighed.

"Well?" Megan said, smiling. "That wasn't so bad, was it?" Ben frowned in disagreement. The bell rang again as the red-haired man left the shop too. "Now, don't look so glum. You'll see—once you're out and about, I'm sure you'll have fun. Portia seems really nice."

"Mmm," he replied. It was hard to stop himself from contradicting his mum, but he knew that if they got into an argument, she'd just end up lecturing him about how it wasn't healthy to be a loner. How he needed friends his age. How he'd miss out on all sorts of important experiences if all he did was sit there with his head in a book.

Ben knew his mum wished he was more like other kids, and for her sake he wished he was different too. But every time he tried to behave the way she thought he should, his stomach tied itself in knots.

Dad had never tried to push him into making friends

with other kids. Ben knew his mother was only acting out of love for him, and yet . . . at moments like these, Ben wished his dad were still around. Dad had always understood him.

Sadness settled on his shoulders like a heavy blanket, as it so often did since his father had passed away.

"Ben . . . ," Megan began, but just then something smacked against the shop window with a thump. They both spun around.

"What on earth was that?" Megan wondered aloud, while Ben was already on his way over to the door. Stepping outside, he immediately saw what had happened: a disheveled blackbird was lying on the sidewalk, right in front of the shop. It must have smashed into the window at full speed.

Ben ran over to the bird and squatted down to discover that it was still alive. The blackbird was trying to flutter away, but one of its wings was sticking out at a funny angle.

His chest tightened in pain. That poor bird! Where had it been flying to? He looked up and noticed a sparkle in the windowpane—and then the reflection of the red-haired man, watching him from the other side of the street.

Megan appeared next to Ben. "Goodness me! The poor thing."

Ben was only half listening. He turned around just in time to see the red-haired man disappear around the street corner. For a moment it seemed as if a cloud of golden dust was hanging in the air in his wake. Then Ben blinked, and the cloud was gone. He must have been mistaken.

Peculiar Events

✍ PORTIA ✎

Later that afternoon, Portia sat in the living room at Afallon, drumming her fingers on the arm of her wing-backed chair. She had just gotten off the phone with her mum, and it had been nice to hear her voice—most of all because Gwen had sounded like she was in good spirits again, up for anything. Portia had told her all about the trip to Conwy: the old town filled with the smell of sea salt and spindrift, the giant seagulls, the narrow lanes, and the fish and chips she and the aunts had enjoyed on the harbor.

The day had been a busy one, and Portia hadn't had much time to ponder the events of the previous night, but now her gaze wandered to the closed door of Bramble's study.

Thoughts of the fox had been flitting through her mind all day. The aunts had dodged all her questions about the incident, which obviously piqued her curiosity even more.

Portia got up from her chair and went over to the study door. She was alone in the house—Rose had retreated to her writing shed in the garden to work on an editing project, and Bramble was walking Marlowe—so no one would know if she went into the study now.

Forget it. It's a ridiculous idea, Portia told herself. But then again, it wasn't like Bramble and Rose had explicitly forbidden her to go into the room. And hadn't Rose told her to make herself at home? So, what harm could it possibly do if she took a quick look?

Portia peeked through the open conservatory door to make sure that neither aunt was around, and then she stepped into Bramble's study.

Bramble had an old-fashioned desk: a bureau with a front that folded down to give a writing surface, revealing lots of compartments and drawers behind it. Unlike her car, her workspace was neat and tidy. Notebooks were lined up along the open compartments, a fountain pen and pencils had been tucked into two mugs, and a Welsh dictionary sat at the edge of the desktop. An empty vase stood on top of the bureau next to a shoebox.

Portia placed both hands on the desktop. That's where the fox had been, and that's where Bramble had been poking around right after chasing it away. *Curiosity killed the cat,* said the voice of reason in her head, but she ignored it. The mystery surrounding the fox in the study was just too intriguing.

She felt along the desktop edge with her fingertips until she found a thin join in the polished wood. A smile crept over her face. Bingo. She pushed lightly against it and heard a clicking noise. When she pulled back her hand, the secret compartment slid out from the desktop.

"Abracadabra," Portia whispered. In the secret drawer, she found a flat metal box. Her heart beating with excitement, she opened the lid—and raised her eyebrows in surprise. Inside the box lay an antique, ornately decorated key, with a tatty green silk ribbon tied to it. The wide bit at the end didn't look like it would fit any modern lock. Portia picked up the key and ran her thumb over the knot in the ribbon. Why was Bramble hiding a key? And more importantly, had the fox been looking for it? No way. Impossible.

Portia ran her fingers along the metal. Would Bramble tell her what it was for? Probably not, she decided. Especially since Portia would have to confess to snooping around her desk before she asked. But perhaps there were more clues to be found elsewhere in the study?

She put the key down, letting her eyes wander around the room and over the drawers and compartments, before picking up the shoebox sitting next to the vase. Inside was a wild jumble of odds and ends. On top sat a pincushion with a single needle stuck in it, and next to it a small jewelry box made of blue velvet that Portia opened to discover a silver locket. Inside it, instead of a photograph, there was a flower pressed under the glass. Portia held it up against the light. Unless she was mistaken, they were the faded white petals of a dog rose. Portia put the locket back in its case and continued to search through the shoebox.

Underneath the pincushion were two postcards from a Greek island, and a photograph showing Bramble and Rose at a beach. She put them aside and flipped through a pile of old newspaper clippings. Bramble had kept a book review, and a magazine article with pictures of Afallon's garden. And there was an older cutting with the headline SEARCH FOR MISSING STUDENTS CONTINUES.

Deeper down, she found a photo of Marlowe as a puppy, and another of a group of seven friends in hippie clothes, posing in front of a theatre. And a more serious scene, too: six students in long black gowns, wearing mortarboard caps as if at a graduation.

Portia turned the group pictures over. Something was scribbled on the back of each one: *The Order of the Needle, 1963* on the first and *The Order of the Needle, 1966* on the second. She frowned. What was the Order of the Needle? She inspected the photos more closely. The group of students consisted of five women and one man. Portia stopped short. The woman in the middle looked just like her mother—she had Gwen's pitch-black hair and the same heart-shaped face. But the young woman in the photo was arching her right eyebrow in a way that reminded Portia of somebody else. Then she realized—it had to be Rose on her graduation day. Portia was just about to put the photo aside when she saw another familiar face: Bramble! She was standing next to Rose in the picture, but Portia hadn't recognized her right away. This Bramble was all smiles, with her hair down, wearing an embroidered cap instead of a mortarboard.

Portia saw that she had come to the bottom of the box. She contemplated the keepsakes spread out on the desk in front of her. There was no explanation for the secret key to be found here. Portia picked it up again and weighed it in her hand. Did she dare to keep on trawling through the desk?

The sensible thing would be to tidy up all this mess. *Before* she got caught. Then again, another five minutes of searching might just unearth the clue she was looking for.

She was already reaching for one of the notebooks when she heard the soft jingle of the wind chimes in the conservatory. Portia turned around and then froze. The fox was sitting in the study doorway, looking up at her with pricked ears. No, not at her. . . . He was staring at the key in her hand.

"Portia," Rose called from the conservatory. "Is that you?"

Portia felt a jolt of cold fear shooting through her body. What if Rose found her here? Fox or no fox, she spun around, collected Bramble's keepsakes, returned them to the shoebox, and hurried to place it back on top of the desk. She was about to put away the key as well, when she heard footsteps in the living room.

"Portia?"

She turned around, quickly stuffing the key into the pocket of her jeans. The fox had disappeared once more, and instead Rose appeared in the doorway.

"Ah, *there* you are. What are you doing in here?"

"I was looking for a pen," Portia improvised. She prayed that her body was concealing the still-open secret drawer behind her. "I'm sorry."

"No problem. Take whatever you need." Rose was carrying a bunch of freshly cut roses, hydrangeas, and euphorbias, and now absent-mindedly sucked one of her thumbs, which must have been pricked by a thorn. Portia saw her chance and groped behind her back for the edge of the desk and closed the drawer.

"What do you think?" Rose asked. "Time for dinner?"

"Sounds great." Portia's heart was in her mouth, but luckily, Rose didn't seem to notice anything.

"Wonderful." She pointed at the desk with her elbow. "Could you bring along that vase, please?"

Portia was hoping Rose would go ahead, but she waited in the doorway for Portia to leave the study before shutting the door behind her. The key felt as heavy as lead in her pocket.

✒ BEN ✑

Ben and Megan lived in Trefriw, in a narrow terraced house on the hillside above the church. The entire row had been whitewashed, but the Reeses' house alone had blue window frames and a blue front door.

With their bags of takeout food from the pub in one hand, Megan used the other to unlock the door. Ben slipped past her, holding the cage containing the injured blackbird carefully so as not to shake it.

In the hallway, Megan set the food down on the telephone table: chicken tikka for herself, and fish and chips for Ben. She threw the keys into a little wicker basket and peeled off her denim jacket.

"Dinner in five minutes?" she asked.

"Let me just take the blackbird upstairs," said Ben.

"All right, but hurry up. Otherwise your chips will get soggy, and you know there's a No Returns policy."

Ben grinned and went upstairs with the cage. His room faced the street. It wasn't exactly big to begin with, and the piles of books on the floor, as well as on the shelves and the desk by the window, made it seem even smaller. There were posters on the door and above his desk, but the wall next to his bed was still covered by the forest his parents had painted for him when he was little.

Ben placed the blackbird on his desk and pulled away the cloth he had used to cover the cage. The bird immediately started hopping from one perch to the other, trying to flap its wings.

"Easy," Ben said softly. "No one here is going to hurt you." He stood still and waited a moment until the bird had calmed down. The vet, Dr. Davies, had splinted its broken wing.

"It's a miracle that it's still alive," he had said. "Most birds that fly into windows get a concussion and die."

His mother had shot the vet a sharp look, and Dr. Davies had instantly turned bright red. "This little fellow is looking quite tough, though," he had hastened to add. "He'll be flying again in no time, easy-peasy!"

That kind of exchange between his mum and Dr. Davies was nothing new to Ben. Since his dad had passed away the previous year, grown-ups seemed to think they had to handle him with kid gloves. Ben wasn't exactly annoyed by it—he simply didn't like all the attention.

He took off his backpack, pulled out the bag of birdseed he'd just purchased, and dug around for the small plastic bowl and water bottle that Dr. Davies had given him. On the wall next to him, shaggy, round-eyed monsters peered out from between the trunks of red- and green-leaved trees. *Where the Wild Things Are* had been his favorite book when he was little. He had asked his dad, Tom, to read it aloud to him so many times that one day, Tom had looked Ben in the eyes and said, "If you want to spend that much time in a story, boy, you've got no choice but to learn how to read yourself." Three months later, Ben was reading the book aloud to his dad. Every now and then, Tom had needed to help him with longer words, but from then on they'd worked their way through dozens of books together, taking turns to read aloud. Tom's well-worn copy of *The Hobbit* still lay under Ben's pillow. Even though he had not opened it for a while, he could still hear his dad's voice as he read Bilbo's adventures to him: *In a hole in the ground there lived a hobbit.*

Ben put the plastic bowl on the desk and filled the bottle on the side of the cage with fresh water. The blackbird nervously scuttled back and forth on his perch, but it didn't seem too panicky anymore.

"You'll feel better soon, I promise," Ben assured the bird.

"Ben!" his mother called from downstairs. "Soggy chips in T-minus ten seconds."

Ben ripped open the bag of birdseed, poured a generous amount into the little bowl, and carefully placed it in the cage.

"Enjoy," he said, and headed downstairs.

INTERLUDE

Night had fallen on Trefriw like a cloak of black velvet. Around midnight, the clouds parted to reveal the full moon, which bathed the town in an unearthly, milky shimmering light. The moonlight flooded into Ben's room, wandering over the sleeping boy's body and along his blanket, grazing the palm trees on the wall and illuminating the birdcage on his desk.

The blackbird was awake. It sat on its perch looking out through the window. Down there, in the street, a shadowy figure was moving about. Someone walked along the row of parked cars: a tall figure, striding with soundless ease. Below Ben's window, the figure paused, and glanced up.

The blackbird's neck feathers bristled. Moonlight sparkled on its head, and silvery rays ran down its plumage like rivulets of rain. A shiver went through the bird. It ruffled its feathers, puffing them out in all directions. Then, in the blink of an eye, a tiny man stood on the perch instead of the blackbird. His hair was as dark and shiny as the blackbird's feathers of which his robe was made. His legs and feet were bare, and he held his splinted broken arm tightly to his chest.

Ridik ap Mwyalchod stepped closer to the cage bars. On the street below, the night wanderer put a cigarette between his lips. A moment later, the flame of a lighter and then the glow of the cigarette lit up the man's narrow, pointy face and head of red hair. He visibly relished taking a deep puff before tucking his free hand into his trouser pocket.

"Robin Goodfellow," Ridik whispered. "What are you up to?"

The man sent a smile toward the window above, as if he had heard the question. He raised the hand holding the cigarette and drew the shape of a key in the air in front of him.

"No." Ridik clutched the cage bars.

The cigarette held between two fingers, the man sauntered away down the street. The shadow that followed him was far too small for a man his size.

The Human Door

Portia sat on the wall by Afallon and checked her watch for the fifth time. It was ten past eleven, and Ben had not made an appearance yet.

Portia's backpack sat by her feet—she had packed it the evening before: a map, a few plastic bags for collected leaves and flowers, and her journal, of course. That morning, she had added two sandwiches, a thermos filled with tea, and a cloth to use as a picnic blanket. It would be such a shame if all that effort had been for nothing.

She tilted her face toward the sun. Perhaps she could just take off on her own? Rose was out shopping in Llanrwst, and Bramble was at her desk, working on her newest book. All morning, Portia had been nervously waiting for her to notice the key was missing, but so far luck seemed to be on her side. She was gambling on Bramble taking Marlowe for his walk again later that day. She would put the key back then. And in the meantime, there was no point in her sitting about twiddling her thumbs.

Portia let her legs dangle over the wall. The morning sky was bright blue, not a single cloud in sight. In the meadow near the lane, a few early butterflies were flitting about, while a bluish haze of morning mist still lingered at the edge of the woods. Portia took a deep breath. It was too beautiful a day to waste indoors. There were meadows and paths waiting to be explored.

She was just getting up when she noticed the fox crouching at the northern end of the wall, underneath a blackberry hedge. This time she was not surprised by its appearance.

"You just can't stay away, can you?" Portia expected him to bolt at the sound of her voice, but far from it. He just sat there, his bushy tail neatly curled around his legs. Portia couldn't help but smile. Would he let her come closer?

She slid cautiously off the wall. Suddenly the fox began to move. But it didn't run off. Instead it started trotting casually toward Portia. She stopped in her tracks. Such a strange animal! Was it tame, perhaps? Otherwise, there was no explanation for how it was behaving.

The fox stopped right in front of her. Portia hesitated briefly, but then squatted and held out a hand. It retreated at first, but then came forward and nudged her jeans pocket with its muzzle. She raised her eyebrows. Did it know that she had the key in her pocket?

The fox backed away, staring her in the eyes.

"Are you really after Bramble's key?" she asked.

The fox's right ear twitched.

Portia rose, glanced back toward the house over her shoulder, and then fished the key from her pocket. The fox stayed calm, but Portia could see it was pressing its paws into the grass just a little deeper. Portia let the key dangle from her finger on its green ribbon. The fox took a step closer.

"Blimey," she whispered. But if she had thought this fox couldn't behave any weirder, she had thought wrong. It sidled past her and peeked through the gate up toward the house. Having made sure they weren't being watched, he came back, brushed past her legs, crossed the lane to the edge of the meadow, and looked back at her expectantly.

Portia watched all this with increasing fascination. What was happening here was basically impossible. A tickle stirred underneath her breastbone, and the desire to follow the fox pulled at her like the wind tugging a sail. But she mustn't give in to that wish. That would be absolutely ridiculous, perhaps even dangerous.

Then again, what was the worst thing that could happen if she did follow him? Just a little way, just to see what he would do next. Bramble and Rose didn't have to find out. They would think she was out and about with Ben.

I'll just follow it a little way, she thought. The voice of reason in her mind was about to protest, but Portia had made her decision and silenced it. She looked back to the house one last time, then picked up her backpack. Was it her imagination, or did the fox curl its lips into a smile?

"Go on, then. Show me where you want to go," she muttered.

The fox crossed the meadow, slipped underneath a fence, and went on into the woods. The further they went, the faster it trotted. Every time Portia dropped behind, it paused and waited; it clearly wanted her to keep up, and it was obviously leading her somewhere. They left the shelter of

42

the forest, went down a broom-covered slope, then skirted the shore of a lake, before diving back into the woods. From there on, the going got steadily steeper, and Portia worked up a sweat. The fox ran up the hillside ahead of her, slipping nimbly between rocks and tree trunks. There was no path, but Portia wasn't worried about losing her way. Down below, the lake glittered like a mirror between the trees. She was confident she would be able to find her way back again at any time.

In fact, she was feeling more and more at ease, walking through the beautiful, unfamiliar landscape. Aside from herself and the fox, the hillside was deserted. No hikers in colorful jackets, no groups of students out for an excursion. The only sound was the faint whine of a chain saw coming from the other side of the hill, but soon that faded away too.

Portia and the fox climbed still further up the hillside. The tree trunks were covered in thick, shaggy moss now. Ferns sprawled between rocks, and the ground was a soft carpet of dead leaves.

Glancing down to the side, Portia realized that the lake had disappeared, hidden by a mass of rocks and ferns. She stopped, but then heard the fox yapping a little further ahead. Portia set off again, following the sound of its call. Scrambling up the slope, she skirted round a large rock, and then at last she saw it.

In a clearing fringed by oak trees and dense undergrowth loomed the remnants of a gray stone wall. Portia stepped closer. A pair of oak trees had grown up against the wall, framing an old door like two columns.

The fox was pacing back and forth in the doorway. As Portia approached, it stopped and stood still, with only its bushy tail twitching to and fro.

Portia ran her fingers over the door. The wood was rough and worm-eaten, covered with a wrought-iron pattern of leaves. From the center of the door hung an iron ring, with a rusty lock below it. She touched the lock with her fingertips and glanced down at the fox.

"Let me guess," she said. "That's what the key is for."

The fox's ears twitched. Portia pulled the key from her pocket. Walls like these often ran around the grounds of old manor houses. But why would Bramble hide the key to a remote country estate in her desk? And what was hidden behind the door? Portia took a step back and tried to see whether there was another way to get around the wall—but a mass of blackberry bushes formed an impenetrable natural barrier. The only way to the other side was through that door.

Portia weighed the key in her hand. Now that she was here, she might as well see if it fit. She put the key in the lock and looked at the fox. It didn't move, but its eyes seemed to shine. Portia turned the key, pulled at the iron ring, and opened the door.

She was hit by a gust of cold air that filled her nose with the scent of damp grass. Goose bumps ran down her neck, and the hair on her forearms stood on end. Was this how an archaeologist felt when they pried open the door to a pharaoh's sealed tomb?

She had barely gotten the door open when the fox dashed past her, leaping across the threshold in a flash of red fur.

Portia hesitated. She could feel her heart beating against her ribs as another gust of cold air came rushing through the doorway. She felt as if she were standing in the middle of a hurricane, and if she let go, she would be whirled away by the wind.

What if there was a magical place waiting on the other side? A secret place, that she would be the first to discover? That was nonsense of course, but her heart still raced faster at the idea. She spared a brief thought for Bramble and Rose, and for her mum, who would be worried sick if she got lost somewhere in the Welsh wilderness. She should really go back. But every centimeter of her body was longing for an adventure, however small.

The fox barked on the other side of the wall. It was strange, but despite all her worries, Portia had the feeling that she was in the right place at the right time. She pulled the key from the lock and stepped through the arched doorway to the other side. She didn't bother closing the door behind her.

ॐ BEN ॐ

Ben stood at the counter of the pharmacist in Llanrwst, waiting for Mr. Duke, the pharmacist, to come back from his storage room. In front of him on the countertop stood the carefully covered blackbird's cage. The bird seemed calm just now, but Ben expected it to start fluttering again at any moment.

When he had come back into his room that morning after breakfast, the bird had been hopping about so frantically that Ben was worried it might hurt itself. Megan was already on her way to the bookshop, and Ben had been planning to cycle to Afallon—but the bird just wouldn't settle down. Flapping its healthy wing, it had bashed its body against the cage bars again and again. In the end, Ben couldn't take it anymore. After throwing on a jacket, he took the cage and headed into Llanrwst.

As he arrived at the pharmacist, he realized he should have called Afallon. Was Portia waiting for him? Probably. If he hadn't made a terrible impression yesterday, he must have done now. He told himself he didn't care, but that wasn't entirely true.

Behind the counter, Mr. Duke's trainee was sorting pill packages on the shelves while humming a tune. Ben caught himself tapping his fingers to it. Then Mr. Duke returned, a little bottle in his hand.

"Here you go," he said. "That's much better than what young Davies prescribed."

Ben had stopped by the vet's office first. Dr. Davies had told him there was nothing more he could do but had sent Ben to the pharmacist to pick up a sedative for the bird.

Ben looked skeptically at the little bottle in Mr. Duke's hand.

"What?" Mr. Duke snapped. "It's valerian. Works just as well as that chemical brew that whippersnapper of a vet recommended. And it's far less harmful."

Ben was already familiar with Mr. Duke's tirades—he had

a habit of complaining about both doctors and vets.

"Amateurs, the lot of them." Mr. Duke pulled the cloth off the birdcage. The bird sat staring at them from its perch. "Now, just you be reasonable and let us help you," he said, pouring a few drops of valerian into the bird's drinking water. Then he covered the cage with the cloth again, and Ben felt himself relax.

"You can keep the bottle. But it's for the bird only, got it? Don't even think about taking a little sip."

"No, absolutely not," Ben assured him. Then he pocketed the little bottle and made a bolt for it.

Outside the pharmacist, Ben strapped the cage to his bike rack. The bird stayed calm. Perhaps the valerian was already working? He tucked the cloth in place and set off home.

Pushing his bike down the street, he wondered how he was going to confess to his mum that he had flaked on Portia. He knew exactly how she would react: she'd make him go and apologize.

Ben was already imagining that ordeal in excruciating detail when he saw a solution to his problem further down the hillside. The Afallon women's old Nissan was sitting in the supermarket parking lot, and Rose was just stepping out of the shop, a shopping bag in each hand. Ben's heart leapt. He would explain to Rose why he hadn't been able to make it to Afallon today, and she would pass on his apology to Portia. Perhaps Mum would be satisfied with that?

Yeah, right, thought Ben. Still, he couldn't miss this opportunity. He hopped onto his bike and sped down the steep road. Down in the parking lot, Rose had finished packing her shopping into the trunk and was walking to the driver's side. She was going to leave before he could get there! Ben bit his lower lip, plucked up some courage, and began frantically ringing his bike bell.

He had just called Rose's name when the bird started panicking. It chirped and flapped about so fiercely that its cage started to shake and rattle behind Ben's back. Startled, Ben twisted around to look, but as he did so, he jerked the handlebars, causing the bike to fishtail. The back wheel skidded out to one side, sending the bike, Ben, and the cage hurtling to the ground.

Someone called out to him, but Ben didn't care. He got back to his feet, ignoring the stinging pain in his arm.

The cage had landed on its side next to the bike, still covered by the cloth. Ben's fear at what might have happened to the bird clutched like a cold fist at his insides.

"Ben!"

He turned around to see Rose running toward him, her skirt flapping around her legs. Still slightly dazed from his fall, he stepped over the bike and squatted down next to the battered cage. The fluttering sounds had stopped. His heart pounding, he pulled the cloth aside, expecting to find the bird lying there with a broken neck. Tears blurred his eyes, but he quickly wiped them away. When he lowered his hand, what he saw made him freeze; instead of the bird, a tiny man was kneeling inside the overturned cage.

The ground seemed to shift beneath Ben's feet.

"Oh, Ben, are you all right?" Rose crouched down next to

him, putting her hands on his shoulders. "Ben, what . . . ,"
she began again, but then fell silent. Ben knew why. She
had seen the man in the cage too. The tiny, impossible
man, who raised his head at the sound of her voice, then
struggled to his feet. He was wearing a robe as black as the
blackbird's plumage. He held his right arm—*his wing*, Ben
thought—pressed protectively against his chest.

I must be concussed, thought Ben. He was clearly halluci-
nating. That was the only possible explanation.

The man in the cage turned toward Rose and gave a digni-
fied bow. "Viola Rosethorn," he said in a voice surprisingly
deep for a man his size. "It pains me that we meet again
under such circumstances, but I am the bearer of terrible
news." He stepped nimbly across the grid at the bottom of
the cage until he was holding the bars in his tiny fists. "And
time is short."

The birdman can talk, Ben thought. *Of course he can*. He
wasn't even surprised to hear him call Rose "Viola." Even
stranger was Rose's reaction.

Her hands slid off his shoulders. She reached out to touch
the cage with her fingertips.

"Ridik ap Mwyalchod, my old friend," she said in a hoarse
voice. "What happened?"

The birdman leaned forward and placed his uninjured
hand against Rose's finger. "It's Goodfellow," he said. "He
has opened the door."

Between Worlds

Rose raced along the winding lane. Ben sat in the Nissan passenger seat, pressing his feet into the bottom of the footwell as if he might be able to brake the car himself if he pushed hard enough. His hands were cupped in his lap, where Ridik ap Mwyalchod sat on his upturned palms. The tiny man felt warm against his skin, and his robe was as soft as a bird's feathers. His mere existence was so incredible that Ben could hardly tear his eyes away. The boy's left forearm was badly grazed, but he barely felt the burning pain.

He stared and stared at Ridik. He was holding a magical creature in his very hands! A living, breathing magical creature! He hadn't felt such a tingle of excitement in his stomach in a long while.

When he was little, his parents had always prepared a surprise for his birthday. A bunch of colorful balloons, a dragon carved from a cucumber. Mum and Dad had always had the best ideas. On his fifth birthday he'd gone out fishing with his grandfather and discovered a forest on his bedroom wall when he got home. His parents had been standing in the doorway, his dad with a splash of paint on his cheek.

When he looked at Ridik, he felt the same excitement as he had that day when he had stepped into his room to see the Wild Things romping among exotic palm trees on his wall.

"You must be mistaken," said Rose from the driver's seat.

"I'm afraid not," Ridik replied. "I can feel the shift in the air."

"He can't have opened the door," Rose insisted. "There's no key."

Ben looked down at the tiny man, who gave no reply.

"Ridik?" Rose pressed.

"Goodfellow always said he didn't believe you really got rid of the key."

"But we did!" Rose exclaimed. "Dear Lord, we'd have been foolish to keep it."

"And you took care of it yourself?" Ridik asked, a hint of hope in his voice.

"Bramble did," Rose said. "She threw it into the lake."

"Did you see her do it, Mistress Rosethorn?"

"Well, no, I . . ." Rose broke off. She stared straight ahead through the windshield, a realization visibly dawning on her. Then she sank down slightly into her seat as if someone had placed a heavy weight on her shoulders. "No."

She turned the Nissan off the road and onto a dirt track leading into the woods. It was an access path that only foresters were allowed to use, but Rose didn't seem to care.

"Rose?" asked Ben. "Can I ask you a question?"

Rose chuckled drily. "I'm sure you have plenty of questions, Ben," she said. "But even if I could answer all of them, you probably wouldn't believe me."

Ben looked back to Ridik. "I'm not sure about that."

Rose shook her head. "Where should I begin? With the Door Between Worlds? The key? The Gray King?"

"Perhaps we might begin with me?" Ridik asked softly. He turned around and looked up at Ben. "Allow me to introduce myself. My name is Ridik ap Mwyalchod. The blackbird's son. Scout of the Adar."

"The Adar?" Ben repeated. He knew enough Welsh to understand the word. "Scout of the birds?"

"Indeed."

Ben was about to ask more questions, when suddenly he remembered something. He had seen Ridik before! There was a drawing of a tiny man in one of Bramble's books who looked just like him!

"*In the Forest of Talking Birds*!" he exclaimed. "The blackbird scout Bramble wrote about . . . That was you, Ridik. . . . I mean, that was you, Mr. ap Mwyalchod, wasn't it?"

Ridik smiled. "It was an honor to serve as inspiration for one of Mistress Brambleblossom's characters."

"But then . . ." Ben's thoughts turned somersaults in his head. "Everything else in that book, the flying frogs, the fairies, that's all real as well? Bramble didn't just make it up?"

"Oh, she does have a very vivid imagination, I will say that," Ridik said, and smirked. "But she's also well versed in the art of describing things she's seen with her own eyes. She has the heart and talent of a true bard, no doubt."

"That's true enough," Rose said darkly. "She's always been a good storyteller."

Ridik flashed her a glance. "I'm certain she had a good reason for not telling you about the key, my lady."

"You mean a good reason for lying to me," said Rose. The crease between her brows deepened. "That's why Robin has been trying to break into our house all this time. That's why he stole from us. *Damio*, Bramble! How could anyone be so foolish!" She pounded the steering wheel with the heel of her hand and stepped on the accelerator, making the engine roar. "If Robin leaves the door open . . ."

". . . then all of our struggles have been in vain," Ridik replied, finishing her sentence. Then he doubled over, his face contorted in a grimace of pain.

Ben moved his thumb a bit so Ridik could lean against it. Then he looked over at Rose. "What door?"

✍ PORTIA ✎

Portia followed the fox through a meadow of wildflowers, then a grove of oaks, going further and further into the hills. *I'll keep going until I can see the next road.* That's what she'd told herself when they went through the door, but by now they'd been walking for ages without a road in sight. At first, the thrill of excitement had drowned out everything else, but now she was conscious of a small but growing feeling of unease in her belly.

Perhaps it was because the weather was beginning to turn. Dark clouds were gathering overhead, there was a chilly edge to the wind, and Portia thought she could smell a hint of rain in the air. They'd also been traipsing up and down hillsides for what seemed like forever without stopping for a rest. Portia had no idea how long they had been walking for. When she checked her phone, she saw that the display was pitch black. The battery must have died. If only she'd remembered to charge it last night.

She really wished she knew what time it was.

The hillside they were walking up now was getting more and more wet underfoot. The grass was giving way to clumps of wild heather, with large boggy puddles in between. The mountains lay beyond the treetops like sleeping giants. They had definitely inched closer now.

Portia looked up at the sky. The clouds were blocking out the sun, so it was impossible to tell how low it had sunk. Had Rose and Bramble realized by now that she had set off on her own?

She stopped, gnawing nervously at a fingernail. For the first time, she was really aware of the stillness surrounding her. There was no birdsong, no revving of distant engines. Nothing but the sound of heather quietly rustling in the wind. Goose bumps crept across her skin, making her wish she had brought a jacket. She looked around her, trying to see which direction they had come from, but the oak grove was nowhere to be seen, and she had left no footprints on the soft ground between the clumps of heather. Had they been walking across the marshy hillside in a straight line or in an arc?

She would have loved to turn around now, to follow her tracks all the way back to that strange door, and to Afallon beyond. But she was long past the point where she could still have found her way home.

ঔ BEN ঙ

"Damn it, Robin." Rose stared at the open door in the crumbling wall, with clenched fists. Ridik, still standing on Ben's palm, gasped with shock.

Ben looked around him. He knew these woods. His parents had brought him here to forage for mushrooms a few times. He'd never seen that door on any of their trips, though. It wasn't that surprising—there were no walking trails leading to the clearing where it stood.

"How long has the door been open?" Rose asked.

"Hard to say," Ridik replied. "But I wouldn't be surprised if Goodfellow is nearly at the second door."

Doors leading to other worlds. Kingdoms full of fairies and other magical creatures. It all sounded like something from a book to Ben, not like real life. But he had witnessed Ridik transform from bird to man with his own eyes—that sight had shifted the boundaries between *impossible* and *possible* in his head. It was an amazing feeling, even though Rose was clearly very worried about the open door, and Ben realized that he should be too.

And yet—when he looked through the door, he felt a warm thrill of anticipation deep inside.

Rose whipped out her cell phone and began writing a text message.

"The second door," Ben began. "Does it really lead to Faerie?"

"Oh, yes," Ridik said. "The door in front of you was built by druids, wise women and men in ancient times. It leads from the Human World into the Borderlands. The second door awaits at the border of my world. My home. Faerie, as you call it."

Ben was eager to ask more questions, but Ridik peered over the edge of his palm, down at the forest floor. "Could you please put me down?" he asked.

Ben squatted and let the tiny man walk from his hand to the ground. Ridik walked back and forth through the carpet of long-dead leaves. He seemed to be searching for something. Ben stepped closer to the door and lightly brushed it with his fingertips. The doorframe was twined about with brambles. Beyond it, the forest gave way to a meadow. High grass swayed gently in the wind. Above, a pair of white butterflies tumbled in the air.

The Nissan trunk slammed shut. Ben flinched guiltily, pulling his hand back from the door. He hadn't seen Rose go back to the car. Now she came back across the clearing with a rake in her hand and a face as dark and menacing as a storm cloud. Ben's gaze had wandered back to the door when he felt a tugging at this trouser leg.

He looked down to see Ridik clutching the hem of his jeans in one tiny hand. He stared up at the boy, a solemn look on his face.

"Better keep your distance, young Ben."

"But are the worlds beyond the door dangerous?" Ben asked.

"Every world has its own danger," Ridik said. "But in the Borderlands between the worlds anything could happen. There the Gray King awaits, and who can tell what else might emerge from the cracks between the Here and There."

These words made Ben's blood run cold. "Why is this Goodfellow opening these doors?"

"Because he wants to go home," Ridik said simply.

Ben frowned. He had assumed that Robin Goodfellow was the villain of this story—but it almost sounded as if Ridik had some sympathy for the key thief.

"Why did he leave the Human Door open, though?" Ben wondered aloud.

"Because he's angry," said Rose. "He has been for forty years."

She had pulled the metal head from the wooden shaft of the rake and began to carve something into the wood with a pocketknife.

"If Goodfellow's going to get to the second door soon, shouldn't we hurry?" Ben asked.

"We?" repeated Rose. "No chance. You're going home now,

Ben." She blew a few wood shavings off the shaft and put her knife away before resting her hand on Ben's shoulder. "It's bad enough me dragging you all the way out here into the woods after the fall you've had. I'm certainly not going to take you any deeper into this whole mess."

Ben opened his mouth to argue, but she shook her head. "No. The only foolish human passing through this door today is me."

Ben felt a wave of disappointment rolling through him. Then Ridik cleared his throat.

"That's not quite true, Mistress Rosethorn," he said.

Rose stared down at him. "What are you saying?"

"Goodfellow was not alone," replied Ridik. "I found human footprints."

"Bramble?" Rose's hand tightened on Ben's shoulder.

"No, these footprints are too small. They belong to a child."

"Portia," groaned Rose, screwing her eyes up and raking her fingers through her hair. Alarmed, Ben looked back toward the door. How had Portia fallen in with such questionable company?

"Who is this Portia?" asked Ridik.

"My great-niece," explained Rose. "She must have found the key among Bramble's things. I wondered what she was up to in that office!"

"Do you think Goodfellow has persuaded her to help him?"

"My guess is that he tricked her. That would be just like him." She swore again. "Ben is right—we have to hurry.

Perhaps we can reach them before he rouses the Gray King from his sleep."

With each word Rose spoke, Ben's disappointment grew. How often had he dreamt of climbing into one of his books? Of exploring foreign lands, riding a dragon, or swimming with mermaids? And, just when he'd found out that those fantastic worlds were real, he was supposed to just turn round and go home? To the dog-eared old copy of *The Hobbit* tucked underneath his pillow? To his dad's favorite mug gathering dust on a shelf in the kitchen?

Something snapped inside him. Suddenly the idea of walking away from all this seemed unbearable. He clenched his fists and screwed up all his courage.

"I'm coming with you."

"What did you say?" asked Rose distractedly.

Ben thrust out his chin, determined. "I'm coming with you," he repeated.

"Ben, we don't have time for—"

"If you won't take me with you, I'll just follow you," he cut in.

Ben had never argued with a grown-up like this before. He could feel himself going red, and a prickly sweat broke out on his brow. But he forced himself to look Rose in the eye.

"This day just gets better and better," murmured Rose. "Ah well." She beckoned Ben over and rested her hand on his shoulder once more.

"When we are on the other side of the door, you do everything I say, okay? No hesitating, no questions. Understood?"

The relief made Ben's knees feel as wobbly as jelly. He nodded.

Rose gave his shoulder a quick squeeze. "Good. Stay close to me," she said, her voice softer now. Then she looked down at Ridik. "Think you can catch up with Goodfellow?"

"I can try," he replied. "Young Ben, kindly pick me up so that I can sit on your shoulder."

Ben did as he was told. "Are you going to shape-shift again?"

Ridik smiled. "I will have wings, yes. And so will you."

Rose took Ben's hand in hers. "The scouts of the Adar possess the gift of swiftflight," she explained. "As soon as we pass through the door, Ridik will grant us magical speed. It will be as if we were wearing seven-league boots." She turned to Ridik again. "Will you be able to cope with your broken arm?"

"I'll manage," he said.

"Then let's go." Rose gripped the rake shaft in one hand and Ben's hand in the other. Together they walked toward the door. Rose went through the archway first. Ben felt a shiver of excitement as he stepped through in turn. He heard Ridik whispering words in an unknown language, followed by what sounded like the beating of an enormous wing. Then a current of air sucked him forward through the doorway.

The Faerie Door

The clouds were so low that the mountaintops in the distance had disappeared behind a shroud of mist. The wind was whistling more fiercely across the heather now, carrying the smell of brackish water to Portia's nose.

Her feet were hurting, but she kept on walking. She still hadn't given up hope of coming across a road or a house. Portia stepped over a tuft of heather and up onto one of the grassy tussocks that stuck out of the marsh.

She caught sight of the fox up ahead, and then for the first time she saw where it must be taking her. Beyond the high moor a long, low rocky slope rose out of the heather like a sea monster's scaly back. And standing right in the middle of the slope was . . . Portia felt as if the ground was giving way beneath her feet. Cut into the rocky hillside was a second door.

She marched on mechanically, until she fell to her knees in front of the door. There was no crumbling wall this time. Instead two rough-hewn stone pillars protruding from the ground, with a third pillar resting on top as a lintel. The wooden door itself was inlaid with carved, knotted patterns. On either side of the doorway grew a rowan tree, their intertwined branches forming an archway above the stone pillars.

The fox was sitting underneath the left-hand tree, watching Portia expectantly. Portia stared right back.

She felt sick with exhaustion and fear. She had no way of getting her bearings and finding her way back home to Afallon. Another door was all there was. A spark of fury flickered in her chest. Fury at herself for not turning around when there was still time. For being foolish enough to follow the fox in the first place. And at the fox, too, who didn't seem to care about her suffering, and who was probably even taking pleasure in having tricked her.

Portia scowled down at the fox. "I don't know what's going on here," she said, "but I've had enough. I'm going back." As she spoke, her resolve strengthened. The fox narrowed its eyes to mere slits.

Portia struggled to her feet. "I'm going back," she repeated, turning to leave. She'd go back to the cottage and make herself a big mug of tea. Then she'd snuggle up in Rose's reading chair, and for the rest of her vacation she'd look for adventures only between the pages of a book.

"Please don't do that." Portia flinched so violently at the sound of the voice that she almost fell to her knees again. She jerked around, her heart hammering in her chest.

The fox was nowhere to be seen. Instead a man stood by the door. He was tall and slender, wearing a white shirt and sandy trousers with blades of grass sticking to them. His hair was the same shade of coppery red as the fox's fur.

Portia's mouth was suddenly bone dry. *No. What you're thinking is impossible. It can't be real.*

The man took a step toward her, and she backed away.

"Hey, there," said the stranger, smiling. "We've been such good friends up until now, haven't we?"

Portia's head was spinning. She wanted to run, but her legs felt as heavy as lead.

"I won't stop you from going home," the man assured her in a voice like honey. "I won't keep you. We just need to unlock this door." He squatted down in front of Portia and held out his hand. His eyes were the color of dark amber.

Fox eyes, thought Portia, and shuddered.

"The key," he said. "Please."

With trembling fingers, she produced the key from her pocket. The man snatched it from her hand, pressed it to his lips, and briefly closed his eyes. Then he rose and walked back to the door.

"Do me a favor, Portia," he said without turning around. "Go back to the women in Afallon and tell them the key is truly gone now. They no longer need to lie about it." He pushed the key into the lock and placed the palm of his hand on the door.

"What?" Portia croaked.

"They won't have much time for regrets," he said. "Before the fog rolls in."

He turned the key in the lock and opened the door. A gust of wind hit Portia in the face. The red-haired man glanced up to the sky. He hesitated for a moment, then took the key out of the lock and stepped through the doorway.

Traveling with Ridik was the most peculiar thing Ben had ever experienced. In one sense, he felt as if he were standing still while the landscape rushed past him. In another, it was as if he were striding into a strong wind that parted and flowed around him like water.

There was one last wingbeat; then suddenly Ben was standing by Rose's side on a wide-open moor. He staggered, unsteady on his feet, as if he had just stepped off a ship onto solid ground—although this particular ground didn't feel very solid. Were those tufts of grass and heather really moving under his feet, or was it just his wobbly legs?

A small hand grabbed Ben's shoulder. "Here we are!" said Ridik, panting.

Ben jerked up his head. Right ahead of them, on the edge of the moor, a rocky ridge rose from the ground. In it stood a door framed by two trees. And in front of the door stood a man who looked as if he was just about to pull it open.

"Quick!" Ridik's voice sounded like a rasping caw. Rose started running, and Ben stumbled after her. Then he noticed the small figure with a head of black curls standing stiffly to one side of the Faerie Door. *Portia!*

The man stepped through the doorway and made to pull it shut behind him.

"Robin!" Rose yelled. "Don't do it!"

Portia spun around and stared first at Rose, then Ben. She looked exhausted, pale, and disheveled. Ben stopped at her side, panting heavily. Portia gently touched his arm, as if she couldn't quite believe that he was really there.

"He's got the key!" Ridik shouted.

Rose rushed toward the archway and seized the edge of the door with both hands. The man on the other side let out an angry howl and fiercely tried to yank the door shut, but Rose dug her heels into the ground.

"Robin, please," she pleaded, "give me the key!"

For a moment, there was silence. Then they heard a voice so deep, it sounded like a growl: "The key. So that's why you're here."

"Robin . . ."

"All these years," the man said. "All these years, you swore there was no way back."

"But I didn't know!" Rose exclaimed. Her left foot was being dragged across the ground now, but she didn't let go of the door. "Robin, I really didn't know."

"So she lied to you too? Well, well. A fine companion you picked."

Rose would not be deterred. "I'm begging you," she pleaded. "You know very well what will happen if the door to our world remains open."

All of a sudden the door flew open, sending Rose tumbling backward. She scrambled back to her feet. A tall, slender man, Robin Goodfellow stood in the doorway, towering over Rose by at least a head. His hands were raised in front of him, his fists clenched. A memory flashed through Ben's mind. It was the man from the bookshop!

The man who had been watching Portia, right before Ridik had crashed into the window.

"Perhaps that's exactly what I want," Robin hissed. "Perhaps it would only be fair for you to realize what it feels like to lose your world."

Rose stood tall. She was silent now, watching Robin intently. He stared back, his chest rising and falling, as if his rage was billowing inside him like a storm. Was he going to attack Rose? Ben found he was clenching his own fists, his fingernails digging into the palms of his hands.

"Come on now," whispered Ridik, and then Robin finally dropped his hands to his side. Without a word, Rose held out her own hand for the key.

"Hmmm," Robin bristled, as if disgusted by the whole situation. Then he curled his lips into a smile that was entirely devoid of friendliness.

"Portia!" he called. "Thank you for your help." He threw the key toward her, and it landed right by her feet. Then he turned to face Rose one last time. "Don't ever come back here."

"We won't—" Rose began, but Robin cut her short.

"But of course I'm well aware how much your word is worth. *We're not leaving anyone behind.* I wonder whether Hermia believed you too?"

Rose flinched as if he had slapped her. Then Robin stepped backward through the archway and pulled the door shut with a bang.

⌒

For a moment, Ben and the others stood in silence. Then Rose came alive with a jolt, marched over to Portia, and picked up the key that lay on the ground in front of her. She pushed it into the keyhole and turned it twice, before pulling it free and stuffing it into her skirt pocket.

Ben looked about him, taking in their surroundings properly for the first time. The moor lay in a saddle-shaped depression between two ridges whose tops were shrouded in clouds. The wind had dropped, and the air felt damp. If he was reading weather correctly, they would soon be immersed in a gray soup of fog.

Portia was the first to move. She sat down on a flat rock, curled up with her head resting on her knees, as if she was refusing to acknowledge the whole crazy situation. Ben felt as if he should go over and comfort her, but what could he do really? Give her a pat on the back and tell her to cheer up?

Rose beat him to it anyway. She knelt down in front of Portia and cupped the girl's head in her hands, gently brushing the hair from her face. "Oh, Portia," she said softly. "Girl, what on earth are you doing here?"

Portia mumbled something that Ben couldn't make out. She raised her head and opened her mouth as if she was about to tell Rose everything—but then her gaze wandered back to Ridik. She shook her head in disbelief and buried her face in her palms. "It's all a bad joke, isn't it? It must be."

Rose gave her a quick hug. "I promise I'll explain everything as soon as we're back home," she said. "Okay?" Then she looked at Ridik.

He nodded. "We shouldn't waste any more time."

While Ridik got to his feet, Rose held out a hand and pulled Portia back to her feet. "Now, this may feel a little strange," she warned.

Portia shot Ben a questioning, almost desperate glance, but he had barely opened his mouth to reply when the strong winds of the swiftflight surged about them.

The Gray Riders

The world dissolved into a swirl of wind and flowing colors. Portia held her breath as she was yanked over the shifting landscape below like a fish on a hook. Only a few seconds later, with a wingbeat as loud as a thunderclap, the world snapped into place again. Portia stared about her, wide-eyed. The moor had disappeared. She was standing in a grove of gnarled oak trees.

A wave of nausea rose in her stomach, making her gasp. She held on to the straps of her backpack, closed her eyes, and took deep breaths. In, out . . . In, out . . .

"Are you okay?" someone asked.

Portia opened her eyes to see Ben's concerned face. "Yeah, fine. Aside from the fact that I've lost my mind."

Ben ventured a cautious grin. Portia smiled back, and the urge to throw up finally went away. She took a breath of cool air, brushing the curls from her forehead with a trembling hand. She recognized the oak grove they were standing in. Just past it was the meadow, and beyond that, the first door that she had opened for the fox. The fox who had turned out to be a man.

She turned to face Ben. "I'm not imagining this, am I? This is all really happening."

Ben nodded, and then glanced at the tiny man crouching on his shoulder.

"I am very sorry," the man croaked weakly.

Rose joined them and held out her hand. "No reason to apologize, Ridik. You've taken us far enough. Thank you."

The tiny man briefly pressed his forehead against the back of her hand and gave her an exhausted smile. Rose smiled back before marching toward the edge of the forest at a brisk pace. "Let's go."

Ben followed her without hesitation, and Portia followed in his wake. She still didn't understand how the others had found her, or what was going on. Why was Rose accepting everything so calmly? Yes, she seemed tense, but otherwise completely unimpressed by all the miniature humans and the foxes turning into people. It even looked like she was friends with the tiny person sitting on Ben's shoulder. And then there was that broomstick-like staff that Rose was carrying like a samurai sword. Who *was* Rose, really?

At the forest's edge, Rose came to a halt and raised her hand. Ben stopped immediately, but Portia passed him to stand by Rose's side. Wisps of gray fog were drifting across the meadow like soap bubbles on bathwater.

Rose bit her lower lip and drummed her fingers on the staff, lost in thought. On the other side of the meadow, no more than fifty meters way, the door in the wall was waiting for them.

"We're not going to make it," the tiny man said. What had Rose called him? Ridik?

Rose came to life again. "We have to." She turned to Portia and Ben. "Stay close behind me."

Portia shot Ben a questioning glance, but he just shrugged. He obviously didn't understand what was going on any more than she did.

One by one, they stepped out of the safety of the woods.

They began to walk across the foggy field, cleaving through curtains of mist. With every step, the haze grew denser, until they could barely make out the door on the other side of the meadow. Then, about halfway across, Rose stopped.

"They're here," she murmured.

To their right, from somewhere in the swirling mist, came a whinnying sound, followed by the muted drumming of hooves. Portia was instantly covered in icy goose bumps.

Ridik straightened up and stared intently in the direction of the sounds.

"What on earth?" Portia said in a low voice. She reached out and took Ben's hand. He jumped in surprise before giving her fingers a reassuring squeeze.

Rose raised her staff to her lips and seemed to whisper to it. As she spoke, a web of glowing blue veins appeared on the wood, like the veins of a leaf.

Ben gasped. Portia just stared, wide-eyed. This couldn't be happening!

"Rose—" she began, in a small, frightened voice, but the older woman cut her off.

"Keep calm," she said, stepping in front of Portia and Ben, holding the staff ready at her side. Portia noticed blue lines glowing on the inside of her wrist as well. *Her tattoo*, Portia thought, but then all thoughts were washed away like a sandcastle by the tide.

Just a few meters away from Rose, a horse emerged from the mist, snorting and pawing at the ground with its gray hooves.

"Nazgûl," mumbled Ben.

Portia shuddered. The rider was wearing a hooded robe. Both man and horse looked as if they were made of fog, their outlines fraying at the edges like skeins of smoke.

Just then a dog appeared at the horse's side. Portia backed away automatically. It was a big, wiry beast with a long snout, a white coat, and ears as red as if they had been dipped in blood. Its eyes blazed like headlights on a foggy night.

Ben flinched at the sight of the animal too, and Portia heard Ridik breathing heavily on his shoulder.

"To the door," Rose said calmly. "Now."

She had barely finished speaking when the rider raised a hand, and the dog bolted forward across the meadow toward them. Ben was squeezing Portia's hand so hard, it almost hurt. They both stumbled backward and froze, unable to run.

Rose stood stock-still, not moving an inch. Only when the dog was almost upon them, about to spring, did she spin around, whipping her staff through the air and hitting the beast in its flank. The pattern on the staff glowed brightly, glittered—and then, suddenly, the dog was gone.

"Watch out!" Ridik yelled.

While Rose had been fending off the dog's attack, the rider had spurred his horse toward the door. Rose ran across the meadow to block his path. The rider pulled hard on his reins, making the horse rear up, its hooves beating the air. Rose swayed backward and struck out with her staff, hitting the horse on the leg. The blue pattern glowed brightly once more, and a fizzing sound rent the air. The rider grabbed at Rose, but she ducked underneath his arm, caught hold of his robe, and pulled him from his saddle. As he fell, Rose swung her staff again, and this time the horse burst apart in an explosion of fog and smoke. Then, before the rider could get to his feet, she spun around, raised the staff over her head, and thrust it down. There was a flash of blue light, and the rider vanished, as if he had never been there at all.

Portia stood in silence, open-mouthed. Ben let go of her hand and took a few dazed steps toward Rose. Fog surged and broke around her, like waves against a rock.

"Rose?" Ben had hardly uttered her name, when from the depths of the fog came a thundering sound of hoofbeats, growing louder and louder.

That's not just one horse. That's a lot of horses, Portia thought. *And they're all galloping our way!*

"Too late!" Ridik said, his voice a warning. "Too late!"

Just then a rider burst out of the fog, tearing toward the open door. He was too fast and too far away for Rose to stop him. Roaring with frustration, she spun around. "Ridik!"

The tiny man stood up on Ben's shoulder, holding his

arms out straight from his body. His cloak of feathers seemed to puff up for a moment before he leapt into the air and shifted into his blackbird shape in the blink of an eye. Portia could hardly believe what she was seeing. As swift as an arrow, the blackbird man shot toward the gray rider. Rose was running too, her staff held firmly in one hand and the other thrust into her skirt pocket.

The key, Portia remembered, and that thought finally jolted her back into action. She grabbed Ben's sleeve. "Come on! Quickly!"

For a moment he stared at her, frozen, but then he too seemed to come to his senses. They set off running across the meadow toward the door. Portia's backpack banged awkwardly against her back as she ran, but the straps were done up too tightly for her to just drop it.

In the meantime, the blackbird had caught up with the rider. It flew a tight circle around the horse's head, making it shy up, before the bird dove toward the rider's face, its tiny claws outstretched.

"Ridik!" Ben stumbled, but Portia grabbed his arm and pulled him to his feet again. Another dog appeared, tearing past them so close that Portia felt a buffet of air as it barreled by. It wasn't after them this time. It was making straight for—

"Rose!" Portia yelled. Up ahead, Rose had reached the wall and slammed the door shut. She spun around just as the dog leapt. This time the beast caught her staff in its fangs, splintering the wood, but Rose swung her weapon in a wide arc, flinging the dog away from her. Barely had it landed when it scrambled to its feet and leapt again, but this time Rose was ready. She thrust the staff into the dog's body, and it vanished in a blaze of blue light.

At the same moment, Ben cried out in alarm. Portia whirled around to see a second horse rearing wildly as the blackbird kept up its darting attacks on its rider. Struggling with the reins, he lashed out frantically until finally one of his blows hit home, knocking the bird from the air.

"No!" Ben yelled, and started to run toward the fallen bird.

Rose swore and pulled the key from her pocket. Before Portia had time to realize what was happening, Rose had locked the door and was sprinting over to Ben, who was kneeling over the blackbird. The gray horse was still agitated, and Ben would have been crushed under its hooves had Rose not arrived in the nick of time to snatch the reins and drag it aside.

As she did so, the rider sent a long streak of fog lashing toward her like a whip. Rose cried out in pain as the gray tendril coiled around her forearm. She pulled herself away, tearing free of the foggy rope just as the rider prepared to attack again.

Portia ran over to Ben too, even though the further away she got from the door the louder the alarm bells rang in her head. *This is bad. This is very bad,* she thought despairingly. They needed to get away from here and back through the door before more of those riders showed up.

Ben was crouching in the grass, bent over Ridik's body. As Portia reached him, she saw that he was holding the blackbird in his hands. Portia felt a stab in her heart when she noticed his twisted wing, but there was no time for sorrow now. She grabbed Ben's arm and pulled, but he didn't budge.

"Come on!" she hissed. But Ben didn't even lift his head. Frantically she looked over to Rose for help, but she had her hands full. The rider was sending whip after foggy whip toward her, like a knife thrower at a circus. Rose was managing to dodge his attacks, but in doing so she was retreating further and further from the door. Panic rose in Portia's throat, but then she understood that Rose was deliberately steering the rider away from her and Ben. As soon as she had drawn him far enough, she caught one of the nasty fog whips on the tip of her staff. The rider tried to retreat when he realized what was happening, but his own weapon would be his undoing. Portia could see now that those swirls of fog were a part of the rider, attached to him like an octopus's tentacles. And one of those tentacles was tightly coiled around Rose's staff.

Rose smiled, grim and determined. She clutched the staff more tightly, and the wood started to glow. The rider squirmed, but it was too late. A pulse of blue light shot along the fog tendril; then Rose tore the staff free and leapt forward. While still in midair, she struck out with her staff, swinging it in a glittering arc through horse and rider. Both dissolved in a puff of mist, but in the distance yet another bank of fog was already building, threatening to cut off their escape in no time.

"Ben!" Portia pleaded desperately. "Ben! We have to get away from here!" She might just as well have been shouting at a rock. He didn't move an inch.

Then, suddenly, Rose was by her side. As she squatted down in front of Ben, she noticed the lifeless blackbird in his hands. Shining tears welled up in her eyes, but she wiped them away.

"We have to leave. Now!" she told Portia, who managed to nod in reply.

"Ben," she urged. "Ben, come on!"

Finally Ben raised his head. He was crying, and Portia felt his sorrow like a weight on her own heart. Rose held his face with both hands and looked him straight in the eyes. "No hesitation, no questions," she said.

Ben let out a long, shaky breath. Then he got to his feet.

Portia looked back toward the door—but where the wall had stood before, there was now only a swirling bank of gray fog. Portia could make out ghostly shapes stirring deep within the murk, and could hear a terrible scratching sound, like claws scraping on a wooden door. Her blood ran cold.

"We can't go back now," Rose sighed. She took Portia by the hand and pulled her toward the oak grove, gently pushing Ben ahead of her. "We have to get to the Faerie Door. That's our only chance."

"But . . . ," Portia began.

"It's no good, my dear," she said, and this time her voice cracked. "There are too many of them."

They reached the edge of the oak grove, and Rose gave Ben a gentle shove into the safety of the trees. Portia glanced back one final time before she followed, and what she saw made the blood curdle in her veins. Out in the meadow, more and more shadowy figures were emerging from the fog. There were no horses now. Instead the creatures were on foot: gray ghosts in tattered robes, all swarming toward the closed door like moths to a flame. And then, from somewhere beyond the meadow, came the long, drawn-out call of a hunting horn.

Dead End

The journey back to the Faerie Door seemed never-ending. Ridik had sped Ben on his way earlier, but now the bird's lifeless body weighed as heavy as a rock in the boy's hands.

Rose led the way, striding determinedly ahead. Portia looked exhausted and was trailing behind.

They had long left the oak grove behind, and the lush meadows were giving way to rockier ground as they drew closer to the mountains. After a while, Rose shot Portia a worried glance. "We're taking a break," she announced.

A withered rowan tree rose from the grass nearby. It seemed a good spot to rest.

Portia dropped to the ground in front of the tree. Rose sat on a flat rock nearby, and Ben did likewise, carefully balancing Ridik on his thigh. Rose raised one hand, hesitated briefly, and then touched his plumage with her fingertips. She swallowed, as if fighting back tears. "*Swirne saff*," she said softly.

Safe travels, Ben translated. Tears welled up in his eyes, but he didn't make a sound. He had to pull himself together, he told himself. He had only just met Ridik, after all. But the sight of the blackbird's lifeless body was rattling a door hidden deep inside him, one he'd kept tightly locked since his father had passed away. Rose put an arm around his shoulder, but he stiffened at her touch. It reminded him of all the other hugs he'd had to put up with. There had been a seemingly endless line of aunts and cousins at his dad's funeral, all squeezing and patting him. He had wanted nothing more than to run out of the brightly lit living room and into the safety and solitude of the forest on his wall.

Rose took her arm away. She didn't ask him to put Ridik down, and Ben was grateful for that. Portia gave him a look full of compassion, but he avoided meeting her eyes.

Rose rubbed her face with both hands and ran her fingers through her hair. Her forearm bore a narrow gray mark where the rider's whip had caught her. When Rose caught sight of it, she snorted dismissively, as if it were a trifling annoyance.

"Does it hurt?" asked Portia.

"No."

Portia frowned, incredulous. "How did you know how to do all that stuff?" she asked. "The fighting, I mean. And . . ." She swept her hand through the air. "What *is* all this?"

"It's a very long story," Rose sighed. "But I should at least tell you the most important part." She rubbed her face again, then folded her hands in her lap.

"Bramble and I were in our last term at university," she began. "The plan was to go on a trip after our graduation, but we didn't have any money. So we and a group of friends decided to earn some by helping to clear out a big country estate near here. I remember when we walked into that house, the great hall with its enormous fireplace and beautiful wainscoting—it was as if we had traveled back in time."

A faint smile stole over her face. "We were absolutely fascinated by all the bric-a-brac that had piled up in those old rooms. Chests, porcelain figurines, antique weapons, tapestries . . ." She paused for a moment, as if summoning up the courage to tell the next chapter of the story. "On the second day, our friend Hermia came across a little casket," she continued eventually. "In it, we found a diary, a hand-drawn map of the area around Trefriw, and a very old key."

Portia gasped.

Rose nodded grimly. "Yes, exactly. *That* key." She brought it out of her pocket and turned it around in her fingers. "The diary belonged to a certain W.H.," she went on. "He was a folklore collector. You know, one of those people who go around collecting and recording myths and fairy tales. Apparently, he had come to Wales because of all the stories about fairies who were said to inhabit these parts. It seems he had brought the key along himself, although the diary didn't reveal who gave it to him or where he got it from. Anyway, W.H. came to these parts because he had heard there was a magical door somewhere around here, which could be opened by that key. And behind that door was the Fairy World. The *Otherworld*, as we call it in Wales. At first, he was convinced that those stories were mere fairy tales. But then, about ten pages into his diary, he changed his mind."

"He found the door," Ben said.

"Precisely. He found one door leading out of the Human World, and then another leading to the Otherworld. And the map supposedly showed the location of the first door."

Portia gave a faint snort of disbelief, as if to say that this all sounded rather unlikely to her.

Rose just smiled. "Well, we didn't believe it at first either. But we also thought it would be fun to try to find the door using the map, so we took the key and set off."

She fell silent, gazing off into the distance. "It was all true," she said. "Every bit of it. Fairy Queen Titania's underground palace, the magical lanterns in the trees, the Pale Tower."

Rose closed her eyes, as if recalling the beauty of the Otherworld. Portia flashed Ben a skeptical glance, but he just shrugged. He believed Rose.

Portia leaned forward. "So, if the first door leads out of the Human World, and the second into the Fairy World, where are we now?"

"In the Borderlands between the worlds," Rose replied. "And we should not be here."

"The Gray King . . . ," Ben began. Ridik had mentioned his name during the journey through the woods, but hadn't said much more.

"Errm, who?" Portia asked, a hint of desperation in her voice.

"The Gray King," Rose repeated. "The ruler of the Borderlands. Those riders at the door to the Human World? They were his hunters."

Portia fell silent again, a tense look on her face.

Hunters, Ben thought, feeling the flesh on his neck crawl. "And who are they hunting?"

Rose held up the key meaningfully. "The king senses it whenever anyone opens one of the doors," she explained. "Like a wolf getting the scent of a wounded animal. For him, the Borderlands are like a prison. The king wants to get out, into the Human World or the Fairy World. And wherever he goes, he brings with him the fog of forgetfulness. Once released, the fog will devour any trace of life it comes across, until all lands are empty and silent."

She gazed over their heads as she spoke these last words. Ben turned around to see wisps of fog rising through the canopy of the oak wood they had just come through. Was that the fog of forgetfulness Rose was talking about?

"We saw it happening back then," Rose went on. "We left the doors open, and the king led his army into the Otherworld."

"But why didn't you just shut the doors behind you?" Portia asked.

"Because we were fools," said Rose mournfully. "Careless. We didn't have the faintest idea about anything. And some of us obviously haven't changed." She stuffed the key back into her skirt pocket. "Bramble was supposed to throw the key into a lake, so we would never again be tempted to open the doors. And I thought that she had done it. All these years . . ." Rose paused for a moment, then carried on in a strained voice. "We tried to make up for our mistake. Ridik fought the Gray King's ghostly army alongside us back then. So did Robin Goodfellow. In the end, both were stranded in the Human World. Robin wanted to go back, but we decided it was too risky, so we destroyed the key. Or at least I thought we did. Robin never forgave us for that."

Portia was biting her lower lip, still seemingly wrestling with her doubts. Ben believed everything Rose had told them, but his excitement at the discovery of these new worlds was fading. Now that he held Ridik's lifeless body in his hands, he knew: no matter how many worlds existed, death had a place in every single one.

Portia stood up. She picked up her backpack, rummaged around in it, and brought out a blue cloth.

"Here you go," she said. "For Ridik."

Surprised, Ben accepted the gift, and gently folded Ridik into the soft fabric. It felt right, covering him like that. Respectful somehow.

Rose waited for him to finish; then she got up as well. "We have to get moving."

Portia looked up at her. "What's your plan?"

Rose was just about to respond when they heard the long, drawn-out howling of a pack of dogs from across the plain below.

Rose pressed her lips together, determined. "First of all, we have to get to the Faerie Door."

✍ PORTIA ✎

When they reached the moor, the ridges on both sides were already smothered in fog. Scraps of white mist drifted like smoke over the heather. Portia tripped over a grassy tuft and fell to her knees in a boggy puddle.

Rose was by her side in seconds and helped her to her feet. "Are you okay?"

What Portia really wanted was to burst into tears, sink to her knees again, and never get up—but she nodded anyway. Even though nothing was okay. Her mind was a muddle and she couldn't think clearly. She didn't know how she'd manage to take a single step more, and her throat was aching from all the sobs she was fighting so hard to hold back. Without another word, Rose drew her into a hug.

Portia's first reaction was to try to squirm free of the embrace, but Rose held her tight. "There, there," she said softly.

For a few seconds, Portia felt protected from everything that was happening. She leaned her forehead against Rose's shoulder and closed her eyes. *Don't panic*, she told herself over and over again. *Don't panic*. Rose was here, and she knew what to do.

Behind them the fog hounds' howling swelled, only to fade once more. Rose gently eased out of their embrace, and pressed the key into Portia's hand. "Take this," she said. "Now run to the Faerie Door and make sure you get through. I'll lead the pack away from your trail."

"What? No!" Portia tried to give the key back, but Rose grabbed her hand and closed her fingers around it.

"Take it," Rose insisted. "Seek shelter in the Other-world. And look for Robin Goodfellow. I realize he made a rather poor first impression, but I know he'll help you."

Portia opened her mouth to speak, but Rose had already turned to Ben. "Take Ridik back to his world. And remember to close and lock the door behind you."

"But what about you?" Portia insisted. Panic was roaring like a storm in her ears now.

Rose wouldn't look her in the eye. "I'll catch up with you as soon as I can."

"But if we lock the door behind us . . . ," Ben began.

Rose shook her head vehemently. "You have to lock that door." Her lips curled into a sad, thin smile. "We have no choice now," she said. "Tell Robin . . . tell him I'll fix everything."

The baying of the hounds seemed terrifyingly close now, and once more the call of the hunting horn rang out across the moor. Every single hair on Portia's neck stood on end.

"You have to go now," Rose urged. Ben just stared at her, but Portia looked over Rose's shoulder and saw a flood of fog surging toward them. How many hunters were hidden within the mist? A dozen? A hundred?

"Portia!" Rose's voice cut through the air. Portia squared her shoulders and fought down the panic raging inside her. Her stomach was twisted into a painful knot, but she grabbed Ben's hand and pulled him along with her.

Portia had no idea how, but they made it to the door. Panting and sweaty, she and Ben found themselves between the two rowan trees at the portal to the Fairy World. With a trembling hand, Portia put the key into the lock and turned it. The door opened easily, but rather than walking through it right away, they both turned around.

A delicate mist had fallen onto the moor like a veil. Rocks, heather, and grass had all vanished in the haze, while to the west a fogbank cut off their view entirely. It seemed as if the moor was surrounded by a white wall of nothingness—but the nothingness was moving.

"Come on, come on," Portia muttered under her breath as she stared at the approaching white wall, willing Rose to come running out of the fog. At least they could no longer hear any sounds of the hunt. Maybe her aunt's foolhardy plan had actually worked?

"Portia?" Ben sounded nervous.

Portia didn't dare take her eyes off the fogbank. "She'll make it," she said. She *had* to make it.

Ben rested his hand gently on her arm, and just then Portia saw what she had been hoping so much to see. A shadow was moving deep inside the rolling mist! Someone was coming toward them, a single figure cutting through the gray-white soup. She felt a wave of relief wash over her . . . only for it to evaporate a moment later.

The figure that emerged from the fog was not Rose. It wasn't riding a horse either, though it was as gray as the hunters that had attacked them at the door to the Human World. Whatever it was, it was tall. Taller than a normal human. Its body was shrouded in a long coat, and where its face should have been was a gleaming white stag skull, which peered out from underneath the edge of a hood, with black antlers branching out to either side. When it was less than a hundred meters away, the creature paused. Some of the fog swirling around it solidified into the shape of a dog. A second hound quickly materialized in turn, and then a third.

Where was Rose?

"Portia!"

She whirled round to see a stunned Ben staring at the ground. Thin tendrils of fog were rising from the grass and curling around their ankles.

"The door!" Ben shouted in warning. A few white fingers were already snaking their way toward the archway.

Portia hurriedly pulled her foot away from the groping fog, glancing nervously back at the moor. The hounds were already edging closer.

Ben grabbed her arm. "We . . . we have to go."

"No! Have you lost your mind? Rose is in there somewhere!" Portia clenched her fists stubbornly, but Ben tugged at her sleeve.

"Portia, please," he pleaded. Just then, as if they had been waiting for a signal, the dogs set off toward them.

Portia gasped in fright, stumbling backward against the archway. She felt Ben's fingers gripping her arm as they fell through the doorway together, and he tore the key from her hand. Behind them, the dogs were getting closer and closer as the fog thundered toward them like a tidal wave.

"Rose," Portia whispered, just as Ben slammed the door and turned the key in the lock.

Ridik's Final Journey

The door to the Fairy World had opened into a dark tunnel that burrowed into the ridge, before emerging onto a bracken-smothered plain. A few wisps of fog that had drifted through the tunnel after them disappeared into the ferns, but Portia immediately charged after them, kicking and scuffing at the ground until every trace was gone.

Ben had turned around to discover two stone columns, covered with an ornate pattern of knots and ribbons, flanking the entrance to the fairy tunnel. But all he could really see in his mind was Rose, walking alone toward the fog.

We left her behind. The thought made him numb. How had everything turned into such a terrible mess so quickly?

Ben turned his back on the tunnel once more and forced himself to take a closer look at their surroundings.

A circle of half a dozen standing stones protruded from the mass of ferns. Portia was standing in the middle of it, in front of a mossy pile of rocks, but she didn't seem to be paying the stone circle any heed. Instead she had taken off her backpack and was rummaging around inside. As Ben arrived at her side, she pulled out a map, which she proceeded to unfold and study intently. Ben was baffled. Did she really think the Otherworld would be on an ordinary map?

As he thought about it, he realized how serious their situation was. Not only had they lost Rose, but now the way home was blocked too! And while Ben was stranded here . . . and while the Gray Riders were roaming the Borderlands between the worlds . . . his mother must have been waiting and waiting for him to come home. He felt a lump in this throat at the thought of her watching for him through the bookshop window.

Then he glanced down at the little bundle in his hands and swallowed a sob. Rose had asked him to take Ridik back to his world. He had no idea what awaited them here, but honoring her wish and paying his last respects to Ridik was the least he could do.

Ben walked to the pile of rocks and touched the soft green cushion of moss covering it. It gave way under his fingers, warm to the touch as if it had been storing sunlight all day long. He knelt and placed Ridik on top of a rock, carefully folding back the cloth so his head was resting on the moss. *You're home now*, he thought. Ben felt tears pricking at his eyes, but this time he held them back. Then he rose and went over to Portia.

She was still studying the footpaths and forests on her map. "Do you know your way around here?" she asked. "Is there a path leading from this side of the moor back down to Trefriw?"

Ben raised his eyebrows. "I don't think that's how it works," he said. "We have to go back through the doors to get home."

Portia huffed defiantly. "No thanks," she muttered, clenching the map tighter in her hands. "We'll have to find shelter before it gets dark," she continued without looking up. "Do you know what time it is? My phone died."

Ben glanced at his watch. It had stopped. Did the Otherworld stop all human technology from working?

Portia looked around then, not waiting for his reply. "If we head west, we should come to Lake Crafnant. There's a hikers' hostel there, I think." She stared at the map, seemingly not even interested in what he might have to say. "We'll have to walk cross-country, but we should be fine if we use my compass."

Ben didn't know what to say. How could he make her understand that she was wasting her time? Then again, he had no idea what to do or where to go either. He was just about to ask Portia whether she understood that they were no longer in the Human World when he heard a fluttering overhead. Looking up, he saw that a pair of chaffinches had settled on one of the standing stones.

Portia had jammed the folded map under her arm and was rummaging around in her backpack again. Meanwhile, more and more birds were arriving to perch on the rocks: blackbirds, finches, tits, and even a spotted woodpecker. Their shiny, beady eyes were all focused on Portia and Ben. Meanwhile, oblivious to what was happening around them, Portia had found the compass. She held it up for a moment, then shook it despairingly.

"Come on! Work!" she hissed.

"Portia?" Ben said softly.

But Portia was intent on the compass, and only looked up when Ben touched her arm. He gestured at the stones around them, and Portia's eyes widened in surprise.

Just then, a female blackbird dropped from her perch and swooped toward them. Ben and Portia broke apart and backed off as the bird glided between them toward the mossy pile of rocks. Just before she reached the rocks, she gave a quick flap of her wings and changed shape. There was a blur of brown feathers before a tiny barefoot woman landed lightly on the moss next to Ridik's body. As if that had been a signal, the other birds shed their feathers too. Within moments, there were tiny people sitting or kneeling on top of all the standing stones.

Portia stood dumbstruck, the compass still in her hand. Ben gazed around him at the wonderful gathering. "*Yr Adar,*" he said under his breath. The Bird People had arrived.

The blackbird woman slowly circled Ridik's body. Then she crouched, touched his wing, and whispered something Ben couldn't make out. A ripple passed through Ridik's black plumage; then the feathers receded into his body with a rustling noise. The scout of the Adar lay on the moss in his human form, clad only in his coat of black feathers, his skin as white as snow. A murmur passed through the audience seated on the rocks.

"What happened?"

"Preet, what is the meaning of this?"

"Where did he come from?"

"How did he die?"

Ben cleared his throat and stepped forward. "Ridik fell in battle with the Gray Riders," he said in a thick voice. As soon as the words left his mouth, he felt foolish and theatrical. The Adar stared at him as if they were surprised he could speak at all.

"The Gray Riders," a podgy little man in a robe made of yellow and blue feathers repeated. The others whispered nervously among themselves.

"The Gray King's riders!" a woman cried, and then another called out, "So the Gray King has returned?"

"No," a third voice cut in. "That can't be. He is sleeping!"

Then the blackbird woman addressed Ben directly. "Is the door closed?"

Ben nodded quickly. "Yes. We locked it behind us." He turned to Portia. "Didn't we?"

Portia, still looking stunned, nodded as well.

Two of the Adar shifted back into bird shape and flew off. Those who remained began to yell and argue among themselves. The blackbird woman ignored the uproar. "Do you have the key?" she asked.

Ben and Portia exchanged another look. Portia pulled the key from her pocket, and the Adar fell silent.

"Little humans," the blackbird woman said. "You had better come with us."

The grove of the Adar lay within an oak forest just a few miles from the border of the Otherworld. The trees did not grow tightly there, but their crowns spread out to form a thick, dark green canopy.

Up high in the trees the Adar had built their homes. Round nest-like dwellings, tiny huts, and open platforms nestled in the crooks of branches. Since their world was hidden from the sky by the forest canopy, it was filled with gloom and shadow, and the Adar had hung lanterns all about, so the treetops were filled with tiny glowing lights.

There was a guest hall for visitors, too. A dome made of braided willow branches, standing by the bank of a broad stream; it reminded Ben of an igloo. The walls and roof were covered in silvery leaves, and a curtain of twigs hung over the round entrance hole. Inside, the floor was a mossy hollow. There were roots to lean against here and there, and several blue and red cushions scattered in between, some of which already looked a bit rumpled. Carved wooden lanterns hanging from the roof bathed the hall in a milky light.

Ben climbed onto a root and stood on tiptoes to try to get a better look at one of the lanterns. Where was the light coming from? No flame he knew of burned with that strange color. He peered inside, and saw no candle or oil wick. Instead he discovered a cluster of moths with wings that gleamed as if they had been dipped in moonlight.

He gently touched the lantern window and marveled at how one of the moths landed directly on the other side of the glass from his fingertip. Ben wished he had brought along his sketch pad and pencils. He would have loved to draw this place and its inhabitants. The Adar had led him and Portia to the tree town after their encounter at the stone circle. Preet ferch Mwyalchod, the blackbird woman, had shown them to the guest hall, and suggested they rest for a while. News of the two human visitors to the Otherworld must have reached the grove ahead of them. When they had stepped into the willow dome, two bowls had awaited each of them: one filled with blackberries, the other with grilled mushrooms. There were also two wooden cups, which sat next to a spring that splashed gently in the middle of the mossy hollow. While Ben was exploring the dome, Portia stood by the entrance, peering out through the curtain of twigs. Once Ben had finished examining the lantern, they sat down on the mossy floor together.

"Animals that turn into people. Tiny houses in trees. It definitely can't get any weirder," she said in weak voice.

"The lanterns are full of glowing moths," Ben added.

"Of course they are. What else would be in there?" Portia sighed. She rested a hand on her backpack. "That map really isn't any use, is it? The only way back is through the doors."

"I think so, yes." Ben glanced nervously across at Portia. He was expecting her to get angry again, or maybe burst into tears. But instead she was staring blankly into space. Ben carried on, before he could change his mind. "Look on the bright side, though. At least they're doors and not a wardrobe. You know, like in Narnia."

To his surprise, Portia laughed weakly. "Or a rabbit hole, like in *Alice's Adventures in Wonderland*."

She shook her head, as if trying to clear her thoughts. Then she opened her backpack and brought out not only a thermos but two wrapped sandwiches as well.

"I prepared these for our little trip to the stone circle."

She shrugged. "I suppose we did see a stone circle in the end. But I'm guessing it was a bit different from the one you were planning to show me?"

"Oh, yeah. Just a bit." Despite everything, Ben couldn't help but grin.

"Here you go." She handed him a sandwich. "I'm pretty sure that'll fill you up better than a handful of berries."

Ben took the sandwich, so surprised that he forgot to say thank you. He had assumed Portia had only agreed to go to the stone circle with him to be polite. Now it seemed she had actually been looking forward to it, and had even packed a picnic. For both of them. He definitely hadn't expected that. Lifting a corner of the sandwich, he found ham, cheese, salad, and mayonnaise inside—his favorite.

He remembered the blue cloth. The one she had given him for Ridik's body. It must have been meant for a picnic blanket.

Portia unscrewed the thermos and poured peppermint tea into the wooden cups left for them by the Adar. The scent of mint curled toward the ceiling of the dome with the steam rising from the cups. "You're right," she said. "We have to go back and through the door. If only to find Rose."

"Do you think she's all right?"

"Well, you saw how she dealt with those ghost riders. Obi-Wan Kenobi's got nothing on her."

Ben took a bite of his sandwich. Somehow Portia's confidence that they would be able to find Rose and get back home made him hopeful too. Of course they would go back for her.

He was just taking a sip from his mug when a blackbird came fluttering into the dome through the twig curtain, landed on a root, and took Preet's humanlike form. A plump wren followed close behind, landed at her side, and transformed into a stocky, bald man who only came up to the blackbird woman's shoulder.

"Little humans," Preet said. "I hope you've replenished your energy and strength."

"Oh, yes," Portia replied, quickly grabbing a blackberry. "Thank you so much for your hospitality."

"Yes, thank you," Ben hurried to add.

Preet smiled. The blackbird woman had thick brown hair that hung down to her hips, elegantly shot through with streaks of silver. She wore a sleeveless brown tunic, and a shawl made of mottled brown feathers, fastened at her right shoulder by a silver brooch. A tattooed pattern of knots and spirals flowed up her arms and neck all the way to her temples. A similar pattern covered the plump wren's bald head.

"This is Tatap ap Drywod, son of the wrens," Preet said, introducing her companion. "He's a scout, as am I."

"Like Ridik?" Ben asked.

Preet nodded. "Ridik was my uncle," she explained. "When he disappeared, I had only just earned my scout badge." She bowed her head, clearly upset. Tatap rested a comforting hand on her shoulder.

"Now, kindly tell us how you came to be here," Preet said when she had regained her composure. "How did you find yourselves in the Borderlands?"

Portia and Ben looked at each other before beginning to tell their story. Ben told the Adar of Ridik's accident, about his transformation the next morning, and how they had followed Robin Goodfellow and Portia to the first door. But when he got to the part where he had to describe the Gray Riders, he clammed up. Portia took over.

"If it hadn't been for Ridik, the rider would've made it through the first door . . . the door to the Human World," she said. "Ridik slowed him down. And the rider killed him for that."

Ben clutched his cup with both hands, avoiding the Adar's eyes. Portia glanced his way, but thankfully she carried on talking.

"We hurried back to the other door, the one on the moor, but those fog creatures caught up with us. Rose stayed behind to distract them, so we could escape."

"This Rose," Preet interrupted. "Does she know her way around the Borderlands?"

Ben nodded. "Yes, she's been there before. And here as well, actually. Many, many years ago. With Bramble and a few other friends."

"Oh," Tatap said. And then, more excitedly, "Oh! You speak of Viola Rosethorn and the other humans!" He whistled. "I didn't think we'd ever see them again."

"We didn't even know she'd survived the battle against the Gray King," Preet added.

"We knew only that they had driven him into the Borderlands and locked the door behind them." Tatap shook his head in amazement. "Feather and fluff, what news this is!"

"Those were terrible times, when the Gray King came to our world," Preet said gravely. "The fog overran the curlews' dwelling place."

"My grandmother saw it in her nightmares until the day she died," Tatap said. "She witnessed the fog rushing in across the ocean. It was as if the world was dissolving and devouring itself at the same time—that's how she always described it. And now the Gray King has awoken again." He shuddered. "Are you absolutely sure that the door is locked?" he asked.

"Yes," Ben confirmed. "Both the Fairy and Human Doors."

"How long do we have to wait until we can open the doors?" Portia asked. "Until the . . . you know, until those fog things are asleep again?"

"Open the doors?" Preet repeated.

"Yes, how long do we have to wait until—" Portia began, but Tatap cut her off.

"No, no," he said firmly. "The doors must remain locked."

"The risk is too great," agreed Preet. "If the Gray King has awoken, then the Borderlands must be swarming with his riders."

"They may even be waiting on the other side of the door," Tatap said darkly.

Preet nodded.

"But we have to go back," said Portia. Her voice sounded calm, but her tensely clenched fists told a different story. Ben felt ice-cold fear creeping through his body too. He couldn't bear the idea that they might be stranded in this place forever.

"There must be another way," he said. "Perhaps a different door, or maybe a secret path?"

Preet and Tatap exchanged a look. "We're very sorry," Preet said.

Portia fumbled in her pocket, as if to make sure that the key was still there. "What about that fox? Robin Goodfellow?" she wondered aloud. "Rose said he would help us."

"Goodfellow?" Tatap seemed surprised. "Robin Goodfellow has returned?"

"Oh, but of course!" Preet exclaimed. "That makes sense. He disappeared at the same time as Ridik. We thought he'd become lost in the fog, remember?"

"That's right," Tatap agreed. "Stranded in the Human World, the both of them. My goodness. You can't help but wonder who else might show up around here one of these days."

"And Mistress Rosethorn really said you should ask Goodfellow for help?" Preet asked, sounding skeptical.

"Yes," Portia insisted.

"Well now," Preet said, still sounding doubtful. "They do say he had a soft spot for Viola Rosethorn. Perhaps asking him for help might not be the worst idea."

"Whether he will grant it to you, that's a whole other question," Tatap said drily.

"Why? What's wrong with him?" Ben asked.

"He was . . . or rather, he *is* a trickster. He's a trouble-maker in the service of Oberon, the Fairy King," Tatap explained. "I for one wouldn't trust him. Presumably we can thank him for the fact that the doors were opened again?"

"Yes," Ben confirmed. "Ridik thought he must have wanted to get home."

"That sounds just like Uncle Ridik," Preet sighed. "He always did believe that there was something good in everyone."

A solemn moment of silence followed. "So many years," Preet said at length, dabbing at her eyes. "Ah, my heart is breaking just thinking about how he couldn't come home for so long. He must've been so lonely."

Tatap took her hand. "At least he's returned home now."

Preet patted his hand and turned to Ben. "Thank you for bringing him back to us. From here, his soul can embark on its next journey. That would mean a lot to him."

Ben nodded, a lump in his throat.

From outside in the forest came the blaring of a horn. Preet and Tatap stiffened. "The time has come to bid Ridik farewell," Preet said. She turned to Portia. "If you really want to try your luck asking Goodfellow for help, Tatap and I would be happy to take you to him. We can leave tomorrow morning."

Portia managed a strained smile. "Thank you."

"And until then, you're our guests, of course," Tatap said. "Eat well, rest well." He smiled. "You look as if you need it."

INTERLUDE

The stone circle beyond the Faerie Door lay deserted. The Adar and the Human children were long gone. Now the sun had set, and fog began to rise amidst the bracken. At first just a few gossamer wisps snaked upward between the ferns, but then the mist thickened until the ground inside the stone circle resembled a round white pond. For a moment, the fog was still; then its surface began to ripple and churn. From the center of the maelstrom, a shape materialized, like the prow of a ghost ship emerging from the sea.

The clouds parted, and the moon cast its silvery glow onto the circle. The woman standing in its center was shrouded in a long black veil that covered her face like a delicate cobweb. A crown braided of bare winter branches rested on her head, and a horn carved from a giant boar's tusk hung from her shoulder. Her hands were hidden by gloves. Fog surged about her, and when it cleared, two pale, growling hounds stood at her side.

The woman turned to gaze toward the tunnel leading to the Faerie Door. She could sense that this passageway was closed, but there was still a faint silver-bright trace of the World Key lingering in the air. She turned to face the woods, toward the path leading to the tree town of the Adar. She raised a hand, and the dogs trotted forward. The Gray King's huntress followed in their wake.

Gwil Glumheart

At dawn the next day, Ben and Portia were waiting at the outskirts of the Adar's dwelling place. A shallow brook meandered by their feet. The water gave off an earthy woodland scent as it gurgled between the rocks.

The graze on Ben's arm was itching. He automatically reached for it with his hand, before stopping himself at the last moment. The night before, an Adar healer had smeared a red salve onto the wound and urged him not to scratch it while it healed.

Portia was carrying her backpack again. She looked a bit pale, but was holding on to the straps tightly and looked eager to get walking. Ben's muscles were sore, but it seemed all of yesterday's exertion had hardly affected Portia at all.

Ben sighed wistfully. He had read so many books about adventures in magical worlds—but in those stories people never seemed to get blisters while they were on quests.

Nearby, a small flock of young birds was splashing around in the shallow water near the bank. They chirped and laughed while effortlessly shifting shape: one moment fluffy little birds, the next looking like tiny children.

"Well, welcome to Wonderland," Portia said.

The corners of Ben's mouth twitched into a smile, just as a blackbird and a wren came flying toward them.

Preet and Tatap landed on a rock next to Portia and transformed into human shape. "First the good news. We know where Goodfellow is."

Portia pursed her lips. "And the bad news?"

"He's at the Fairy Queen's court," Tatap said. "And Titania bears no great love for humans."

Ben and Portia exchanged a worried look, but Preet raised her hand reassuringly. "Don't worry. We have a plan." She glanced over at Tatap, who grinned.

"We're taking you to meet a salamander."

Apparently, all of the Adar's scouts had mastered the art of swiftflight. This time Ben took the journey through swirling winds and colors much better. When Preet ended their magical flight in a distant part of the forest, he was able to stand upright without staggering, and he hardly felt dizzy either. Ben was still taking in his new surroundings while Preet gave him her instructions. "Gwil is down by the clay ponds," she said. "You keep back for now. I'll fly ahead and prepare him for your visit."

With that, she transformed into her feathery form and flew off ahead. Tatap stayed on Portia's shoulder as they slowly followed on foot.

"It's been some time since we saw humans on our side of the door," Tatap explained. "And Gwil Glumheart . . . well, he's a rather skittish salamander."

"Magical creatures who are scared of us?" Portia said. "Shouldn't it be the other way around?"

Tatap laughed. "Don't be so surprised! You're as wondrous to us as we are to you. But have no fear, Gwil is a decent fellow. He works as a scribe at Fairy Hill. There's no one better to take you to Goodfellow." Tatap pointed to a boulder up ahead. "Here we are!" At his bidding, Portia and Ben hid behind the rock and cautiously peered around it.

Beyond the boulder, the forest opened into a clearing. The ground was thick with plants with fanlike leaves, and pale yellow blossoms that seemed to float around their stems like little stars. Amid the plants stood a strange figure, gazing at the ground in concentration. Gwil Glumheart was a thin, hunched little man, the size of a human, if a rather short one. He had his back to them, but Ben could see that he was bald. Gwil wore a long robe of faded black cloth and fingerless gloves. In one hand he held a basket filled to the brim with the fanlike leaves, and in the other a small sickle.

Preet had landed on a rock rising from the plants and shifted back into her human shape.

"Gwil Glumheart!"

At the sound of his name, Gwil turned around, surprised. "Scout Preet!" he cried. "What a pleasure!"

He went over to her, and they both bowed. Then Gwil set his basket aside and sat down in front of Preet. Only when he was at eye level with the scout did they begin to talk.

Ben leaned forward, straining to hear their conversation, but Gwil and Preet were too far away for him to catch more than a few snippets.

"What are they saying?" asked Portia. Ben just shook his head, but Tatap squared his shoulders.

"Get ready," he whispered.

Just then, Preet turned toward them and chirped loudly.

"Come on now, let's go," Tatap urged.

One by one, they stepped out from behind the boulder and into the clearing. Gwil Glumheart looked over at them, confused. Then his eyes widened in shock. He leapt to his feet, stumbled backward, fell over his basket, and sprawled headlong in the plants.

Portia, Ben, the two Adar, and Gwil sat in a circle in the clearing. Preet was telling Gwil all that had happened, with some help from Ben and Portia, while Gwil dabbed at his forehead with a handkerchief. They saw now that he wasn't just bald. His eyebrows were missing too, and his skin was waxy and pale.

"So there's a key again," said Gwil, after Preet had finished speaking. She looked over at Portia, who reached for her pocket, but Gwil held up his hand. A black tattooed line encircled his wrist like a bracelet.

"No need, I believe you!" he said. "Oh dear. I fear this is not good news. The Gray King? Oh dear, oh dear." He dabbed his lips with his kerchief.

Preet tried to get to the point. "Gwil, these humans would like to return home."

Gwil's eyes widened again. "Yes. Of course. Yes. But I'm afraid that won't be possible."

"Viola Rosethorn advised them to seek Robin Good-fellow's help," Tatap added.

"Goodfellow?" Gwil repeated incredulously. "What was she thinking?"

"We don't know," Preet said. "But we must help these two in some way or other. Could you guide them to Fairy Hill, perhaps?"

"Oh, Titania won't like that one bit."

Gwil blinked, and it took Ben a moment to realize that he didn't have human eyelids. Instead a sort of filmy membrane flicked quickly up over his eyes from below—like a salamander's eyes.

"Why doesn't Titania like humans, anyway?" asked Portia.

"Actually, there was a time when she was quite fond of visitors from the Human World," Tatap said. "She would sometimes even send out her fairies to lure mortal musicians and poets to Fairy Hill."

"But that has changed," Preet added.

"Yes." Gwil nodded gravely. "Since the humans left open the doors and let the Gray Riders into our world."

An uneasy silence descended upon the group, until Ben spoke up. "Do you mean Rose and her friends? I think she was really sorry about it all. And she did everything she could to stop it from happening again."

"Totally," Portia agreed. "If she hadn't been so determined to stop those ghost riders, she'd be here with us."

"I did like Viola Rosethorn and the others," Gwil said.

"All their stories from the other side . . . I could've listened to them for hours and hours."

"And they loved our world," Preet added. "Do you remember the stories that Mistress Brambleblossom used to tell about it?"

"Oh, yes," Gwil said. "She's a true poet!"

"Indeed, I am surprised she didn't accompany Viola Rosethorn to the Borderlands," Preet said. "Please don't tell me her soul has traveled on?"

It took Ben a moment to understand that Preet was talking about Bramble. Rosethorn and Brambleblossom. Rose and Bramble. The Afallon ladies' nicknames came from the Otherworld.

Portia had apparently come to the same conclusion. "No, no," she hastened to say. "Bramble . . . I mean, Olivia, is fine. But I'm sure she's very worried about us." She looked around the circle pleadingly. "Please! We really must go back. If only to find Rose."

"And we have to hurry," Ben added. "We need to get to her before those Gray Riders do."

Gwil looked at Preet, but she ignored him. "You're right," she agreed. "We can't let her down."

Gwil seemed hesitant, but then he nodded in agreement. "All right." He crumpled his handkerchief and stuffed it into the depths of his robe. "We'd better be on our way then, I suppose."

The Hollow Hill

Preet gave Ben a feather from Ridik's coat as a parting gift, a token of the Adar's gratitude for bringing him home. While Gwil was helping him attach the feather to the collar of his T-shirt, Portia sat cross-legged on the ground with her hand in her jeans pocket clutching the key.

"I'd stop doing that if I were you."

She guiltily pulled her hand from her pocket and looked down to see Tatap standing next to her knee, gazing up at her solemnly.

"Fairy Hill is no place for humans," he warned. "Especially not now Titania regards them as a threat." He placed a small hand on her knee. "Don't tell anyone about that key."

Tatap's warning echoed in Portia's head as Gwil led them deeper into the woods. The forest was dense now, and barely any light filtered through the thick canopy of leaves above their heads. There were no paths to follow, no maps, and their compass didn't work either. On top of that, every step took them further away from the door, and Rose. Portia chewed on her lower lip as Gwil explained his plan.

"Fairy Hill—we call it Bryngolau—has several minor entrances," he said. "For servants and such. If we keep our wits about us, we may be able to get in without the fairies even noticing."

"Aren't there any guards?" Ben asked.

Gwil shrugged. "Well, it's been a while since there's been anything to guard against. Not since . . ." He stopped himself.

"Not since the Gray King's last attack," Portia said, finishing his sentence.

Gwil nodded, a pained look on his face. "Yes, and since that attack Titania has distrusted all humans." He shook himself like a dog trying to scare away a wasp. "Maybe we'll be able to smuggle you past her. Perhaps we'll get lucky!" He didn't sound confident.

Portia had a picture of Titania in her mind by now, and it was anything but encouraging. She imagined her a bit like Maleficent, the evil fairy from *Sleeping Beauty*: tall and severe, with sharp cheekbones and a bluish tint to her skin.

What kind of a place had she ended up in? Portia stopped in her tracks. She tried to take another step, but all of a sudden the thick green undergrowth seemed to be pressing in on her. Her chest felt tight, and she could barely breathe.

"Portia?" Ben turned around, looking surprised.

"Just a minute." Without waiting for a reply, she pushed off the path and into a clearing of waist-high bracken. She had to get out of there, if only for a moment, before Gwil and Ben noticed that she was losing it. She trampled a path through the ferns to a rock, then sat down with her back to it. She closed her eyes and breathed shakily in and out. She thought of her mother, sitting at the kitchen table, her face pale, turning an empty cup round and round in her hands. Was this how it felt to be caught in one of her mum's gray moods?

Breathe. Just breathe.

A mosquito buzzed next to her ear. She shooed it away, then reached into her pocket, pulled out the key, and pressed it against her chest. There was a way out. As long as she had the key, there was a way out.

Breathe. She exhaled slowly and felt herself begin to relax. More bugs buzzed around her head. Portia sighed, swatted at the mosquitoes, and opened her eyes again. Then she returned the key to her pocket and went back over to Gwil and Ben on wobbly legs. The two of them had been resting on the ground, but when Portia stepped out from the bracken, Gwil jumped to his feet, a worried look on his face.

Portia frowned. Another one of those annoying insects landed on her shoulder, and she swatted it away without even looking. "What happened?" she asked. "Is something wrong?"

"Good question," said a voice like a tinkling bell.

Ben's jaw dropped, and Portia spun around. Behind her stood a dainty girl with a head of wild silver hair. She was a few centimeters shorter than Portia, and her short green dress was as delicate as a dragonfly's wing. Her eyes were the same shade of green and gleamed like two candle flames behind colored glass.

Portia stumbled backward, bumping into Gwil.

"What is that?" she said under her breath.

"A fairy," he whispered.

Something whirred past Portia's ear. She stared in disbelief as another tiny creature with dragonfly wings landed on a frond of bracken. A plume of blue smoke rose into the air, before falling to the ground like a waterfall. In the dragonfly creature's place now stood another girl, this one with sky-blue hair.

"Peaseblossom," said Gwil, greeting the blue fairy in a husky voice, before turning to her companion. "Cobweb. Allow me to introduce you to Portia and Ben, from the Human World."

The blue fairy smiled, revealing a set of sharp pearl-white teeth. "Guests for Queen Titania! She'll be so pleased to hear it."

Peaseblossom skipped ahead of them with a featherlight step, while Cobweb brought up the rear. When Portia risked a glance behind, the fairy glared at her, so she quickened her pace until she caught up with Ben.

"Is this how you imagined fairies would be?" she asked under her breath.

Ben looked over his shoulder. "I thought they'd be nicer."

"What are we going to tell them if they ask what happened in the Borderlands?" she whispered.

"No idea," he replied quietly. "But we'd better not mention the key. Preet warned me. Titania still blames humans for endangering the Fairy World."

"Tatap told me the same thing." Portia felt Cobweb's gaze burning into her back like a laser beam. She had to fight the urge to reach for the key again. Suddenly she remembered how she had pulled it from her pocket when she had stepped off the path earlier. Those bugs buzzing around her head—those had actually been fairies, hadn't they? What had they seen?

Portia walked on in silence. She didn't tell Ben that the fairies might already know about the key. What would they do if they found out she had awoken the Gray King? At least they had locked the door leading to the Fairy World, so Titania wouldn't be able to use that against them. Even so, Portia was beginning to feel queasy.

After some time, the forest gave way to a wide clearing. A glade of foxgloves lay ahead of them. From the midst of the purple flowers rose a rocky, moss-covered hill. On top of the hill a leafless tree stretched its bare branches to the sky.

Peaseblossom spun around. "Welcome to Titania's court," she exclaimed excitedly.

"Where is this palace supposed to be?" Portia asked Ben.

"Inside the hill, I suppose?" he replied. "Fairies always live inside hollow hills in fairy tales."

"Less talking, more walking," said Cobweb, chivying them along, and she gave Ben a little shove between the shoulder blades.

They marched through the foxglove glade in single file. As soon as they passed into the shadow of the hill, the air grew chillier and Portia got goose bumps all over. The closer they got, the sharper and more jagged the rocky hillside looked. Portia nervously wet her lips with the tip of her tongue, but kept walking until she saw the archway in a rocky crevice up ahead. Beyond the archway was an inky black void, as if night itself awaited them in the hill. The sight hit her like a blow in the chest, and the next moment Cobweb gave her a dig in the back for good measure.

"Keep moving," she hissed, and before Portia could brace herself, the shadows beneath the archway had devoured them.

The Audience

ᴗᴑ PORTIA ᴖ

The darkness was so impenetrable that even the air itself felt heavy. Portia groped along a damp rock wall with her fingertips. She was afraid of losing her bearings, but then she saw a weak light up ahead. Shortly after that, they emerged from the tunnel onto a balcony. Ben, Gwil, and Portia went up to the balustrade and gazed around. The hill really was hollow—high above them, roots snaked across the roof of a great cave, covered in white and gold glowing moths, like fairy lights. The light of their fluttering wings pulsed in ripples over the rough rock walls.

It's like we're underwater, Portia thought. Then she looked down and gulped.

The balcony loomed over an abyss. Here and there the light of a moon-moth drifted down into the dismal depths, but the bottom remained shrouded in darkness.

"Oh, man," she groaned, trying to catch Ben's eye. She saw his face in the flickering moth light. His eyes were wide and his pupils looked pitch black. But was it out of fear or amazement? Just then Cobweb cleared her throat impatiently, and they began their descent.

A spiral staircase wound down the rock wall, leading them deeper and deeper into the earth. As they walked, they passed moss-covered pillars that lined the stairs like a cloister in a monastery.

Portia's nerves were all on edge. Until now, she'd never been afraid of the dark. But Fairy Hill's darkness felt different, menacing somehow, as if the rocks themselves were whispering to her.

Several bends later, they finally reached the bottom. As Peaseblossom hopped off the last step and onto the ground, a labyrinthine pattern of quartz-crystal veins began to glow beneath her feet.

Portia looked all around her. Several doorways were cut into the rock walls. She could make out groups of shadowy shapes moving about beneath the archways. Then one of the shapes came out of the darkness toward them.

Portia's whole body stiffened. The woman—if that's what she was—seemed to flow across the floor. Her silk dress billowed around her like the wind made visible. Her long hair drifted in coils about her head as if she was underwater. And her face . . . her face was too long and thin to be human. She passed by Portia and the others without sparing them a glance. Portia's blood ran cold.

Only when Ben gave a little moan of fear did Portia tear her eyes away from the mysterious figure. More figures had stepped forward out of the shadows, and several pairs of glittering eyes were examining the newcomers.

Peaseblossom seemed about to run to one of the groups, but Cobweb grabbed her by the collar of her dress. "Find Titania and tell her who we've brought."

"But—"

"Now!"

Peaseblossom pouted but shifted into her miniature shape with a *Puff!* before flying away. Portia remembered how she had swatted the tiny bright-eyed fairy with her hand, and it made her feel sick again.

"You stay here," Cobweb commanded, before marching over to a group of fairies.

Portia watched her with growing unease. "I think they saw the key."

"What?" Ben spun around. "Are you sure?"

"No, I'm not." Portia bit her lip and made a decision. "You take it."

"What?"

"If they saw me with the key, they're bound to ask me about it. So you take it."

Ben looked like a rabbit in the headlights, but when Portia subtly passed him the key behind her back, he closed his fingers around it.

"They'll take you to Titania," Gwil said in a high-pitched voice. "Oh dear!"

Portia wished his fear wasn't as obvious as it seemed to her. Her stomach felt as if it was filled with cement.

"What are we going to do?" Ben asked.

Before Gwil could reply, Cobweb came back. "Don't you have anything else to do, Glumheart?" she snapped.

Gwil cowered, staring at his feet. "Well, I thought . . . ," he began, but trailed off. Ben swiftly went over to his side, took his hand, and squeezed it firmly.

"Thank you, Gwil," he said. Gwil winced and opened his mouth as if about to reply.

"Chop, chop! We don't have all day!" Cobweb growled, cutting him off.

With one last glance at Ben and Portia, Gwil went off toward one of the archways, clutching his basket of leaves.

Ben stared after him anxiously. Portia felt her heart begin to beat faster too. Gwil had wanted to help them, but she was pretty sure Cobweb had the opposite in mind.

Cobweb led them hurriedly along a dimly lit tunnel until they came to another archway. Portia frowned. There was an unusual scent in the air—sweet and flowery and some-how . . . strange.

Before she could work out what it was, Cobweb shooed them through the arch.

They had barely passed through when Peaseblossom came running toward them from the opposite direction. "She's expecting you," she panted, out of breath.

Before Portia knew it, the fairies had seized her and Ben and marched them forward into a great vaulted room.

No sooner had Portia passed through the doorway than a flower-shaped lamp began to glow overhead. Moon-moths flew up in all directions from its glass petals, illuminating bushes of irises and white chalice-shaped lilies.

They were in an underground greenhouse! Giant plant

pots lined a winding path of pale stone slabs. Wild vines with beautiful flowers tumbled from the ceiling, while everywhere delicate flower lamps glowed amid the tangled foliage.

Portia was no gardening expert, but she was pretty sure plants didn't normally grow so lushly underground. She could hear water burbling somewhere, and a dragonfly buzzed past the tip of her nose.

Soon they left the plants behind and found themselves at the center of the room. In the middle of the floor was a round pond. More dragonflies buzzed over the large lilies growing along the water's edge. The fish that swam below the green lily leaves glowed pink, blue, and purple, like underwater shooting stars. Thick Irish moss grew all around the pond and carpeted the wide steps rising on the far side. On the steps a group of fairies was lounging on pillows, talking in whispers. They all turned to look at Ben and Portia, but their blank dolls' faces showed neither curiosity nor surprise.

"This is definitely not weird," Portia muttered under her breath. Ben could only manage a wordless whimper. Then somewhere beyond the steps a little bell chimed, and the fairies went back to their conversations as if nothing had happened. Portia felt the soft hair on the back of her neck standing on end.

Cobweb led them past the pond and up the steps to a raised gallery. There they found a chaise longue uphol-stered in a fabric of magnolia flowers, and lying on it a fairy dressed all in white.

"Titania," Ben whispered.

Portia couldn't help but stare.

Titania—for it could be none other than the Fairy Queen—rose from her bed. She was only inches taller than Portia, and her face was that of a child. Her long chestnut hair hung in pretty curls behind her little pointy ears. Portia had expected a woman clothed in the kind of splendor befitting a queen, but instead Titania wore a plain, straight-cut white dress under a robe of the same color. Only when she stepped closer did Portia realize that the garments weren't so simple after all. The sleeves of the robe were embroidered with hundreds of tiny pearls, while the dress underneath seemed to be woven from shimmering flowers.

Cobweb and Peaseblossom curtsied before their Queen, and Ben and Portia did their best to imitate them. Portia felt very silly doing so, but Titania gave them a warm smile.

"So it is true, then," she said. "We do have visitors from the Human World." Her eyes wandered from one to the other of them. "Portia. And Ben?"

"Yes, Your Majesty," Ben said in a quiet voice and lowered his gaze.

Titania laughed, clearly pleased. "Such good manners. Please be seated."

They sat down on two cushions made of blue silk, while Titania lowered herself onto the edge of her chaise longue. She wore no shoes, and her bare feet dangled just inches above the ground. As far as Portia could see, the only blemish on her pristine appearance was her fingertips, which were as black as if she'd dipped them in ink.

Peaseblossom joined them, sitting on a cushion in front of the chaise longue. Titania raised a hand, and a servant came forward. The girl appeared to be a salamander, like Gwil. She had no eyebrows, and her head was wrapped in a sky-blue scarf. She carried a silver tray of glasses filled with a red liquid. Titania took a glass from the tray before it was offered to Portia and Ben. As the girl held out the tray, Portia caught a glimpse of a tattoo on her wrist. It was the same as Gwil's. Perhaps all salamanders had the same tattoo?

As the guests reached for their glasses, Titania beckoned Cobweb over and whispered something into her ear. Cobweb bowed her head and rushed away. Shortly after, the melody of a lute filled the air.

Titania watched Ben and Portia in silence. She seemed to be waiting for them to drink, but Ben simply held his glass in his hand, and for some reason Portia also hesitated to sip the red liquid.

"Well," Titania said after a while. "Do you want to tell me how you were able to cross the border to my kingdom?"

Ben and Portia exchanged glances before recounting their story for the third time. This time, though, they held some details back. They told Titania that they had stumbled into the Borderlands unwittingly, and that Rose had made sure the doors were closed behind them, but the Gray King's servants had somehow become aware of their presence.

Titania listened with a friendly and attentive expression. When they mentioned the Gray Riders, the salamander servant girl began to tremble so violently that the glasses on her tray rattled and clunked. Titania, on the other hand, remained unmoved. Ben was recounting their flight across the moor after the first battle, when he faltered. Portia quickly took the story up.

"We made it to the Faerie Door, but the riders were right behind us." She forced herself to hold Titania's gaze. "Rose wanted to be sure we would escape, so she sent us through the door and stayed behind." As she spoke, Cobweb came back and sat down behind her. Portia fought the urge to move away from her. "She held off the Gray Riders. Didn't she, Ben?"

"Yes," Ben confirmed. "She . . . she wanted to make sure the fog couldn't get into the Fairy World."

Portia looked at him out of the corner of her eye. He was telling the story in a way that suggested Rose had been trying to protect the fairies rather than just her and Ben. It was a good idea, but would Titania buy it?

"Viola Rosethorn," Titania said pensively. "I thought she would already have departed on her next journey. Humans don't live very long, do they?"

"No," Cobweb replied. "Not particularly." Was it her imagination, or did Portia detect a note of satisfaction in Cobweb's voice?

Titania took a sip of her drink, a soft silver glow in her eyes. "What about the key? Where is it?"

Portia was feeling more and more uncomfortable about lying, but she could still hear Tatap's warning echoing in her ears. "I don't know," she said. "Rose probably still has it. She locked the door from her side."

Titania exchanged glances with Cobweb. A drop of sweat trickled down Portia's spine. *Don't clench your fists,* she told herself. *Stay calm.*

"Would you mind emptying your pockets?" Titania asked. Cobweb instantly took a step toward Portia, but Titania raised a hand to stop her. "I'm sure young Portia here needs no help."

Relieved that she had given the key to Ben, Portia got to her feet and turned her pockets inside out to show that they were empty. Titania seemed neither surprised nor disappointed. Portia hoped she'd forget about the key now, but instead the queen shifted her attention to Ben.

"And how about you, young Ben? Would you mind emptying your pockets as well?"

Portia felt a hot flush of fear. Her heart beat wildly as she watched Ben get up and turn his pockets out too.

The key wasn't there.

Portia tried to hide her surprise and look unflustered as she tucked her pockets back into her jeans. Cobweb's face fell as Titania slid from her chaise longue and took Portia's hand. Portia winced in shock, but the queen smiled. She seemed glad the interrogation was over too.

"Do accept my apologies for the inconvenience," she said. "When it comes to the Gray King, we really can't be cautious enough." She waved the servant over and set her glass down on the tray. "Awel, be a dear and bring me some tea, will you?" she said. "I need something to calm my nerves after all this excitement."

The servant bowed her head and hurried away. Titania

turned back to Ben and Portia. "You've seen the Gray King's riders. You understand why I had to ask those questions, don't you?"

"Of course!" Portia managed to splutter. Titania was so different from what she had imagined. Portia was puzzled by her friendliness and had no idea how to deal with it. Still, the squeeze of her hand was warm and comforting, and her smile seemed sincere. For the first time since arriving in Fairy Hill, Portia began to relax.

Titania gave Portia's hand a pat before letting it go. "Now then. What do you wish to do? May I be of assistance in any way?"

Portia was speechless. In all their frantic preparations for this encounter, it had never even crossed her mind that Titania would grant them a wish. Had Tatap and the others been wrong about the Fairy Queen?

Ben cleared his throat. "We'd like to go home, Your Majesty."

"Of course you would," she said, sounding understanding. "But without the key, it won't be possible. I'm afraid you'll have to wait for Mistress Rosethorn to take you back."

That was a reasonable suggestion. Too bad it would never happen. Portia nervously plucked at the hem of her T-shirt. This was a dead end all of their own making.

"I will send two of my fairies to stand guard at the door," Titania continued. "They can welcome Mistress Rosethorn as soon as she appears and escort her here." She clapped her hands. "Until then, please make yourselves at home," she said. "It's been a while since we've had Human visitors.

Peaseblossom!" The blue-haired fairy leapt to her feet. "Take these two to Mistress Quickly. Have them clothed. Show them the guest quarters. And tomorrow, we'll have a celebration in their honor!"

Peaseblossom was far more pleasant company than Cobweb. She was much more curious, too—she cheerfully quizzed them about the Human World as they walked through Fairy Hill. Ben answered all her questions, but Portia was still thinking about their audience in Titania's water lily chamber. Maybe they should have told her the whole story after all. She remembered Titania's friendly words and kindly expression. Why would she deceive them?

". . . very good that Mistress Rosethorn locked the door behind herself," Peaseblossom was saying. That made Portia's ears prick up. Actually, where *was* the key? She glanced at Ben, but he gave her a brief shake of the head.

"It's so very dramatic," Peaseblossom continued, "how she took on the Gray Riders—a lone figure on the great bleak moor!" She turned a corner, then led them down a flight of stairs.

"Perhaps I should take you to our scribes," Peaseblossom said. "They could immortalize Mistress Rosethorn's sacrifice in verse. Turn it into an epic poem. What do you think?"

Portia was just about to tell her what exactly she thought, when Gwil appeared at the bottom of the stairs. Ben's face lit up, and Portia felt relieved too.

Peaseblossom frowned, but then skipped toward the salamander with a few quick steps. "Gwil! What are you doing here?"

Gwil was out of breath and dabbing his forehead with his handkerchief again. "The guest quarters for the humans are ready," he panted.

"What do you mean?" Peaseblossom asked, clearly confused.

"But that was Her Majesty's order, wasn't it?"

Peaseblossom glanced over at Ben and Portia. "Yes, that's right. But I thought . . ."

"May I take the humans there now?" Gwil said, looking at Peaseblossom expectantly.

The fairy was twirling a strand of her blue hair around her finger. "Well, now, that's really quite perplexing. Titania wanted me to take these two to Mistress Quickly."

"Oh, that's not a problem at all," Gwil replied promptly. "The sewing room is on the way."

Peaseblossom bounced on the balls of her feet, seemingly undecided. Gwil clutched his handkerchief so tightly that his knuckles went white, but the fairy didn't notice.

"Very well," she said eventually. "I'll go and tell Prickle-thorn and the others about our guests from the Human World. I bet they're bursting with curiosity." She smiled from one ear to the other. "You'll be the talk of the celebration tomorrow!"

With that, she twirled around once before shifting shape in a puff of blue smoke and buzzing away.

"Oh, thank the spirits," Gwil groaned. "If Awel hadn't

told me that your audience was over, I'd have missed you."
Ben was still standing a few steps above Gwil, so he reached
down and patted the salamander's shoulder gratefully.

"Thank you, Gwil," he said. "Have you got the, errm . . . ?"

"Oh. Yes." Gwil glanced around quickly, then pulled
the key out from underneath his robe and pressed it into
Ben's hand.

"What?" Portia stared at Ben. "When did you give him
the key?"

Ben smiled bashfully. "When Cobweb sent him away. I
guessed nobody would expect Gwil to have it."

Portia whistled admiringly. "Great idea!"

Ben's smile grew even wider.

"Ahem." Gwil cleared his throat. "We should get going.
It's quite a way to Goodfellow's quarters."

Ben tucked the key into his jeans pocket, and they set
off on their way.

Shape-shifters

Robin Goodfellow's quarters were located deep inside the hill, far from Titania's water lily chamber. Portia walked at Ben's side, barely noticing her surroundings. She was trying to stay positive, but the further they advanced into Fairy Hill, the more she began to doubt their plan. If you could even call it that.

"Everything okay?" Ben asked.

"I'm not sure," she replied. "Are we doing the right thing?"

"What do you mean?"

"Finding Robin Goodfellow. I mean, he's the reason we're stuck here in the first place."

"But Rose said he'd help us."

"I know, but I'm still not sure." Portia remembered the cold smile on Robin's face when he spoke to Rose about finally understanding what it feels like to lose your world.

Ben fell silent for a moment. "But what else can we do?" he sighed eventually.

Portia shrugged. *We could ask Titania for help*, she thought, but kept that to herself.

"Here we are!" Gwil stopped in front of an archway and pushed aside a curtain hanging over the entrance. "Hello?" he called. When no one answered, he stepped inside.

Ben looked quizzically at Portia, but she just shrugged and went in after Gwil.

Robin's quarters looked more like a burrow than a human home. Then again, he wasn't human, was he? *Trickster. Troublemaker*—that's what Tatap had called him. *Scoundrel*—that had been Bramble's verdict.

Behind the curtain was a single room about twenty paces across. To their left, the embers of several logs were smoldering in a fireplace. The shelves along the walls were crowded with jars, colorful little glass bottles, and sealed clay pots, while bunches of dried herbs were hanging from the ceiling. Despite herself, Portia was intrigued. It was like a wizard's kitchen!

"It looks as if he'd never been away," Ben observed.

Gwil shrugged. "Goodfellow was King Oberon's right hand. When he disappeared, Oberon gave orders to maintain his quarters."

"But Oberon isn't here?" asked Ben.

"Oberon is traveling. Has been for years," Gwil explained.

On the other side of the room, a narrow bed sat in an alcove. Portia went over to it, passing between the fireplace and a rough wooden table. In a nook in the wall above the bed stood a vase of wild yellow roses. Next to it lay a locket on a silver chain. Curious, Portia picked it up, but before she could open it, a voice said, "Well, well, look at that. You just couldn't resist, could you?"

Portia hastily put the locket back in its place and turned around.

Robin Goodfellow was leaning in the doorway, observing them coldly. He wore a gray waistcoat over a fresh white shirt and light-brown linen trousers. On his feet were the same dusty leather shoes he had been wearing in the Human World.

"Goodfellow!" Gwil croaked. "We . . . we need to talk to you."

"Do you now?" Robin said, feigning interest. He walked over to Gwil and stood so close that the salamander flinched.

The corner of Robin's mouth twitched. He turned toward Ben and Portia. "Tell Rose she can keep her self-righteous nonsense to herself. You know, all that talk of how the risk of opening the doors is too high."

He strolled over to the fireplace, squatted on his haunches, and then took a steel teakettle and hung it above the fire. Robin appeared to be completely indifferent, as if none of this was any of his business.

"Actually, we can't tell her," Portia said. "She stayed behind on the other side."

Robin froze.

"The Gray Riders attacked us," Ben cut in. "Rose stayed behind to hold them off."

Turn around, Portia thought. *Turn around and say something.*

Instead Robin simply got to his feet and walked wordlessly to one of the shelves. Portia could sense her dislike toward him like a bitter taste on her tongue, but Ben was persistent. "She told us to look for you."

"What fantastic advice!" Robin opened a clay pot, took a mug from a shelf, and threw in a pinch of herbs. Ben and Portia exchanged a look, but she didn't trust herself to speak. She knew that if she said anything now, she would end up exploding and venting all her anger. Then she remembered Preet's words: *They do say he had a soft spot for Viola Rosethorn.* Well, it seemed the Adar had gotten that completely wrong.

"Please," Ben said. "Rose said you'd help us. We need someone to take us back through that door."

Robin snorted dismissively. "A foolish idea. Unless you fancy serving as the Gray Riders' quarry." He turned around and headed back over to the fireplace, but Portia blocked his path.

"Then we'll go through a different door."

Robin's face darkened. "You just don't get it, do you?" he asked in a menacingly calm voice. "There's nothing I can do to help. And Rose can't be saved."

"That's not true!" Ben protested. He stood shoulder to shoulder with Portia. "If the Gray Riders haven't caught her, she might be waiting right on the other side of the door."

"And if they did catch Rose," Portia added, "then she'll need someone to rescue her! We have to do something!"

Robin shook his head. "It doesn't matter how fast or how slow you are. Rose is long gone. Whoever is taken by the fog either disappears or is doomed to lead a miserable existence as a Mistwalker. Hasn't Gwil explained to you what that means?"

Portia pressed her lips together. *He's lying*, she thought.

Robin's eyes glittered with anger. "The fog devours all the memories and thoughts that make you the person you are. What remains looks like the person you once were—but a Mistwalker is nothing but a shell, a mere shadow. They breathe and move around, but no one who's become a Mistwalker will ever recognize you again. You can't help Rose. Rose is dead. One way or the other."

"No!" Ben cried.

Robin gave him a look that was somewhere between disgust and sympathy, then turned and squatted down by the fireplace again. "Rose has long owed a debt to the Gray King. And now she's had to pay it."

Ben's breathing was so heavy that his whole body shook. Portia finally boiled over with rage. "This is your fault!" she yelled. "You woke up that gray whoever-he-is on purpose."

"Portia," Ben warned. But she wasn't listening.

She slapped Robin's shoulder. "If it wasn't for you, none of this would've happened!"

Robin laughed bitterly. "Oh, but I think perhaps you're forgetting one little detail. Without *you*, I wouldn't have gotten my hands on the key."

Portia flinched as if she had been struck. "I had no idea what was going to happen."

"True," Robin said. "And yet still off you went, as carefree as a little lamb, opening doors and not thinking about the consequences. Who does that remind me of, I wonder?"

A knot of frustration burned in Portia's chest. *No crying,* she told herself. No way was she going to cry in front of this scoundrel. "But we have to get home!" she exclaimed.

"This is your home now," Robin snapped. "You'd better get used to it. I'm sure Titania will put you to work in the scullery."

Robin was clearly finished with the conversation. He turned his back and stared down at the smoldering embers in the fireplace. Portia's eyes burned with tears. She had to admit that he was right. She was just as much to blame for the situation as he was. Even so, she felt like shoving him into the mantelpiece. Gwil placed a hand on her shoulder and stepped between her and Robin. "Let's all calm down," he said. "I'm sure we'll find a solution."

"If I were you, I'd keep my mouth shut," Robin snarled.

Gwil stiffened, but he persisted. He took another step closer to the fireplace as Robin poured steaming hot water into a mug.

"None of us wants to let the Gray King cause trouble here again," he said soothingly, "but I'm sure we could still help Mistress Rosethorn, if only you would—"

In a flash, Robin spun around and threw the boiling water into Gwil's face. Portia and Ben screamed. There was a hiss, and a cloud of steam filled the air. When it had cleared, a little salamander was sitting on the ground, just where Gwil had been standing.

The Salamanders
of Bryngolau

Ben carried Gwil around Fairy Hill on the palm of his hand. In his salamander shape, Gwil had black skin with yellow spots, a long tail, and tiny feet.

"Why doesn't he shift back into his human shape?" Portia wondered aloud.

"Perhaps he doesn't feel like it?" Ben suggested. "Or maybe he just can't?"

Judging by the glum way the salamander hung his head, the second guess was right. Nevertheless, he guided them through the warren of tunnels, halls, and servant quarters like a little living compass. At every turning, he pointed his head in one direction or the other, until they reached a brightly lit cave with a pair of brass scissors hanging above its entrance.

"Is that the sewing room?" Ben asked. Gwil nodded, white eyelids twitching over his eyes.

They stepped inside and found themselves in a cave that looked more like a bazaar. Rolls of fabric in all colors of the rainbow were piled up next to the entrance. There were shelves filled with folded cloth, and two half-finished dresses draped on mannequins. Dozens of lanterns hung from the ceiling.

Two women stood next to one of the mannequins. The shorter of the two—young, with a bushy red braid—was holding a basket filled with flowers made out of cloth, while the second, somewhat older, woman attached a flower to the shoulder of the dress. When Ben and Portia approached, the redhead gasped, and the other woman spun around to face them.

"Sweet spirits!" she exclaimed. "So it is true! Humans!"

Portia guessed this was Mistress Quickly, the head seamstress. She seemed to be a salamander as well—at least she didn't have any eyebrows, just like Gwil. Mistress Quickly was wearing an elegant turban made of purple fabric. She had rolled up the sleeves of her dress, and a pincushion was strapped around her wrist.

"Hello," said Portia, and the two women looked at her as if horns had just sprouted from her forehead.

Ben cleared his throat. "Mistress Quickly?" he asked. "I believe Gwil Glumheart wanted us to come and find you."

"Gwil?" the older seamstress repeated. Then she noticed the salamander sitting on Ben's hand. "Oh, not again!" She threw the cloth flower back into the basket. "Sian, dear, would you fetch a jar of spring water, please?"

"Yes, Mistress Quickly, of course." The younger woman set her basket down and hurried over to a table.

Meanwhile, Mistress Quickly plucked Gwil from Ben's hand.

"Why doesn't he shift back?" Portia asked.

"Because he's a salamander. We need help to shape-shift," she replied. "Ah, thank you, Sian."

The girl had returned and handed a jar to Mistress Quickly, who gently placed Gwil on the ground. "Heat makes us shift into our animal shape," she explained. "And to shift back into our human shape, we need something cold." With those words, she emptied the contents of the jar over Gwil.

Again there was a hiss, and a cloud of steam, and then Gwil was sitting on the ground—in his human shape.

"Gwil Glumheart." Mistress Quickly put her hands on her hips and sighed. "What kind of a mess have you gotten yourself into now?"

Shortly afterward, Portia and Ben were sitting in Mera-lyn Quickly's living room telling her everything that had happened. Meralyn and Gwil sat in two flowery armchairs while Portia and Ben shared a sofa. On a round table between them stood a porcelain teapot decorated with a pink peony pattern. The teacups were made of porcelain as well, but were all patterned differently. There were oatcakes with clotted cream and blackberry jam, and thick slices of toasted bread. They were also offered butter, salt, and pickled parsley to go with it, which was surprisingly tasty.

After all the excitement of their ordeal, Portia had worked up quite an appetite. As she devoured the last crumbs of an oatcake, she took a closer look at Meralyn Quickly. The head seamstress was taking a sip of tea, and Portia noticed the stamp of a famous porcelain brand on the bottom of her cup. She started.

"Is something the matter?" Meralyn asked.

"No, not at all," Portia said hurriedly. "I was just wondering . . . is the crockery from the Human World?"

Meralyn smiled. "It is indeed! You wouldn't think it today, but once upon a time there was plenty of exchange between your world and ours, even though most people on your side had no idea."

She put her cup back down, her pearl bracelet gleaming in the light of the table lamp.

"Some of the things humans introduced us to are now being made here as well," she went on. "Obviously not by the fairies. But many shape-shifter families do good business with human inventions. Especially since the doors have been closed."

Gwil was still stirring his tea even though the sugar must have dissolved long ago. "It is safer that way," he said.

"Yes, because of the Gray King," Meralyn agreed. "But this closing-the-borders thing doesn't seem to be working, after all. And now the Gray King has awoken again, and poor Mistress Rosethorn is stuck in the middle of all that chaos." She shook her head. "What a tragedy."

Portia put the cookie she was just about to bite into back on the plate. "Was Robin telling the truth?" she asked. "Is Rose gone for good?"

"Oh, I wouldn't give up hope so easily," Meralyn replied. "I'm sure we'll think of something."

"You'd help us?" Ben was surprised.

"But of course," Meralyn shot back.

"But won't Titania be angry?"

"Salamandrau help when others hesitate," the older woman said proudly. "And no matter what Titania thinks, we don't always have to dance to her tune."

Gwil cleared his throat, and Meralyn put her hand on his. "If we're careful, of course," she said reassuringly. She let go of his hand and reached for her teacup again. "It'll be a challenge, admittedly. We know very little about the Gray King, his fog, and its effects." Meralyn looked at Gwil, and he nodded.

"When the Gray King last attacked, a party of hare merchants was on their way to the Night Market," Gwil recalled. "The fog must have surprised them during their journey, and they never arrived at their destination. Their families looked for them, but there was no trace of any of the missing ones. But then one of them showed up again after all. Branys was his name. Two of his cousins found him wandering in the woods and took him home." Gwil was trying to hold Portia's gaze, and she forced herself to look him in the eye as he spoke.

"He did not remember his family. He did not speak," Gwil continued. "He did not react when they asked him questions, and whenever they took their eyes off him, he began to wander off and drift away, westwards."

"Like a cloud of fog," Meralyn said sadly.

"What happened to him?" asked Ben.

The salamanders faltered. "Well, one morning he

disappeared," Gwil said eventually. "His grandson had been sitting on a chair in front of the house all night. He swore he hadn't opened the door, yet his grandfather was gone, and there was nothing but cold dew on his bed."

"So Robin is right, after all," Portia said flatly.

Ben wanted to reach out and take her hand, but thought better of it.

"Perhaps," Meralyn said, "but perhaps there's still hope. Branys was missing for a whole moon before they found him. Rose has only been lost for a short time. And she's smart. It's quite possible that the fog hasn't overpowered her yet."

"But what if it has?" Portia asked.

Gwil shrugged. "There are stories of Mistwalkers who have been saved, even after falling victim to the hold of the fog."

"Every child knows the story of Ifor and Nerys," Meralyn confirmed. "It took place in the times of the Gray King's first attack on our world. A young warrior by the name of Ifor was swallowed up by the fog and disappeared. His sweetheart, Nerys, went after him and brought him back. They were missing in that fog for a whole moon, but when they finally returned, both were unharmed."

"How did they manage it?"

"The story goes that Nerys placed her own heart in Ifor's hand, so his memories of her came back."

Portia snorted. "Well, if that's all we have to do!"

Meralyn smiled. "The part with the heart is probably a metaphor. You know, a flowery description of what actually happened. Bards love things like that. Whatever Nerys really did . . . well, we'd have to look into that."

Gwil's eyes widened. "Oh, but of course!" he exclaimed. "World's End!"

"World's End?" Portia repeated incredulously.

Gwil nodded. "When humans were still traveling between the worlds, they and the Salamandrau elders created a place where all knowledge from both worlds was gathered," he explained. "It's a library, and its name is World's End. If there's a solution to your problems, that's where you'll find it."

Meralyn nodded eagerly. "Yes, that's a great idea. Actually, I know someone who might be able to help you—Tegid, the librarian there. Gwil, you'll take the children to the library, won't you?"

"Me?" Gwil turned pale.

"That's all well and good," Portia interjected. "But even if we do find some kind of miracle cure for the fog in this library, how will we make it through the Faerie Door? Titania has sent guards to watch over it."

The confident glow quickly disappeared from Meralyn's face. "I hate to say it, but Titania's right—the Faerie Door must remain closed. If the Gray Riders are roaming the Borderlands, their bloodhounds are surely lurking near the door."

Portia was about to object, but this time Meralyn beat her to it. "There's actually another door," she said. "In fact, Mistress Rosethorn and her friends used it all those years ago. She may have found her way back there again."

Ben sat up straight. "Where is this door?"

"It's inside the Pale Tower," Meralyn replied.

"How lovely," Portia sighed.

"The Pale Tower is where the Gray King sleeps." Gwil nervously cleared his throat. "Well, rather, where he was sleeping."

"You said Mistress Rosethorn intended to set things right, didn't you?" Meralyn asked.

Ben nodded.

"Which could mean that she is trying to put the Gray King back to sleep. And what better place to try that than the place where she succeeded once before?" Meralyn drummed on the table with her fingertips. "The Pale Tower would be well within reach of World's End."

Portia stared at the salamander. "Just to be clear—are you suggesting that we go through a door leading straight into the Gray King's living room?"

"He won't be expecting that," Meralyn said.

Portia clenched her fists. "Well, a lion wouldn't expect me to just go wandering into its den either," she replied. "He'd still eat me, though."

Ben made a noise somewhere between a cough and a nervous laugh.

Gwil ran a hand across his bald head. "You're right. Of course you are." He looked at Meralyn, who gave him an encouraging smile. "It's the best path for you to take right now. Unless you've got a better idea?"

"Titania!" Portia said immediately. "We'll tell her the truth and ask for her help."

The salamanders remained silent, but they looked doubtful.

"She seemed quite reasonable earlier," Portia insisted.

Meralyn sighed. "Well, she is . . . as long as she's hoping to get something from you."

Gwil turned to Ben. "What do you think?"

Ben frowned. "I don't know . . ."

"You all said it: if we want to save Rose, we have to be quick," Portia said. "Otherwise, we'll lose our best chance of finding her."

"But don't we need to know the best way first?" argued Ben. "Or what we should do if the fog has already stolen her memories?"

"But maybe that hasn't happened yet! What if she's waiting for us? If every second counts?" Portia was on the edge of her seat, gripping the table. Libraries, faraway fortresses—all that would take way too long. She wanted to do something right now, to go back to that door, and undo everything that had happened. Robin had been right: if it wasn't for her, Rose would be safe. She had stolen the key. She had opened the door to the Borderlands. Just to satisfy her curiosity. And if Rose never came home, it would be Portia's fault.

She felt as if her stomach was turning into a tight fist. She would put everything right. She just *had to.*

Ben stared at the table.

"Ben?" Portia asked desperately.

"I like Gwil's idea."

Gwil gave him a shaky smile. Portia could barely believe what she was hearing.

"Portia?" Meralyn asked.

Portia stared at their faces. She remembered saying goodbye to Rose, remembered the warmth of her hug, and the cold when Rose had turned around and marched toward the wall of fog all by herself. She could feel that they were running out of time, could practically hear the ticking of a clock in her head. "No," she said eventually. "There are too many 'maybes' for me." She avoided the salamanders' disappointed looks, cleared her throat, and tried to sound confident. "I'm sorry. I just think we have a better chance if we ask Titania for help."

An uncomfortable silence descended.

"If we find a cure for the Mistwalkers at the library, couldn't we send a message to Fairy Hill?" Ben asked suddenly.

"Yes, certainly," Gwil said. "Tegid has a few carrier pigeons. They could be back here in no time."

"That way, we could try to help Rose in two different ways," Ben suggested, turning to Portia. "You ask Titania for help. Then if you find Rose and she's all right, everything is fine. But if not, we can send you the instructions for the cure."

Portia bit her lip. She disliked the idea of splitting up from Ben just as much as the idea of going further away from the Faerie Door and Rose. But if that was the only compromise Ben was willing to agree on . . .

"I just don't know," Meralyn cut in. "I really wouldn't trust Titania, if I were you. Portia, are you sure you want to try asking her for help?"

She was not. But panic was gnawing and pulling at her, and the idea of fairy warriors confronting the Gray Riders seemed somehow more reassuring than her wandering into the unknown. "Yes," she replied eventually.

Meralyn sighed. "Okay. Then I'll help you prepare for the audience, and Gwil will go with Ben."

"There's just one problem," Gwil said. "If Portia wants to go through the Faerie Door and we want to go through the one at the Pale Tower . . ."

". . . then we'll need two keys," Meralyn said, finishing his sentence.

"Oh," Ben said. "I didn't think of that."

Meralyn smiled. "Don't you worry. That's one problem we can solve right away."

Merron Pathfinder

Meralyn disappeared to an adjoining room and returned a few minutes later with a bottle, two glasses, and a small leather-bound book. She pressed the book protectively against her chest until she had set down the bottle and the glasses and taken a seat. Then she brushed some crumbs off the tabletop, cautiously put down the book, and opened it to the first page.

"This is my great-grandfather's journal." She touched the dense handwriting with her fingertips, tracing each line, a bitter smile on her face. "Merron Pathfinder was his name. Although, the fairies had a different name for him."

"Merron the Reckless," said Gwil glumly.

"He was given that name after he took on the fairies—and then lost in spectacular fashion." Meralyn uncorked the bottle, and the sweet scent of blackberry wine tickled Portia's nose.

"What happened?" she asked. Next to her, Ben leaned forward to get a closer look at the book.

Meralyn raised just one shoulder. "Well, there are many stories, but they agree on one thing. Merron crossed the border between the worlds without permission."

She poured wine into the two glasses and pushed one over to Gwil, who took a generous sip. "Since the first doors were created, the fairies have decided who should be allowed to pass through them," he explained.

"Merron wasn't happy with the fairies' reign," Meralyn said. "He wanted to decide for himself where he should travel, whom he should meet. He had a dream that all Salamandrau might one day be able to wander between the worlds, gathering knowledge from beyond our borders."

"Of course the fairies didn't care much for that dream," Gwil said.

Meralyn nodded sadly. "So he decided to make his own key."

"And did he manage it?" asked Ben.

"Yes, and he wrote the secret down in here." Meralyn closed the book and handed it to Gwil. "It seems we are in luck. According to Merron, a key can only be crafted by the dwellers of two different worlds working together."

Gwil let out a sad whimper. "Apologies," he mumbled, and took another sip of wine.

Meralyn smiled, but her features now looked strangely hard, like marble. "If Titania knew of this book's existence, she'd throw all of us into the deepest of the Fairy Hill's dungeons."

Should she really be asking Titania for help? Portia wondered. She wasn't sure, but she ignored the doubts she felt stirring in her gut. "Is that why you don't make keys anymore?" she asked.

Meralyn snorted. "If the fairies didn't have such control

over us Salamandrau folk, one of us would surely have made another key." She sounded as if she would have liked to be that rebellious salamander herself. "But our hands are tied, in the truest sense of the word."

"After Merron . . . after he . . . ," Gwil began, but he couldn't finish the sentence.

"The fairies caught and punished him," Meralyn said tersely. "And with him, all the Salamandrau."

She loosened her wristband to reveal a tattoo like those Portia had seen on Gwil and Titania's servant: a black ring around the wrist.

"This is the mark of our servitude," she explained. "It means we have to serve and obey Titania, and we are not allowed to leave Bryngolau without her, or her permission."

Portia frowned. "You really can't leave?"

"No," Meralyn said. "If we tried, the mark would stop us."

Handcuffs, Portia thought, horrified. *The tattoos are handcuffs.*

"Which brings us to another problem." Meralyn nodded toward Gwil.

Gwil placed a hand on his tattoo. "If I'm to take Ben to World's End, then I'll need a spell that stops the mark from working, temporarily at least."

"I think Pricklethorn could cast a spell like that." Meralyn turned to Ben and Portia. "He's Titania's Lord Chamberlain."

"He could," Gwil agreed. "But he won't. Not without a good reason."

"Or a good bribe." Meralyn smiled again, then got up and

opened the trunk next to the sofa. She carefully removed some layers of tissue paper before bringing out a bundle of cloth that she let unfurl in her hands into what looked like a woven starry sky. A sheet of dark blue silk ran down Meralyn's arm, shimmering all over with tiny rhinestones—or were they diamonds? The sight of it left Portia breathless, and she wasn't the only one.

"Pricklethorn has long coveted a garment to rival our queen's attire. I'd say this would fit the bill." Meralyn smiled mischievously, her eyes twinkling. "Provided that he helps us, of course."

Later that evening, Portia lay in bed staring at the ceiling. The guest bedroom Meralyn had shown her to was near the sewing room. She could hear the muffled voices of the seamstresses, still at work. A glass filled with moon-moths stood by the door, glowing softly.

Portia was thinking over her conversation with the salamanders, turning her decision round and round in her head.

I'm making the right choice, she kept telling herself. But then why were there so many doubts gnawing at her?

Portia turned over. Ben's bed was just a few inches away, but a silence as vast as an ocean had grown between them. He hadn't said a word to her since the salamanders had bid them good night. Was it just because he was tired—or because he was upset that Portia was going to leave him on his own?

She wished she could explain, and tell Ben how guilty she felt. She didn't want to put any more distance between herself and Rose, but at the same time she felt she was letting down Ben as well.

After a while, she just couldn't take it anymore. "I wish we could do this together."

Her voice was fading away into the darkened room when at last Ben quietly replied, "Me too."

Portia sat up in her bed. "Then stay! Help me convince Titania!"

Ben lay still for a moment. "Are you a hundred percent sure that she'll help us?" he asked.

She could have lied. Perhaps Ben would stay with her then, so she wouldn't have to confront Titania by herself. But she didn't have the heart. With a deep sigh, she lay down again. "No," she admitted. "No, I'm not."

The silence grew between them again. "If you get home before me, could you please tell my mum that I'm okay?" asked Ben.

The question felt like a little stab in the heart. "Of course," she said. "And if you make it there first, will you do the same for me?"

"I will. I promise."

Ben stared at the ceiling. Portia chewed her lip, filled with indecision. She wished she could tell him about her doubts—but if she did that, he might convince her to come along with him after all. And that would be a mistake. Or would it?

"Portia?" said Ben. "Be careful when it comes to Titania."

"I will," she said.

"I'm serious." He rolled over to face her. "In stories,

humans always end up losing when they make deals with fairies."

"I'll watch out," she promised. "But you be careful too. Stay away from those creepy gray knights. Making yourself invisible should do the trick."

Ben laughed softly. "Well, I've got some experience there. I'm mostly worried that we'll have to walk for hours again tomorrow. I'm so sore. I'm aching in places I didn't even know I had muscles."

Portia couldn't help but grin, despite everything. Ben smiled too. It suited him, Portia thought.

"You can do it," she said, then turned to look up at the ceiling again. She could hear Ben arranging his pillow. She really liked him. He was cautious, but at the same time nothing seemed to really faze him. She was glad he was with her.

For now, at least.

Her smile faded. Sometimes Portia wished she could shut the mouth of her inner voice with a piece of tape.

Departure

After waking the next morning, Ben lay in bed with his eyes closed for a little while. His pillow was marvelously soft and smelled of hay. *I'm in Faerie*, he thought. *At Queen Titania's court.*

When he finally opened his eyes, a moon-moth was tumbling across the dark room. He reached out, and the featherlight moth settled on his hand. Its little feet tickled his skin, and it glowed more brightly. It was like a light bulb you could dim with a switch—just way more amazing. Ben softly blew on its wings, and it fluttered away. He sat up and threw off his blanket. As he moved, the other moon-moths in a jar by the wall woke up, casting their milky light over the walls and ceiling. Ben looked anxiously at Portia's bed. If she was still asleep, the light would surely wake her up.

He was surprised to see that her bed was empty. Ben frowned and got up. He had no idea what time it was, but he felt well rested. More and more moon-moths fluttered about the room until Ben felt he was standing in a cloud of glowing pollen. Portia's backpack was sitting on the stool by his bed. She had attached a note to the safety pin holding Ridik's feather. Ben tore it off and began to read:

For your journey. You can ask Meralyn to refill the thermos. Blister Band-Aids are in the mesh pocket inside. Good luck!

Ben took a moment to process the message. Then he understood. This was Portia's goodbye. And she was leaving him her backpack. He felt a warm glow spread through his chest like sunlight.

Curious, he opened the backpack, and found the thermos, Portia's map, and the promised Band-Aids, as well as a slim red notebook. Ben opened the notebook and found that it was empty—except for the very first page. With a black felt pen, Portia had written *Summer Vacation in Wales* at the top of the page. Underneath, she had glued in a section of a map of north Wales, and a Welsh flag. In the lower corner, she had pasted in the ticket for Conwy Castle with tape, and next to it she had written *Conwy, 10th August*. It was a travel diary!

Ben flipped through the blank pages, thinking how he would have liked to find out what else Portia was going to add to her diary. He could have helped her, could have shown her some exciting places or helped her cut out pictures. Perhaps she would have let him add a few small drawings of his own.

Suddenly he wished he'd had a chance to say a proper goodbye. Or rather, he wished there had been no need for a goodbye. It was a strange feeling for Ben. He never wanted to spend time with his classmates, but he would have liked to get to know Portia better.

～

The dye works were in a big cave in the eastern wing of the palace, where daylight streamed in through gaping cracks in the ceiling.

The cracks provided natural ventilation, which was fortunate, because the cave smelled absolutely disgusting. Large tubs of colored water lined the walls, and the air was thick with the stink of vinegar and urine. The dye workers didn't seem to pay the smell any mind, though. They hustled and bustled everywhere, dipping fabric into the tubs or stirring plants and other ingredients in steaming water. No one paid any attention to Gwil and his companion.

Meralyn had dressed Ben in Fairy World clothes: a pair of comfortable boots, brown wool trousers, a plain shirt, and a scuffed leather jacket that was a few sizes too big. Last but not least, he wore fingerless gloves, just like Gwil's. The only mismatched detail was Portia's green backpack.

Gwil's face wore a determined expression, but his hands revealed how tense he really was. He laced and unlaced his fingers again and again. It was strange, but somehow Gwil's nervousness made Ben feel braver. He was on the brink of an adventure. And he had come well prepared.

"Ah," Gwil sighed suddenly. "There she is."

Ben followed his gaze, and saw Meralyn making her way through the dye workers, easily clearing a path with her long stride. In her hand, she held a folded piece of parchment.

"Has he . . . ?" Gwil asked when Meralyn had reached them.

"He has indeed." Meralyn grinned and handed the parchment to Gwil. "One look at that fabric, and he immediately agreed to allow you some travel time."

"Good, good." Gwil's hand was trembling. Meralyn's expression was serious again. She took his hand and squeezed it gently.

"Good," Gwil repeated. He opened the note and read the foreign-sounding words it contained aloud. A shiver passed through his whole body, and then he sighed, clearly relieved.

"Are you okay?" Ben asked.

"Yes." Gwil smiled faintly and raised his wrist. His tattoo had paled to a gray band. "It feels as if an iron manacle has been removed from my wrist."

"Five days," Meralyn said. "That's as long as I could get."

"Pricklethorn believed the story?" Gwil asked.

Meralyn nodded. "I told him you're going to look for a recipe for cerulean ink at the library. Five days," she said again, and now Ben thought he heard some doubt in her voice. "Long enough for a journey to World's End."

"And for everything else as well. Now"—Gwil looked at Ben—"shall we be on our way?"

Ben was still staring at Gwil's wrist. "What happens if Titania finds out that you took me with you? Won't she activate the mark again?" he asked, concerned.

"She can't," Meralyn said. "For Titania to do that, the bearer of the mark must be there to hear her words."

"And if she does realize that you've come along, we'll be miles away by then," Gwil added.

"Okay," Ben said. "Thank you, Meralyn."

"Oh, don't mention it." She smiled, and then turned to

Gwil again. "Weather permitting, you'll make it to World's End by tomorrow evening. Here." She pulled a little pouch from a pocket of her robe and held it out to Gwil. "Take these with you."

Gwil accepted the pouch and opened it. His eyes widened. "Oh. Oh no. That's not a good idea, Meralyn."

Curious, Ben peeked inside the pouch, but all he saw were a few smooth gray pebbles. "What are they?"

"Ember pebbles," Meralyn replied. "One touch, and they grow as hot as if they've been sitting in a blazing fire."

"No, no," Gwil repeated, and handed the pouch back to Meralyn, closing her hand around it. "I can't have these on me. I . . . I wouldn't be able to restrain myself."

"But you'll need them. Maybe. If you're running out of time."

"What's so bad about a few hot pebbles?" Ben asked.

"If I take one in my hand, I'll shape-shift immediately," Gwil explained. "And I won't be of any use or help to you in my animal shape."

"Well, I'm not suggesting you use them right away," Meralyn said. "But five days isn't such a long time. And if the mark is reactivated—"

"Meralyn!" Gwil protested.

". . . then the pain will return," she said, finishing her sentence.

"Pain?" asked Ben, aghast.

Meralyn nodded gravely. "The mark spell inflicts terrible pain if Titania discovers we have disobeyed her, or if we stray from the hill without permission. Only when we shape-shift do we lose the pain. That's the choice she has given us. Either we submit to her rule completely, or we spend our lives in our animal shape." Her expression softened. "Gwil, take the pebbles."

Gwil blushed. "All right. But Ben should look after them for me." He turned to Ben. "Please don't give them to me until it's absolutely necessary."

Ben took the pouch and put it into his jacket pocket. "Why would you want them earlier?"

Gwil gave a shamefaced smile. "Because we salamanders love fire, and everything that gives off heat. It's in our nature. And sometimes that is, let's say, rather disadvantageous."

Meralyn shot him an amused glance. "Gwil likes the heat just a little too much." Gwil's face was still glowing, but he was smiling too.

"Now then," she said. "That's that." She looked from Ben to Gwil and back to Ben. "Be careful, both of you."

Ben felt a tingling sensation crawling across his skin. They were setting off on a journey. A journey into the Otherworld, where even more wondrous places and creatures must await. This hill of fairies and shape-shifters was just the beginning.

INTERLUDE

A dense blanket of clouds darkened the skies above Bryngolau as the boy and the salamander set off on their journey. They left Fairy Hill by a side entrance, and began trudging westwards.

From the shadow of a rowan tree, the Gray King's huntress watched the pair depart. The fog that followed her everywhere clung to the hem of her robe. Behind her, where the shadows grew darker and the undergrowth wilder, the fog was thicker, and ghostly shapes flitted back and forth in its depths.

She hesitated. Two Human children had come from the Borderlands to the Fairy World. But only one was traveling onward to the mountains. What should she do? She took a deep breath, drawing her black veil close to her face. Then she jerked her head up and sniffed the air. There it was. The faint silvery scent of the World Key. It stuck to the boy and left behind a trace like floating pollen. Her hand reached for her hunting horn, but no—it was still too early to call for her master.

She waited until the boy and the salamander were nearly out of sight, and then beckoned her hounds. A pair of them stepped out of the shadows and strode past her, soundlessly, heads lowered and eyes dimly glowing. The huntress waited a little longer, until the dogs had picked up their scent, and then followed in their wake.

Titania

All day long, curious shape-shifters had been seeking out Portia's company, quizzing her about her world, doing her hair and making her try on different garments as if she was one of Meralyn's mannequins. Now she sat on a bench in the corner of the sewing room, waiting for someone to take her to Titania's celebration. Everyone seemed to have left her alone for a while, and Portia was glad of it—she was so nervous by now that she wouldn't have been able to talk about anything. She was relieved when Peaseblossom finally burst into the room. At least she wouldn't be getting pushed around by Cobweb again.

"Look at you!" Peaseblossom said cheerfully. "All spruced up. With, hmm, leggings! Interesting choice."

Portia raised an eyebrow. Rather leggings than the flimsy, flowy sequined nightgown Peaseblossom was wearing. The fairy's hairdo was even weirder than the day before—piled up high, and braided with a jumble of twigs, feathers, velvet ribbons, and borage blossoms. It looked as if she was wearing a bird's nest on her head.

Portia's outfit was quite simple in comparison; the brown leggings Meralyn had found for her reached just below her knees. The seamstress had also given her a white shirt and a cobalt-blue waistcoat with a cornflower pattern to go with it. The shirt was a bit longer than the waistcoat, hanging down to her hips.

Portia resisted the urge to smooth her clothes. She had hidden the key in the inside pocket of the waistcoat, and was hoping its shape didn't show through the fabric. She had decided she wouldn't play her trump card until she had made her deal with the Fairy Queen. She dried her damp hands on the leggings and trusted that no one would notice how nervous she really was.

Peaseblossom twirled around once before offering Portia her hand. "Shall we?"

Outside Fairy Hill, it was already dark, but the clearing was bathed in silvery moonlight. Peaseblossom led Portia across the foxglove field to a cluster of oak trees. A flight of stairs made of roots led down into a brightly lit hollow, where a lake awaited them, as flat and clear as a mirror. Oak trees lined the shore, lanterns hanging from their branches. More lights had been placed on moss-covered rocks, and bowls filled with whirling moon-moths floated on the lake's surface.

Titania's royal household had gathered by the shore. Portia saw fairies in shimmering garments, with pinned-up hair and floral corsages. Among them, small groups of shape-shifters gathered here and there: fluffy-eared squirrels and short, stocky men with black stripes on their faces. As she descended the stairs to the hollow, Portia passed a young man with a pair of antlers growing from his head. The delicate sound of little bells and harps was coming from somewhere, but the crowd's murmur almost drowned out the music completely.

Peaseblossom guided her straight to Moon Lake. Wooden platforms drifted close to the shore, like big lily pads. More fairies were standing on the platforms, and pale ivory-haired girls swam in the water below.

All eyes were on Portia. She felt as if she were on display. At the same time, she couldn't help but stare back—the assembly of Otherworldly creatures was just too beautiful and peculiar. As she reached the lake shore, a fat toad with iridescent dragonfly wings buzzed right past her face.

No one will ever believe any of this, she thought.

A narrow footbridge led straight out over the lake to a crescent-shaped platform, in front of the dark hillock of an island, where Titania was holding court.

Portia slowed, but Peaseblossom waved her eagerly onward. "Chop, chop! Let's not keep Her Majesty waiting!"

Her Majesty, Portia thought, her blood running cold.

Titania sat on a throne of woven branches. Leaves, mushrooms, and frilly ferns all sprouted from the tangled wood. The branches of an oak tree growing on the island formed a canopy above the Fairy Queen.

Titania looked nothing like the harmless young woman Portia had met the day before. She sat bolt upright on her throne, staring at Portia with her silver eyes. The bodice of her dress clung to her upper body, and a cascade of shimmering flowers flowed from her shoulder to her feet. A stripe of cobalt-blue paint stretched from temple to temple across Titania's face, highlighting the unnatural glow of her eyes. On her head sat a crown of peeled willow-tree branches, and her long hair hung down to her shoulders. Instead of flowers, glittering dewdrops decorated her hair and crown.

Portia approached the platform with trembling knees. What had she gotten herself into?

Cobweb stood at Titania's left side. On the queen's other side was a rotund fairy man in a long robe dyed in shades of blue—presumably this was Pricklethorn, the Lord Chamberlain.

"Curtsy!" Peaseblossom hissed in a low voice.

"What?"

"Curtsy!" she repeated, before bobbing respectfully before the queen. Portia tried her best to copy her.

"Portia Humanchild." Titania's voice echoed across the lake. She raised her hand and beckoned Portia to come closer. Her fingertips had been dipped in silver-blue paint.

Portia walked up to the throne, trying hard to ignore Cobweb's stony expression. Titania was smiling at least, although her smile seemed a bit cold and formal. "Welcome to the dance of the fairies. Do you like it?"

At first Portia couldn't speak. She swallowed before managing to choke out a few words. "Yes, very much. Your Majesty."

"If I remember correctly, there were two of you. Where's your companion?" asked Titania.

There was no turning back now. Portia could only

hope that Ben and Gwil had put some distance between themselves and Fairy Hill by now.

"Ben is on his way to the World's End," she said. "He wants to help Rose, so he's gone to find out whether it's possible to bring someone back from the fog."

Portia stood stiffly, feeling her heartbeat pounding in her throat. Any moment now, Titania would surely explode in anger and have Portia thrown into the dungeons. But instead, the Fairy Queen raised her hand and let a moon-moth land on a fingertip.

"Surely the boy has not gone all by himself," she said. "Who's showing him the way?"

"It's Gwil Glumheart," Cobweb cut in. "It was he who brought the humans to your court in the first place."

"Is that true?" Titania asked.

Portia nodded. There was no sense in denying it, but she felt a wave of heat rising from her neck to her face. Far too late, she was realizing that she had underestimated the danger to Gwil and Meralyn. Even if Titania never found out about Merron's book, the salamanders had still acted without permission. What would Titania do? Punish Meralyn and Gwil for treason?

"So Glumheart has left the Hill." Titania turned to the Lord Chamberlain. "Did you grant permission?"

Pricklethorn lowered his head, his face bright red. "Yes, my queen."

"Interesting." Titania flicked the moon-moth from her fingertip. She gazed thoughtfully at Portia. "You and the boy are clearly rather fond of Viola Rosethorn."

Her tone was friendly, but still Portia felt a bead of sweat running down her back. "She's my aunt," she replied. "And she saved our lives. Please, Your Majesty. I know everyone's saying we can't help her. But we've got to try at least."

Titania settled back on her throne. "I do understand, child," she said. "Everyone who remembers the Gray King's last attack knows what it feels like to lose someone to the fog. And if there's an answer to your questions anywhere, then it's at World's End. There's one thing I don't understand, though. How do you plan on reaching Rose, since the key is with her, in the Borderlands?"

It felt as if the key was burning a hole in Portia's pocket. She really did want to tell the truth, but now that she had the chance, she didn't dare.

"Are you hoping that Rose is still herself enough to be able to open the door to our world?"

"No, Your Majesty."

"Could it be that you haven't told me the whole truth?" Titania asked. "Perhaps my Cobweb was not mistaken, after all, and she did see the key in your hand?"

Portia looked up, her face ablaze with fear, but Titania was smiling, and this time her smile seemed warm. "I thought as much," she said. "And I understand that you wanted to be careful. You didn't know me and couldn't have known how I would treat you. As I remember, humans are fond of telling stories about cunning fairies and their tricks."

Portia lowered her head, and at long last the knot in her chest loosened. "We shouldn't have lied, Your Majesty. I'm sorry."

Titania nodded. "I do hope you understand me as well," she said. "My folk have suffered greatly at the hands of the Gray King's army. And the World Key poses a great risk. Especially if it is used several times in a short period. But I also understand that you want to help Rose. And I'm sure you want to go home."

It seemed as if all Portia's worries had been for nothing. "Yes," she said, feeling so grateful, she would have liked to hug Titania.

"How would you feel about a deal?" Titania asked. "I'll agree to help you. And when you have the key again, you'll hand it over to me, and I'll keep it safe."

Did Titania think the key was still hidden somewhere? That would have been a good idea, actually. She could hear Ben's warning in her head: *In stories, humans always end up losing when they make deals with fairies.* Titania's offer sounded straightforward, but it was better to play it safe. She tried to sound as confident as possible. "If I agree, will you allow Gwil and Ben to finish their mission? And there won't be any punishment, either?"

Titania raised an eyebrow. "Punishment," she repeated, glancing at Pricklethorn, who looked increasingly pale. "Very well. I agree. I'll allow them to do what they need to do. You have my word."

Portia hesitated for a moment, but then she took a step forward, holding her head high. "Then I accept the deal."

Titania clapped her hands. "Wonderful," she said. "Then let's set the seal on our agreement. Pricklethorn?"

The Lord Chamberlain reached inside his robe and

handed Titania a silver bracelet. "This bracelet shall be my pledge," she said solemnly. "I hereby swear to get you home safely." She leaned forward and held the bracelet out to Portia. Portia took it, and Pricklethorn gestured for her to put it on her wrist.

Titania smiled again. "Your turn now. Will you reveal where you're hiding the key?"

Portia pulled the key out of her waistcoat pocket. Pricklethorn drew in a sharp breath, but Titania remained calm.

"As promised." Portia held the key up, and Titania took it nonchalantly. Then with a thin smile, she leaned back in her throne, twirling the key between her sparkling blue fingertips. "Such a tiny thing," she mused, "and yet it does so much harm. Cobweb!"

"Your Majesty."

"Make sure that the human child is taken home."

Portia frowned. "Right away?" she asked, taken aback.

"But of course," said Titania, in a friendly voice.

"Don't we need to get ready first?" Portia asked. "I don't know . . . gather provisions? Get together a troop of warriors, or something?"

"You'll hardly need provisions. It's not far to the servants' quarters."

"What?" Portia stared blankly at Titania. "I thought you were going to take me home."

"And that's exactly what I intend to do." Titania smiled again, but this time there was no warmth in her expression. "Bryngolau is your home now, human child."

Portia felt an icy chill run through her. "You promised to help me!"

"Oh, yes," Titania agreed. "I'll help you find your place in my world. I'll help you survive here. Instead of imprisoning you in a cloven oak tree, as anyone who is a threat to my people deserves." She leaned forward. "Did you truly believe I'd let you open the doors?" she hissed. "Never again will I allow any human to put my people in danger."

"But . . . I didn't mean to . . . ," Portia stammered.

"You didn't mean to what? Lead the Gray King right to my door? Lie to me?" She sat bolt upright on her throne, glaring down at Portia. "You did well to ask for forgiveness for your human friend and the salamander. I wasn't expecting that. Too bad you didn't ask the same for yourself."

Portia backed away, but Cobweb was standing close behind her and grabbed her by the arm and held her with an iron grip. Portia stared about her wildly, desperately looking for someone to help her. She saw Peaseblossom gaping at her, wide-eyed, her hands pressed to her mouth.

"You tried to betray me, and thereby you broke my laws," Titania roared. "From now on, you'll work off your debt as my servant in my service. *Caethiwa!*" The final word rang out like a bird's cry.

The last syllable had barely left Titania's lips when a blazing pain burned into Portia's wrist. She screamed in shock and jerked her arm up. The bracelet that Titania had given her began to smoke, and then melt on her skin like mercury. It burned. Oh, it burned so much! Portia watched aghast as the silver sank into her skin, leaving behind a smoking band around her wrist. Her eyes filled with tears, and she fell to her knees. She clasped her wrist with the other hand, but the mark that the bracelet had burnt into her skin couldn't be wiped away.

Titania slipped from her throne and strode past her to the edge of the platform. Through the blur of her tears, Portia saw she was holding the key between her fingertips.

"No!" she croaked.

"Get used to kneeling before your queen," Titania said, and threw the key into the lake.

The Library

Ben was grateful for Portia's Band-Aids. He and Gwil had been wandering the mountains beyond Fairy Hill since the previous afternoon and had slept only for a few hours before climbing another mountain pass at dawn. They walked on narrow trails, cut across scree-covered slopes and barren plains, and followed mountain streams through deserted groves of oak trees.

Soon they left the mountains behind and trudged across wild grassland, heading toward the coast. As evening fell, a drizzling rain swept in from the west, and soon enough their clothes were dripping wet.

At first, Ben had bombarded Gwil with questions about the Fairy World, but now he was too tired talk. He was as filthy as a sheep, and smelled like one too. Ben longed for Ridik's magical swiftflight, and cursed himself for having the fabulous idea of walking to World's End with Gwil. Walking to the end of the world—that's exactly what it felt like.

"Not long now," Gwil assured him. "Look."

He pointed forward. In the waning light, Ben could make out a dimly gleaming strip of sea and a hill rising above a bay like the shell of a tortoise.

"World's End," Gwil said.

Ben could only manage a weary nod. The last stretch of their journey seemed to drag on agonizingly. When they finally reached the shore, the last rays of sunlight were dying, and the tortoise-shell hill was blending into the gray twilight.

Gwil headed toward a clump of dark trees at the bottom of the hill. Amid the trees stood a low dwelling with a conical thatched roof. As they drew closer, Ben could make out a vegetable garden behind a wall, and a rough stone hut. As they passed, he saw through the gaps in the walls goats moving around inside.

"Almost there," Gwil mumbled.

As they approached the house, the door swung open and a figure stepped out with a lantern in his hand.

"Who's there?" a voice called.

"Ho, Tegid!" Gwil replied. "It's me, Gwil." He and Ben kept walking as Tegid came toward them. They met at the edge of the vegetable garden.

"Gwil Glumheart!" The librarian of World's End grasped Gwil's hand and smiled broadly. "So good to see you, my friend."

"Likewise," Gwil replied. "It's been far too long since I paid you a visit."

"Very true," Tegid said. Then he turned back toward his house and beckoned them to follow. "Come in, come in. I just put my supper on the stove. Looks like I should throw some more carrots into the stew!"

∽

Ben had never been happier to walk into a house. A house with a roof to keep out the rain, and with a fire crackling in a fireplace.

It seemed as if Tegid had made himself quite comfortable at World's End. The ceilings were low, and the stone floor was covered with thick rugs. A ladder led up to the loft, where Tegid had his bed as well as a space for visitors.

When Ben was settled in a chair by the fireplace, snug in a set of dry clothes provided by their host, it seemed as if all was right with the world, at least for now. Tegid handed him a bowl of stew, and he let out a satisfied sigh.

Tegid grinned. "Long journey, eh?"

Ben nodded, already enjoying his first spoonful of stew. Tegid chuckled and brought Gwil a bowl too, before settling into the last free chair in front of the fireplace.

The librarian was a good head shorter than Gwil, and somewhat plumper too. His figure seemed even rounder thanks to the thick swaddling of clothes he wore: leather slippers, linen leggings, a dark brown gown, and a chunky gray woolen sweater. The whole outfit was topped off with a green woolly hat.

Ben took another spoonful of the stew and felt his whole body warming up. Tegid was a good cook; there were turnips, carrots, onions, parsley, and garlic in the stew, with a handful of dried plums that added a sweetness to the broth, and a good pinch of pepper—enough to make Ben's eyes water.

Gwil told Tegid their story while they ate. When they had finished, he nodded.

"So the Gray King is awake again, then. Well, I've always thought it was just a matter of time."

"The door is closed now," Gwil said.

Tegid tutted. "Yes, and poor Mistress Rosethorn is stuck on the wrong side of it."

"Do you know Rose?" Ben asked.

"A little. I knew her friends better. Three of them came to visit World's End, all those years ago."

Ben swallowed a mouthful of stew. "Ridik told me that Bramble and Rose fought the Gray King back then."

"Oh, yes, indeed they did," Gwil confirmed. "Side by side with the badgers and Titania's fairy warriors. Until a messenger from the Adar arrived to announce that their friends had figured out a way to kill the Gray King here in World's End. Then they rode to the Pale Tower to attack him at the heart of his power."

"That's not quite true, actually," Tegid cut in. "We didn't know how to kill the Gray King back then, either. Or even whether it was possible to do so. We did figure out how to stop him, though."

"Really?" Ben said. "How?"

"By stitching a rune charm into a cloth and throwing it over him. In this way a spell was cast that put him into a deep sleep. But you need one piece of crucial knowledge for the spell to work: the Gray King's real name."

"And what is it?" Ben asked.

Tegid leaned back. "In the stories we tell our children, the Gray King came out of nowhere. He's a creature of the in-between, we say, a being made of fog and dark thoughts." He paused and smiled sadly. "But that's not true. The Gray King's real name is Arawn. And Arawn is the ruler of Annwn."

Ben flinched.

"So the human folk still speak of Annwn?" Tegid asked, seeing the boy's reaction.

Ben gulped. "Where I'm from they do."

"And what do they say?"

"They say it's the land of ghosts. The . . . the Underworld." Ben remembered the day he had read about Annwn for the first time. He was ten years old and had found a book of Welsh mythology in the library.

Tegid nodded. "It's *one* of the Underworlds, yes. The one that's closest to us."

Gwil set down his bowl. "Arawn is the ruler of Annwn, just as Titania and Oberon are the rulers of our world. But he left his kingdom a long time ago."

Tegid rubbed his chin. "I have no idea why he turned his back on Annwn, but something must be driving him to cross the borders into other worlds."

"He doesn't just cross over—every world he sets foot in is wiped away by the fog if nobody stops him."

There was an uncomfortable silence. There was still some stew at the bottom of Ben's bowl, but he had lost his appetite.

"May I see Merron's book?" Tegid said eventually.

"Of course." Gwil pulled the book from inside his robe, and passed it to Tegid with a trembling hand.

Tegid leafed through the yellowed pages, examining them with curiosity. "Instructions for crafting a World

Key," he read. "Well, that should help you to get into the Pale Tower. Are you planning on banishing him again?"

"No," Gwil replied. "We think Rose has become a Mist-walker, and we want to bring her back."

"Not an easy task," Tegid said. "But I'm sure there's a solution hidden away somewhere in my library."

The research appeared to be a welcome challenge for him. Meanwhile, Ben was still pondering Tegid's suggestion of banishing the Gray King again.

"Why doesn't Titania get rid of the Gray King?" he asked. "If anyone could do it, surely she could?"

"Titania has no interest in confronting Arawn these days," Tegid said. "As long as the doors to the Fairy World are closed, she doesn't care what he does."

Every shape-shifter Ben spoke to seemed to agree that they could expect no help from Titania, and yet Portia was pinning all her hopes on the Fairy Queen. Worry wormed its way into his mind. *How did her negotiations go?* he wondered. *Is she getting the help she was hoping for?*

"As for your plan," Tegid said, "I don't suppose I need to tell you how dangerous it is?"

"We know," Ben said quietly.

"And yet, you still want to try. For Rose's sake." A grin spread across Tegid's round face. "That, my friends, is the stuff that great heroes' stories are made of."

Gwil snorted. "But this isn't a story."

Tegid winked. "Are you quite sure about that?" He got to his feet, scurried to a shelf, and returned with a clay bottle and three little mugs.

"This is what we need right now!" He poured some liquid into the mugs, and the scent of honey reached Ben's nose. "I'll help you two as much as I can." He handed each of them a mug and raised his in a toast. "I know just where to find the books we consulted the last time the Gray King attacked. We'll surely find answers to your questions there."

Ben took a sip and coughed. Tegid's brew tasted sweet, but it burned his lips. "When are we going to the library?" he asked.

Tegid beamed. "A real bookworm, eh?" he asked, and chuckled. "Tomorrow. My lady looks her best in daylight."

INTERLUDE

At dawn, a soft white mist rolled in from the sea. Thick fog swept across the shore to coil around the hills of World's End, smothering all sound.

No one yet stirred in Tegid's house, but a white dog slunk along the wall outside. It moved as lightly as a breath of air, on long, sinewy legs. It paused in front of the door and listened. Gray clouds swirled within its eyes—as if someone had filled two glass orbs with a thunderstorm.

Far away, the sun was rising over the sea, and the mist on the waves began to clear. A bird sang from a nearby tree. The dog flinched, turned, and ran back across the meadow in front of Tegid's house. There, amidst the high grass, stood the Gray King's huntress. The second hunting dog waited by her side.

When both dogs were near, she touched their heads, and they dissolved into fog. She looked at the house. A lantern was burning in one of the windows. The huntress turned and disappeared into the mist.

Her time had not yet come.

The Fairy Curse

Outside, dawn was breaking, but not a single ray of sunlight penetrated the depths of Fairy Hill. Portia flattened herself against a wall and peeked around a corner. At the bottom of a broad stairway, a group of young salamanders had gathered to report for service. Those who were to work in the kitchens tied their aprons, while those who were to serve breakfast to the fairies smoothed out the wrinkles in their headscarves or turbans. Titania couldn't stand her servants looking disheveled.

I hope she chokes on her breakfast, Portia thought bitterly.

Awel, the salamander girl Portia had seen in the water lily chamber, glanced about, looking for Portia, who quickly drew her head back and hid behind the wall. Awel had taken Portia under her wing after the "celebration" by Moon Lake, found a sleeping place in the servants' quarters for her, and explained all the jobs that would be hers from now on. But her words and everything else that had happened since that evening by the lake were just a blur for Portia. She kept touching her wrist, again and again. Despite the burn mark, the skin was still smooth. She couldn't really feel the manacle, but every time she looked down at it, her stomach twisted into a painful knot.

Bryngolau is your home now.

The memory of the gleeful glitter in Titania's eyes left a sour taste in Portia's mouth. She would never give up, and there was no way she was staying here!

She threw a last glance at the salamanders before setting off to make her escape.

Portia didn't know the way out of the Hill, so she chose her route more or less at random, going up staircases when she could, turning and hurrying off into deserted side tunnels when she heard voices up ahead. She forced herself not to run. There had to be a way out. Several even, as Gwil had said: forgotten gates, secret servants' doors . . . She'd keep looking until she found an unguarded exit. A whole choir of doubts was singing inside her head, but she blocked it out.

Away from the main thoroughfares, pathways through Fairy Hill were simply tunnels drilled through black rock. The one Portia was walking down at the moment was gloomy and cave-like, with an uneven floor and rough walls dripping with lime. Whole colonies of shimmering blue mushrooms grew on the rock, bathing the passageway in a watery light. The air felt cooler and more humid, too.

The further she walked, the narrower the passage became—until she had to hold her arms tight to her body to avoid touching the glowing mushrooms. She was about to turn around and go back when she noticed a flight of stairs up ahead.

Portia started with excitement, and accidentally touched

a clump of mushrooms with her elbow. To her horror, the little round heads shuddered, and a hissing noise surged through the passage. Portia clamped her arms to her sides and made a run for the stairs, only to trip over her feet and tumble to the floor when she heard a choir of faint voices whisper: "Don't go."

Portia felt goose bumps creeping up her neck. The voices seemed to be coming from nowhere. Or perhaps they were coming from the walls?

"Don't go," the choir murmured once more.

Portia got to her feet and began to run again, but in her haste she brushed against the soft, cool mushrooms once more. This time the whole wall of mushrooms began to tremble and sway, like the tentacles of a sea anemone, searching for a tiny fish to ensnare.

"Turn back!"

"You're putting yourself in danger!"

Fear clawed at Portia's stomach, but she kept running, her eyes fixed on the stairs. The noise of the voices swelled to a terrible groan, but by then she was hurrying up the staircase.

After a while, the passage became so narrow again that Portia could feel damp moss brushing against her arms. She had left the stairs behind long ago, but still the shaft was climbing steeply. Portia scrambled upward, on hands and knees now, and shuddered each time her elbow scraped against the wall. What if the tunnel got too narrow? What if she got stuck and couldn't turn around? She could feel the fear in her chest, like a trembling rabbit, but she forced herself to focus on the way ahead. She could see a circle of light in the distance now, and slowly but surely it was growing bigger.

Almost there, she told herself. *Almost. There.*

When she saw some green fronds of bracken against a slice of blue sky at the end of the tunnel, her heart nearly leapt out of her chest. She scrambled the final few meters to the way out, which was no more than a hole in the rock, squeezed herself through into the daylight, and slid down a slippery rock face to tumble into a tangle of brambles and bracken. Finally she had solid ground beneath her feet again! Portia almost sank to her knees with relief. She lifted her face to the sky and sucked in a deep lungful of fresh air. A ray of sunlight fell onto her grubby, sweaty features.

She stood there for a few seconds, just breathing in and out. She'd made it. She'd really made it. Once she was sure that her legs would carry her, she began to explore the area. Ahead of her lay a narrow clearing amid the scrub. Beyond that, the woods began. How far would she be able to get before Titania realized that she had escaped? *Far enough*, she told herself.

She'd follow Gwil and Ben to World's End; then they would find Rose together. She knew the library lay to the west—all she had to do was make it to the coast. Then she should be able to find her way.

But Portia had barely taken a step toward the clearing when a searing pain shot from her wrist to her shoulder. She looked down at Titania's mark, and saw to her horror that the edges of the tattoo were glowing golden red. It felt as if stinging nettles were flowing through her veins.

Portia clenched her fists and forced herself to keep putting one foot in front of the other. She would *not* be stopped. She *would* catch up with Ben. She *would*. . . . The next wave of pain made her scream out loud. She staggered forward, but the clearing began to blur before her eyes. *Keep going*, she told herself. *Keep going!* A burst of pain struck her in the chest like a bolt of lightning. Her knees buckled, she pitched forward into the bracken, and the world turned black.

Rune Magic

After a breakfast of porridge and berry jam, Ben and Gwil followed Tegid outside. He led them through the little wood around his house and up onto the hill behind, with the thunderous rumble of waves breaking on the shore accompanying them all the way.

World's End library stood at the top of the hill, next to the edge of a cliff that plunged a hundred meters or so to the waves below. Like Tegid's house, it was a low, round stone building with a thatched dome for a roof. As they climbed toward it, Ben was buffeted by the sea wind. When they drew near, a scattering of jackdaws took off from the roof to soar on the breeze.

At the entrance, Tegid turned to face them, his eyes sparkling.

"Ready?" he asked. And then he opened the door to World's End.

Ben was so excited as he stepped inside that his nails were digging into the palms of his hands, but he was immediately disappointed with what he saw. The library consisted of only one room, with two circular rows of shelves, one nestled inside the other like a tree's rings.

There were certainly plenty of books on the shelves, but not a remarkable number.

Was this really the great library of the druids and salamanders? After everything Gwil and Meralyn had told him, Ben had expected piles of scrolls, folios, and precious old books.

Tegid watched Ben's reaction with a broad smile. "Still not impressed?" he asked. "Then watch this."

He walked to the middle of the room. Dead in the center of the shelf rings was an empty white circle. Tegid stopped at the edge of the circle, and stepped on a rune that had been burnt into the floor. He had barely touched the rune with his foot when a gritty scraping sound filled the room. The white circle sank down and split into two halves, which slid apart to leave a perfectly round hole in the floor. Tegid beckoned Ben over. Ben went to his side and peered cautiously into the hole. Floor after floor stretched out below them. Dozens and dozens of levels of shelves filled with books. They were standing on the top floor of a tower that stretched down into the ground! Light shone dimly into the tower at each level, as if sunlight were streaming in at the sides.

"Welcome to World's End," Tegid said, clearly in good spirits. "Let's see what we can find."

The salamander had not been exaggerating. World's End was a miraculous place. The outer wall of the upside-down library tower seemed to protrude from the cliff face, and on the second floor down, a huge curved window let in plenty of light. There was no glass in it; instead, runes carved into the walls created an invisible shield, protecting the tower against wind, rain, and cold. It looked as if you could step right out of the tower into the sky.

Tegid set to trawling through the library's shelves right away, but Ben stood awestruck, tracing the rune shapes on the wall with his finger.

"Most of us can use runes," said Gwil, standing at Ben's side with his hands clasped behind his back. "Fairies, humans, shape-shifters . . . But making the runes powerful—that takes a lot of practice. You don't only have to see the word the runes are spelling in your mind's eye—you have to see the meaning and purpose too."

"The meaning?" Ben repeated.

Gwil reached out and touched one of the runes. "Let's say you scratch runes into a young tree and speak the rune word *grow*. If it's done correctly, the rune speaker should see an image of a sprouting sapling in their mind. They are not only imagining the tree growing; they can sense it too. If they aren't careful, the sapling might only grow a few leaves . . . or a whole forest might shoot up instead." Gwil smiled. "Everyone knows some rune magic, but some have a special gift for it. Take Rose, for example—she's got a talent for combat and defense runes."

Ben looked up at the lintel of the window, which was entirely covered in runes. "How about you? Can you write runes?"

"Yes," Gwil said. "But I don't really have a talent for magic."

"Hooray!" Tegid's voice came from behind the shelves.

Gwil and Ben exchanged a smile and went over to a worktable by the window.

Tegid emerged carrying a pile of books. "Here you go," he said, enthusiastically plonking the pile down on the table. "These should keep us busy, for starters. And look what else I've found." He reached inside his cardigan and pulled out a slim red notebook with a worn linen binding.

"This was Rose and Bramble's notebook," Tegid explained. "It's one of the rune books they practiced spells and magic with."

Ben was itching to get his hands on the notebook. Tegid noticed his impatience and pushed the book across the table to him.

Ben accepted it gratefully. "Is the rune spell to banish the Gray King in here?"

"No," Tegid replied immediately. "One of the humans stitched that on a cloth."

"A cloth?" Ben asked.

"A charm cloth. She and the others took it to the Pale Tower. Rose must have awakened the runes in the tower to banish the Gray King."

"Do you know which rune spell they used?" Gwil asked.

Tegid plucked a book from the pile and tapped its cover. *"Taliesin's Evening Blessing."*

"Could the thing with the charm cloth work a second time?" Ben asked.

"It could," Tegid said, "but it's too dangerous for you two to try it."

"I know," Ben agreed. "But if we bring Rose back here, she can do it, can't she?"

Tegid rested his chin on his folded hands. "Maybe. But

that's just it, isn't it? *If* we bring Rose back here."

Ben lowered his gaze and felt along the edge of the red notebook with his thumb. Yes. If.

Tegid briefly placed his hand on Ben's. "Don't be disheartened!" he said. "We'll find a way to snatch her from the fog's claws. These few books are just a start, and if we don't find what we need here, we'll keep on searching. There's an answer to everything buried somewhere in this tower."

"Buried?" Gwil asked, worried.

Tegid beamed at him. "Indeed. We may have to go deeper than I've ever been so far to find it."

He didn't sound remotely worried at the prospect.

That afternoon, the salamanders went back to Tegid's house for some tea and a bite to eat. Ben stayed at the desk at the window all by himself. They had pored through three piles of books by now, with no luck.

Ben leafed through Rose and Bramble's notebook. They had copied paragraphs from books about runes and elemental magic, both making notes in the margins commenting on each other's writings. There was even a sketch of a standing stone covered in runes.

Ben flicked ahead until he got to a page that had a number of runes and their respective translations listed in three neat lines. That morning he had made sure to bring Portia's travel diary with him, so he could take notes in it himself. He took it out of his pocket now, snapped off the rubber band keeping it shut, and, using the pen clipped to the front, began sketching one of the runes. Ben liked its shape: one vertical line, and two diagonal lines that jutted out of its side like branches. For some reason, the runes reminded him of the forest on his bedroom wall, where the Wild Things hid. So many times, he had imagined stepping through the painted trees to another world. And that's where he was right now, wasn't he? In another world.

Ben kept browsing, copying combinations of runes at random without giving it much thought. Rose's and Bramble's translations were in Welsh, and he understood most of them. With every rune he copied, his desire to say them out loud increased. He felt silly, but excited at the same time. Ben placed a finger on the last line of runes he had drawn, wet his lips with the tip of his tongue, and then spoke the rune's name.

"Darganfydda." Find.

Ben held his breath for one tense moment, but nothing happened. Disappointed, he breathed out, shaking his head. What had he expected? A tingling in his fingers? For the runes on the page to glow blue, like the ones on Rose's staff?

Ben sighed and returned to Portia's notebook. He was about to sketch a small pile of books when something fluttered into his field of vision from the right. He lifted his head to see a moon-moth tumbling toward him. It landed on the open diary, right on the drawing of the rune he had just read aloud.

Ben didn't dare to take his hand off the page. He didn't even dare to breathe. As he watched, the moon-moth began to glow a deep blue. Its antennae quivered; then it took flight again and fluttered to the middle of the room. It stopped above the stairs leading down, deeper into the tower, hovering in place as if waiting for something. Or someone.

Ben stared, frozen for a few moments, then jumped to his feet and followed the moth as it began to descend the tower staircase. The light coming through the window faded as he went further and further down. The moon-moth flew ahead of him like a particularly keen guiding star. Or perhaps a will-o'-the-wisp, set to lead him astray? At that moment, however, his curiosity was stronger than his fear. Where had the moth come from? Had he summoned it? And what did it want to show him? Trying to solve the puzzle was irresistible. Finally Ben understood why Portia had followed a fox into the wilderness.

With every step, Ben descended further, and the deeper he got, the gloomier his surroundings became. The scent of old leather grew stronger, and Ben noticed that the air wasn't musty or damp. No dust, low humidity: the perfect conditions for a library. His dad would have loved this place.

Ben imagined what it would have been like to tell him about the library, and how he would have set out for World's End right away. As always, he felt a twinge of pain when it struck him that he would never talk to his dad again.

He was still lost in thought when they reached a new level and the moon-moth finally came to a halt. Ben stopped too. It was utterly silent and still down here. He could make out the vague shape of shelves nearby, which ran off and disappeared into darkness.

It wasn't cold, but Ben's forearms were covered in goose bumps. The moth didn't stay still for long and soon fluttered off up one of the aisles that ran between the shelves like the spokes of a wheel. Ben glanced back one last time at the stairs, and then followed it.

As they left one wall of shelves after another behind, Ben felt increasingly ill at ease. How far was the moth leading him? And was it his imagination, or did the tower seem much wider down here than the entrance room on the top? Up there, Ben had seen only two rings of shelves, but down here he had already passed through four of them. He was just thinking of turning back when the moth seemed to reach its destination. In the middle of the aisle, a few feet away from Ben, stood a desk. On it lay a single book. The moth was dancing above it like a tiny star. With his heart pounding, Ben approached the table.

The book's binding was so ancient that the leather looked black. It was scuffed from the touch of many hands—or perhaps the hands had belonged to just one person, who had taken the book from the shelf time and time again. Ben placed his own hand on the cover and felt a gust of air behind his back. He spun around with his heart in his mouth. It had felt as if someone was running up the aisle behind him, but there was no one there. He was alone.

Reluctantly he turned back to the book and opened it. A loose slip of paper fell out from between the pages, and Ben picked it up. There were only two words on it: *Codex Reditus*. They meant nothing to him. Cautiously he began to turn the pages. The scuffed binding was misleading; the book was old, but not ancient. The pages were made of thick cream-colored paper covered in handwritten text—yet another notebook, apparently. One page seemed to have a date written in the corner, but the ink was so smeared that Ben couldn't decipher it. The writing was crammed tightly on the pages, as if the author had been trying to save space. Here and there the lines of text were interrupted by pictures of strangely contorted faces.

The author probably just hadn't been very good at drawing faces, but still those uncannily long heads and black misshapen eyes sent shivers down Ben's spine. As he leafed through the book, Ben found ripped-out pages from other books that the author had collected and added to their own notes. One showed a woodcut of a man sitting on a rock, holding a lute. He was surrounded by animals, who appeared to be crying. Another page was decorated with a colorful image that reminded Ben of illuminated Bibles from the Middle Ages. There were no praying monks or angels here, though. Instead there was a slim man, his head downcast and shoulders hunched, walking toward the left margin of the page. Ben shivered. Another figure, a humanlike creature wearing a robe, was following the man. Or was the creature chasing him? Ben gulped, turned another page, and then caught his breath. He recognized the black door in this drawing. The paper was grooved, as if the artist had scratched the page violently with a quill, many times over. The door looked like a gaping black maw, like an abyss leading through the book to who knows where. As he stared at the page, the moth fluttered over to Ben and landed at the edge of the page. Ben's hands were trembling.

Underneath the black door was just one word. *Annwn.*

Shards

The Fairy Queen was posing on a pedestal in the water lily chamber, trying on the latest creation from Mistress Quickly's sewing room. Around her, a dozen fairies lay or sat on cushions and pillows. A harpist gently strummed at his instrument.

Portia stood next to the pedestal, holding a tray bearing a silver plate filled with pralines. The sweets were covered in white chocolate and decorated with little candied violets. She was tight-lipped with frustration, fighting the desire to hurl the tray across the room.

She had tried to escape three times now. Each time the pain radiating from the mark on her wrist had almost made her lose her mind before she passed out. Then Titania had sent Peaseblossom or Cobweb to fetch her, and as soon as she had woken up back inside Fairy Hill, the pain was gone. But the more often she opened her eyes belowground, the more the walls of Bryngolau seemed to be closing in around her.

Up on the pedestal, two of Meralyn's seamstresses were scurrying around the queen, adjusting and pinning a sky-blue gown strewn with tiny pearls. Meralyn Quickly stood to one side, observing their work.

When the girls were done, Meralyn sifted through the pile of fabrics she had brought along, and chose a long sash made of dark-blue velvet. Then she approached Titania and draped the sash over her shoulder, so that it hung down to her waist.

"I think this would make a lovely addition to the gown, Your Majesty," she said.

"Fine, fine, whatever you think is right," the queen said impatiently.

Meralyn lowered her head in a bow.

Portia wished she could have at least stayed with Meralyn, as she had on her first night in Fairy Hill, but now she was denied even that safe haven—Titania had forbidden any contact with the head seamstress.

After the fitting, the seamstresses gathered their material, curtsied, and left the salon. Portia forced herself not to follow them with her eyes.

Titania stepped off her pedestal and lay down on her divan. She was wearing the simple white dress that she'd had on when she'd first received Ben and Portia. It had all been a trick, Portia realized now. Her harmless appearance was nothing but a mask. Anger simmered in her stomach—at Titania, and at herself for having been foolish enough to trust her. Titania had completely outsmarted her. But if the queen thought she had Portia under her power, then she was wrong.

Portia would never give up. She was going to escape and find Ben and Gwil. Together they would find a way out of this glittering pit. And Titania could burst with rage, for all she cared.

"Human girl!" Titania cried in her most commanding voice. She had stopped calling Portia by her name a long while ago. "Have you grown roots over there or something?"

Portia forced herself to hide her emotions as she went over to the queen. She curtsied silently, offering her the tray. Titania didn't say anything, but Portia couldn't help but notice the amused twitching at the corners of her mouth.

She thinks she has won. Portia's anger left a sour taste on her tongue.

Titania picked a praline, and bit into it with visible pleasure. Then she snapped her fingers, and the harpist switched from a rather cheerful melody to something slow and sweet. Portia was about to back away when Titania addressed her once more.

"Human girl," she said. "What instrument do you play?"

Portia swore inwardly. "None," she replied loudly, before reluctantly adding, "Your Majesty."

"None?" Titania repeated, feigning surprise. "Then you must come up with something else to entertain us. Let me think. You must be able to sing or dance, mustn't you? No? Such a shame."

She daintily brushed a crumb from the corner of her mouth, cocked her head, and looked Portia over. "Are you sure you're really a girl?" she asked, before turning to the assembled fairies. "Humans simply aren't particularly gifted," she explained. "There are some exceptions, of course, but most of them are quite clumsy and ordinary." She examined Portia again. "Rather oafish too, though it's no fault of their own." She beckoned Portia, who reluctantly approached the Fairy Queen.

Titania sighed. "You see?" she said. "That square chin, those eyebrows. No natural beauty, inside or out. We could dress this creature in one of Quickly's most beautiful garments, and it wouldn't make any difference."

Portia's face was hot and aglow with anger. She knew Titania was just trying to provoke her, and yet the queen's words still got under her skin like tiny thorns.

Titania smiled in mock sympathy and placed a hand on her cheek. Portia flinched.

"Human girl," Titania said. "Has no one ever told you that you're not beautiful? I feel I must, since your family obviously couldn't bring themselves to. They must have been trying to spare your feelings, but it's no kindness in the long run. Better to face up to the truth."

Because you're such an expert when it comes to the truth, aren't you? Portia thought bitterly.

Titania turned to her fairies again. "You can always rely on Quickly's judgement. See how she's dressed this creature in trousers. She's just not pretty enough for a dress."

Portia was struck dumb with anger and frustration, but didn't understand why. Why did she care what that harpy thought?

Titania raised an eyebrow and smirked. "Yes, Portia?" she asked. "Did you want to say something?"

Portia ran the tip of her tongue along her lips. "No, Your Majesty." She would have loved to spit all the bitterness she was feeling right in her face.

The corners of Titania's mouth curled into a triumphant little smile. "Well then, don't just stand there gaping. Go and clear the crockery."

Portia left the water lily chamber on shaky legs. She had piled all the teacups, plates, and the silver teapot onto her small tray, and it was now so heavy that she was barely able to carry it. The fairies giggled as they watched her go, waiting for her to drop the wobbly load. She didn't give them the satisfaction, but her composed façade was crumbling, and her fury dwindling under the massive weight of her own helplessness. She couldn't understand how anyone could be so spiteful. Tears burned in her eyes, but she couldn't wipe them away.

She managed to carry the tray all the way to the tunnel outside the scullery, but then one cup skittered off and smashed on the ground. Portia tried to keep the rest of the pile steady, but it was too late; it all came down onto the mosaic tiles with an almighty crash. Portia swore, knelt amid the debris, and began to gather up the broken crockery. By now tears were streaming down her cheeks.

"That's not going to work," someone said above her.

Portia looked up. It was Robin Goodfellow, his hands casually tucked into his trouser pockets. It was too much for Portia. She wiped the tears from her face. "Mind your own business," she snapped. "Ouch!" Portia had cut her hand on a shard of china. Of course she had, what else should she expect? She put the bleeding finger into her mouth and defiantly began picking through the debris with the other.

Robin crouched down next to her. "Is it a human quirk to always do exactly what you shouldn't? Careful!"

Portia jumped to her feet and glared at him. "I wouldn't even be in this horrible situation if it wasn't for you!"

"Careful, dammit!" Robin darted up from his crouched position and kicked a broken cup away from Portia's bare feet. He reached out a hand, but she slapped it aside.

"Don't you dare touch me!" She put her finger into her mouth again and glared at him. "Bramble was right. She should have made gloves out of you."

"Are you sure you're not related to *her*?" Robin asked sharply. "You've got a big mouth anyway, that's for sure."

"I'd rather have a big mouth than a heart of stone."

They stared at each other for a few seconds, like two gunslingers in a Western. Then Robin sighed and raised his hands as if in surrender. "Come with me and we'll get that bandaged up."

For a brief moment, Portia had a vision of the fox sitting under the blackberry hedge. "Ha! Like I'd ever follow you anywhere ever again."

"Oh, come on. . . ." He took a step toward her. She backed away, but he grabbed her arm.

"Do you want to save Rose or not?" he hissed. Portia froze. "Meralyn told me about your genius plan," he said quietly. "Using the World Door at the Pale Tower? I've never heard such a foolish idea. If you really want to go through with it, you'll need all the help you can get." He let go of her arm and raked his fingers through his hair. "And I can't believe I'm really saying this, but I'll help you."

Portia tried to read his expression. She couldn't believe she was even listening to him, after what he had done to her. "Why should I trust a single word you say?"

Robin sighed again. "Spirits, give me strength. For the last time, do you want to save Rose or not?"

Portia hesitated. Then she nodded.

"Great." Robin turned on his heel. "Then come along."

The Book of Return

"*C*odex Reditus," Tegid read aloud. "The *Book of Return.*"

Gwil leaned forward. "That sounds promising."

Ben sat by the picture window and watched as the salamanders examined the black notebook. There were tea and ginger cookies on the table, so far untouched.

"And the moth really led you straight to this notebook?" Gwil asked a second time.

Ben nodded.

"After you spoke the rune?"

Ben nodded again.

Gwil looked him over thoughtfully. Then he smiled. "It was a discovery rune. Who knows, perhaps you have a talent for rune speaking too."

Ben felt his face getting hot, but he was pleased. A rune speaker! Wouldn't that be something.

In the meantime, Tegid was mumbling to himself as he marveled at a particularly chaotic page. "Interesting. Most interesting."

"Have you found something?" Gwil asked. "Something helpful?"

"I'm afraid not." Tegid tapped the book cover. "It's not

about the return of Mistwalkers. This book deals with the question of whether a dead person can return to the realm of the living. Look!"

He pulled out one of the loose pages. "This illustration is from the story of Orpheus. According to the myth, he descended into Hades to bring back his dead wife."

"So we're still no closer," Gwil said, sounding discouraged.

Tegid smiled. "Don't give up, old friend. We're only just scratching the surface."

Gwil nodded, but he still looked glum. He absent-mindedly rubbed his wrist that had Titania's faded yet still-visible mark.

Meanwhile Ben stared at the picture that Tegid had laid on the table. It showed a man walking with head bowed, a woman in a white dress following behind. A hot, tight knot had settled in his chest, and Tegid's words echoed in his head. Was there really a way to bring the dead back to the realm of the living?

"Why that moth would have led Ben to this book in particular is a mystery to me," Tegid said.

Ben wet his dry lips with the tip of his tongue. "The door in that drawing—is that another World Door?"

Tegid creased his pale forehead and flipped back through the book until he reached the picture of the black door. "Yes," he confirmed. "Yes, I think so."

Gwil bent over the book. "Annwn . . . ," he read. "Tegid . . . do you think that's Arawn's door?"

Tegid tapped a finger on the page. "It's possible." His face brightened. "Perhaps that's why the moth wanted you to find the book! You must have been thinking of our destination. It is said that there are two doors in the Pale Tower. One leads to Faerie, and the other to Annwn."

"You said Annwn is one of the Underworlds. Is there really more than one?" asked Ben.

"Oh, yes, dozens!" he replied. "Our Orpheus here, for instance—he wouldn't have been looking for his wife in Annwn. He'd have descended to Hades. Wait!"

Tegid jumped up and hurried over to the rows of shelves, obviously in his element. Ben felt as if he was standing on a thin sheet of ice that was beginning to crack under his feet.

"Is everything all right, Ben?" Gwil asked.

Before Ben had a chance to reply, Tegid came bustling back to the desk carrying a giant book.

"Brace yourselves, friends," he wheezed, and dropped it onto the table, where it landed with a thud. "That," he said, "is an atlas of the worlds. One of the good ones."

Ben forgot his stress of only a moment ago as Tegid opened the atlas and spread out its wonderful pages. The map before them was immensely detailed, drawn in black and blue ink. The cartographer had drawn rivers, mountain ranges, and even waves breaking along the coasts. The page they were looking at showed the region of Faerie they were in. The shape of the land and contours of the coast looked like north Wales, but the fantastical place names were different. . . . The map was also crisscrossed by a veiny network of dotted lines that Ben couldn't quite make sense of.

"We are here," Tegid explained, tapping a peninsula

marked *World's End* with his fingertip. Tegid lifted a corner of the map, and Ben realized it was drawn on tracing paper. He hadn't noticed at first that there was a page of thicker card underneath the map itself. In fact, the whole atlas seemed to be made of alternating layers of card and tracing paper.

"And now, pay attention, my friends." Tegid smoothed the map of Faerie back onto its card underlayer, before carefully pulling out a second map from the pages of the atlas and placing it on top of the first.

The outlines of both maps aligned perfectly. The dotted lines were identical as well, but now Ben could recognize place names on the top map. Harlech. Caernarfon. Those were the names of castles the English had built in north Wales in the thirteenth century.

Ben bent over the map to get a closer look. It looked like a map of Wales in the Middle Ages!

"Wow," he muttered.

Tegid beamed. "Impressive, isn't it. And look at this." He lifted the remaining pages and card dividers in his hand.

As far as Ben could tell, the atlas must have contained more than a dozen maps. *Were they all maps of other worlds?* he wondered.

"Are those all the worlds that exist?" he asked, in awe.

"Sweet spirits, absolutely not!" Tegid said. "This is just a selection from our little corner of the macrocosm. Here we have the Human World, for example," he said, tapping the upper map, "and Faerie is below."

"And Annwn?" Ben asked.

Tegid cocked his head. "Yes, I suppose one could insert a map of Annwn. Arawn's realm is one of the Underworlds of our region, after all."

"But?" Gwil prompted.

"But no map of Annwn exists," Tegid explained. "Or of any other Underworld, for that matter."

"How curious," Gwil commented.

Tegid shrugged. "Not really. Some worlds cannot be drawn on a map. Which must be why so many people are fascinated by them. In any case, this author seems to have been obsessed with the rules governing the passageways between the middle and outer worlds."

"What kind of rules?" Ben asked.

"All worlds have their own laws of nature," Tegid explained. "Their own time, their own moon phases, sources of magical energy, and so on. But they do have a few things in common. For one thing, in every world there are places where the boundaries with other worlds are thin. Some call these places ley lines. Or spirit paths. Or world seams."

He traced a dotted line with his fingertip until he came to a point above a lake, where a five-pointed star had been drawn. Ben frowned, but then realized what he was looking at. He knew that lake! It was right above Trefriw.

"The Human Door!" he called out. "The star marks the Human Door."

Tegid smiled and nodded. "Correct. What you see here is a world seam, and a gate to cross from one world to the other."

Ben's gaze drifted back to the *Book of Return*. "So the door to Annwn must be on a seam too, right?"

"Indeed," Tegid replied. "And you'd need a key for that door, too."

Ben swallowed hard. "But if you had one . . ."

"Then you could cross over to Annwn, yes." Tegid finished Ben's sentence. "But I wouldn't recommend it."

"Why not?" Ben's voice came out in a rasp, but Tegid didn't seem to notice.

"The passageway from the Worlds of the Living to the Worlds of the Dead has its own set of rules." Tegid pointed at the loose illustrated page. "Take our good Orpheus here. According to the legend, he did find a way to get into his Underworld, and he convinced Hades's ruler to give him his wife back. But on one condition: he didn't turn around to look at her until they got back to their own world. And what do you think happened?"

"He turned around," Gwil said.

"He turned around," Tegid confirmed. "He heard her footsteps behind him and turned around, and she disappeared into the Underworld again."

Ben was looking at the illustration and imagined that it started moving, how Orpheus was walking ahead as the woman in white followed him, her gaze full of longing. *Don't turn around*, Ben thought. *Just keep looking straight ahead.*

Tegid closed the atlas with a loud thud, making Ben flinch. "I'll go and fetch us a few more books."

"Wonderful," Gwil sighed, and Tegid gave a determined nod. Then he hoisted the atlas off the table and tottered off to the back shelves. Meanwhile, Gwil gathered up the loose pages from the codex to make space for the next book. Ben should have given him a hand but was finding it hard to concentrate.

His thoughts turned to his father. He couldn't help it. He remembered a trip to the seaside. His parents had never had the money for a big vacation, but whenever possible Tom had loaded the family into the car to drive to the coast for the day.

On that day, the sky had been clear and light blue, like a pane of tinted glass. The wind had whistled across the beach, blowing tiny grains of sand against Ben's calves. His parents had taken off their shoes and rolled up their trouser legs before wading into the water to paddle in the shallows. They tried to convince Ben to join them, but he was too nervous, so his dad started clucking like a chicken, making him laugh. Ben stuck his tongue out, and the next moment Tom came running toward him.

Ben ran away, laughing, but Tom caught up with him, and grabbed and swung him up onto his shoulders.

"Now, my boy. Let's see how big a splash you make."

"Noooo! Nooo!"

Ben laughed and squealed as his dad carried him toward the water. Tom pretended he was going to throw him into the sea for real, but Ben knew that he wouldn't do that. He was holding him tightly and safely in his arms.

The memory was fading, but Ben could still hear the waves, and his father's laughter.

Ben's father wasn't here anymore. That was what Ben had

told himself again and again after the funeral. The grown-ups all kept assuring him that his father was now in a better place, but Ben had never been able to believe that. Some part of him was convinced that after they died, humans simply . . . stopped. The empty space they left behind was just too vast, too bottomless to imagine that they could just be in another room.

But now he realized that everything he had believed was wrong. There *were* other places. And doorways you could pass through to reach them.

Ben's gaze kept drifting back to the codex that Gwil had pushed to the edge of the table. *No distractions*, he told himself. But in his mind's eye he saw the black door leading to Annwn.

A Fateful Sandwich

ᕲ PORTIA ᕥ

Back in his quarters, Robin cleaned Portia's wound. He spread a thin layer of an unpleasant, stinging salve on the cut before wrapping a bandage around her finger. Portia's gaze wandered to the myriad of pots, bottles, and wooden boxes lining Robin's shelves. She suspected they held more than just tea.

"What have you got in all those?" she asked, nodding at the shelves.

Robin put the bandages and salve back in a cupboard. "Medicine," he replied. "Shape-shifting potions, sleeping powder, dream seeds." When he saw the doubtful look on her face, he only shrugged. "Fairies have their elemental magic, druids have their runes. But we shape-shifters know there are plenty more kinds of enchantment besides."

He took another clay jar from a shelf and went over to a small table, where he had placed two teacups and a teapot. The kettle that had been Gwil's undoing during their first visit simmered over the fire in the hearth.

Portia followed Robin to the table, and warily sat down. She was determined not to forget how unpredictable he could be. He seemed friendly now, but who knew what tricks he might have up his sleeve?

"I thought you said there was no way to help Rose."

Robin put three spoonfuls of tea leaves into the pot. "Well, maybe that's not entirely true," he admitted.

"What a surprise."

Robin snorted dismissively, but a smile tugged at the corners of his mouth. He opened a box of cookies and offered them to Portia. When she refused to take one, he sighed, put the box on the table, and went to fetch the kettle from the fireplace.

Portia waited until he had returned. "You also said you wished Rose would suffer the same way you had."

"Wouldn't be the first wish I've regretted." Robin poured steaming water into the teapot. He had bags underneath his eyes, as if he had been sleeping badly.

"So you think we can save Rose?" Portia asked.

"We might have a chance. A small chance." He put the kettle on the floor and settled in the chair opposite Portia. When he held out the cookie box again, Portia took one this time. It tasted spicy, like a gingersnap with a hint of orange.

"There's a story," Robin began. "Well, actually, it's just a legend. It is said there was once a couple who managed to find each other in the fog."

"Yes, Ifor and Nerys," Portia said. "Meralyn told us about them. In the story, Nerys gives Ifor her heart."

"A romantic story, nothing more," Robin said. "However, I've heard elsewhere that a memory can actually bring back a Mistwalker. But not just any memory. You have to remind the Mistwalker of something that's worth staying alive for."

Portia placed her half-eaten cookie on the saucer.

"You've known that this whole time? And yet you refused to help us?"

Robin shook his head. "Even if I'd told you, what memory would you have used to bring back Rose? Do you know her that well?"

The question snuffed out Portia's last spark of hope. "Then there's no way to help her after all."

"Probably not," Robin admitted. "But that doesn't mean that we shouldn't try."

Portia had a lump in her throat again. "Why didn't you tell us before?" she repeated. "Why did you send us away?" *If you had helped us, I wouldn't have made a deal with Titania.*

She didn't say the last sentence out loud, but it hung in the air, unspoken.

For the first time, she thought she saw something resembling regret in Robin's face. "If you carry around anger like that for long enough, it blocks out everything else," he said. "Rose . . . Rose was a good friend before she imprisoned me in her world. A part of me can't forgive her for that. But the thought of her being lost in the fog for good? She doesn't deserve that, no matter what happened between us."

Portia felt like those words had been hard for him to say. But could she trust her feelings?

"Show me your wrist," Robin said.

Portia pressed her lips together and held out her right arm. Robin examined the mark. "Ah. That complicates things."

"You don't say." Was it her imagination, or was there an amused glint in Robin's eye at that?

"Well, yes. But as it happens, I'm pretty good at solving complicated problems."

"I see. And what do you have in mind for this problem? As long as I have that magical mark on my wrist, I can't leave Fairy Hill without permission. And Titania is hardly going to grant me that."

A foxy smile spread across Robin's face. He took down an empty jam jar from the shelf. "Oh, that's easy," he said. "We'll use Titania's own favorite method. Trickery."

It was almost midnight when Titania called for Portia again. Dutifully she set out for the kitchen and then the water lily chamber. This time she was carrying sandwiches and a glass with elderflower cordial on a tray. Robin's empty jam jar was also on the tray, now serving as vase for a bunch of buttercups. Robin himself trotted along at her side in his fox shape.

"I really hope your plan works," she said under her breath. "Otherwise, we're both done for." The fox shot Portia a pointed look, then scampered on ahead of her into the water lily chamber, and disappeared between the flowerpots.

Portia was relieved to see that there were no other fairies in the chamber. The lanterns had been put out, so that the only light in the darkness came from the colorful fish swimming in glowing circles in the pond and a few moon-moths dancing in the air above the gallery where the queen lay.

Titania was reclining on her chaise longue, reading a book. She lazily acknowledged Portia's arrival. "Put the tray down," she said in a bored voice. "No, not there. On the table."

Portia did as she had been told and stepped back. Titania marked her place with a bookmark, and glared up at Portia. "Why are you standing around like a cow chewing its cud?" she hissed. "Get lost!"

Portia bit her lip. "Yes, Your Majesty," she replied, and was turning to go when Titania called her back.

"No, wait."

Titania stared at her thoughtfully. Portia forced herself to appear calm. *She has no idea what we are planning*, she thought. *There's no way she can know.*

Over tea in his quarters, Robin had taken a small glass vial from his shelf of wonders. *A very special seasoning, for the next time you bring her a snack.* Three drops of the clear liquid had been sprinkled onto each of the sandwiches Portia had just served Titania.

She has no idea, Portia repeated to herself. And she could only hope that mind reading was not among the Fairy Queen's skills.

Titania was still looking at her with that alarming scrutinizing look.

"I was expecting you to whimper and whine more."

You'd like that, wouldn't you? Portia thought grimly. Instead she said, "Would it make any difference if I did?"

Titania raised an eyebrow. "Well, well. I thought your new position would have taught you some humility and respect. But apparently you haven't learned your lesson yet."

Portia crossed her hands behind her back to hide her clenched fists. "Whatever you say, Your Majesty." Were her eyes playing tricks on her, or was there a shadow moving behind the lily bushes lining the edge of the chamber?

"Stubborn girl," Titania scoffed. "This won't make your life around here any easier." She opened her book again and reached for a sandwich. Portia could not help herself— mesmerized, she watched as Titania lifted the sandwich to her mouth.

"You're probably trying to work out how to get your revenge on me," Titania said, alarmingly close to hitting the mark. "Feel free to try. I could use some entertainment."

With those words, she took a bite of the sandwich.

Portia held her breath. Titania chewed, swallowed, and took another bite. "Still here?" she asked without looking up. "Honestly, if you keep annoying me like this, there are plenty of . . . of . . ." She broke off in the middle of her tirade. The book slipped from her hand and tumbled to the ground with a thud.

"What . . . ?"

A shudder rippled through Titania's body, followed by a wave of glimmering light that shot over her skin up to her face. Portia gasped in shock. Titania whirled around to glare at her, wide-eyed. She looked down at the sandwich in her hand and then back at Portia.

"You!" she yelled, jumping to her feet, but another shudder of light passed through her, and she fell back onto her chaise longue. There was a sizzling noise, like sparking electrical wires. Titania clutched the chaise longue's armrests tightly, still glaring at Portia. The queen's eyes were now shining with such a bright silvery light that it made Portia's blood run cold.

Titania dug her fingers into the armrest. "I will . . ." But that was as far as she got. Silvery smoke rose from her skin and swirled around her slender shape, turning faster and faster until she was caught in a spinning cocoon pulled tighter by the second. . . . Finally there was a loud bang, and where Titania had been sitting a moment ago, there was now only a tiny figure, fluttering on firefly wings.

Portia snatched the flowers from the jam jar and stumbled backward. In the same moment, Robin leapt out from the lily bushes in his human shape. Grabbing the jar, he swiftly trapped the Fairy Queen inside and screwed on the lid. He muttered a few words under his breath, and ribbons of blue runes glowed on the walls of Titania's glass prison. It was all over in moments.

"Oh, man," Portia managed to croak. Her throat was bone dry.

"Not bad, eh?" crowed Robin, holding the jar aloft. It was filled with smoke and glittery silver swirls as Titania tried to break out. But the glass, fortified by Robin's magic, held firm.

"What is she doing?" Portia asked, stepping closer.

"She's trying to shift back into her old shape." Robin brought the jar close to his face. "I'm afraid that won't work, Your Majesty."

The whirling smoke cleared to reveal a tiny Titania, stomping her foot on the bottom of the jar.

"Let me out! Let me out!" she shouted, her shrill voice audible through the air holes Robin had pierced in the jar's lid.

"No, I don't think we will, actually," said Robin, unperturbed.

She buzzed against the glass like an angry hornet. "LET. ME. OUT."

Robin and Portia exchanged glances.

"What if someone hears her?" Portia said nervously. At that, Titania screamed even louder, hammering her fists against the glass. Robin sighed, and went down the steps to the edge of the pond. He squatted on his haunches and held the glass above the water's surface. Titania fell silent at once.

"What do you think, Your Majesty?" he asked pleasantly. "With a dozen holes in its lid, how long will it take for a jam jar like this to fill up with water?"

Titania remained silent, but Portia could see that she was trembling with rage. Robin held her suspended in the air for another moment, then set the jar down at the edge of the pond. He sat down next to it, and Portia did the same on the other side.

When Titania spoke again, she sounded more composed, but no less furious. "What do you want? I assume there's a purpose to this betrayal?"

"Indeed. And you can make it easy on yourself," Robin said.

Portia held her wrist next to the jar. "The spell on my mark. Lift it."

Titania crossed her arms. "Absolutely not."

Robin placed a finger on the lid and tilted the jar toward the water. Titania cried out. Robin tipped it back. "Would you like to rethink your answer?"

But if he believed that he had intimidated her enough, he was wrong.

"Oh, please," she snorted. "You know as well as I do that drowning me won't break the spell."

Portia glanced over at Robin, who nodded regretfully.

"Better luck next time," Titania sneered. "Now, if you set me free right now, I won't punish you too harshly. The human child can keep serving me. And you, Robin, you can go into exile for a few moons."

Robin gave one of his finest foxy smiles, then got to his feet and picked up the jar. "What a generous offer, Your Majesty. But I'm afraid we're going to pass. As I said, you could have made it easy on yourself. But now it seems you'll have to come with us."

Farewell to World's End

At dusk the sky outside the great window had turned a deep violet. A seagull flew by, so close that Ben felt he could lean out and touch it. He stifled a yawn and was reaching for his mug of cold tea when Tegid came bouncing up the stairs, gathering up the skirts of his robe. "Finally!" he cried. "I knew the books wouldn't let us down!"

Ben and Gwil turned around in surprise, but Tegid was already at their side, excitedly tapping at the open book he held in his hands.

"Olwen Sevenbright!" he said breathlessly.

Ben rubbed his tired eyes. "Olwen who?"

"A salamander folklore expert," Tegid explained. "She found out what the legend of Nerys and Ifor was really about. Look!" He held out the open book. "She writes about the fog that follows Arawn wherever he goes. She says the fog is a part of him—a part of his original world that he can't leave behind. In Annwn, the fog absorbed the memories and emotions of the souls that had passed on. All their longing, fear, sorrow, anger . . . it was all sucked into the fog, relieving the souls of their burdens." He held the book up and read aloud: "Outside of Annwn, however, any living being overtaken by the fog will be drained of all its memories, leaving behind nothing but an empty shell, which will eventually dissolve into the fog entirely."

"But . . . ," Ben began.

Tegid raised his hand and continued reading. "As long as the Mistwalker in question has not yet dissolved, they may be called back by means of a memento. It must be something of great emotional value to the person." Tegid broke off. "That's where the fairy tale about Nerys's heart comes from. Instead of her actual heart, she must have given Ifor something that reminded him of who he once had been."

"Her love," Gwil murmured. "She reminded him that he loved her."

Tegid winked. "You old romantic. Yes, perhaps that's what it was." He looked from Gwil to Ben. "Do you have a memento we could use for Rose?"

Gwil buried his head in his hands. "Oh dear, it's never easy, is it?" he groaned.

Ben, however, had an idea. A memento . . . He bent down and picked up Portia's backpack. Ridik's feather was still attached to the outside, fastened with the bird scout pin.

"Ben?" Tegid asked.

Carefully Ben detached the feather from the backpack. "This was Ridik's feather. He and Rose were good friends. They fought side by side." He handed the feather to Tegid. "Do you think that counts as a memento?"

Tegid twirled the feather between his fingertips. "Hard to say. But, why not? Perhaps the bond of their friendship

215

is strong enough to show Rose the path back to herself?"

"She did love Faerie," Gwil said. "If she associates Ridik with her time here, then it might work."

But they didn't sound fully convinced, and Ben had his doubts too.

"Well then," Tegid said, folding his arms. "It's better than nothing."

Ben and Gwil spent another night at Tegid's house. Ben lay awake for a long time, while the salamanders sat up downstairs carving attack and defense runes into a broken chair leg and a broomstick.

Ben had quickly gotten used to being at World's End. He liked Tegid's house, and the sound of the waves crashing against the cliffs. He would have liked to stay longer, but time was running out. Not only was Rose in need of their help, but soon the spell on Gwil's mark would be activated again.

Even so, as Ben stood in front of Tegid's house the next morning, he hoped that he would get to return one day.

"Here you go," Tegid said, handing Ben his backpack, now stuffed with provisions for the road. "I put the map of the route to the Pale Tower in the side pocket. And don't forget this!" He presented Ben with the rune-carved chair leg. It wasn't exactly an impressive-looking weapon.

"Don't go playing the hero," Tegid advised. "Find Rose, awaken her memories, if necessary, and then get out of the Borderlands as fast as you can."

"That's the plan," Gwil said with a crooked smile.

Tegid placed a hand on Ben's shoulder. "Take good care of yourself."

"I'll try my best," Ben said.

"And if you happen to pass through here on your way back, don't you dare go by without knocking on my door," Tegid said, his voice full of warmth.

"I promise."

Tegid nodded. "Off you go, then! On your way! Time to put your daring plan into action!"

He was still standing in the doorway when Ben turned around for one final look; then they went around a bend in the path, and the house disappeared from view.

INTERLUDE

Morning had broken, but in the depths of World's End, it was still dark. Tegid had set his moon-moth lantern on a table as he cleared away the traces of their work. Humming contentedly, he returned the last book to its place. Ben and Gwil had all they needed to know. It had been proven once again that you could find the answer to almost any problem by looking in the right book.

Tegid smoothed the leather spines of the books with his fingertips, smiled, and went back to his desk. He picked up the lantern and was about to leave when he suddenly froze. In the moon-moths' shimmering light, he could see wisps of gray smoke rising through the floorboards.

Tegid stared at the smoke in disbelief. It was impossible. There was no risk of a fire at World's End—the runes protected against that. Then he understood. This was no smoke. It was fog.

"Oh no," he whispered, and as he did so, he felt all the warmth leave his body.

He raised his lantern. Ahead of him, the corridor between the shelves lay in darkness, but the floorboards were creaking.

As if in a trance, Tegid opened the lantern door. The moon-moths fluttered out toward the black chasm between the shelves, revealing the figure that was waiting for him there.

Motionless, the Gray King's huntress stood between the walls of books. Her black veil trembled with each breath. She did not move, but behind her, the fog gathered and reared up to form a giant hand. No sooner had the moths flown into the cloud than they were snuffed out like candles. In the fading light, Tegid saw fog pouring down from the shelves like a waterfall. He did not move. The time to escape was long past.

Traces of Fog

On the second morning of their journey, Robin and Portia left the mountains behind. They were following the shore of a lake, heading toward the coast. Rain blew in from the west, turning the ground beneath their feet into a quagmire. Portia pulled up the hood of her leather jacket.

Robin had stowed Titania inside his backpack at first, but she had kicked up such a fuss that he had relented and attached the jar to the outside. Since then the Fairy Queen had merely sulked, hissing insults under her breath as they walked.

They were resting beneath a waterfall when she spoke up for the first time in hours. "What exactly are you hoping to achieve with this foolishness?" she asked. "Do you really think you'll be able to hide anywhere in my realm? No matter where you go, my subjects will find you."

"There are other worlds besides yours," Robin said curtly. He took a sip from a waterskin before passing it to Portia.

The Worlds of the Dead, for example, Portia thought. Robin had told her who the Gray King truly was. Arawn, king of the Underworld, who had abandoned the world of shadows and ghosts. Did that make him any less scary? Not really.

"Nonsense," Titania said scornfully. "Without the key, there's only this one world, and my power reaches every corner of it."

Neither Robin nor Portia replied to that, which clearly puzzled Titania. She frowned and looked from one to the other. Portia tried hard to keep a poker face, but something must have given her away.

"You've got a key," said Titania. "Either you've got one or that boy and the salamander do." She stepped closer to the glass wall of her prison. "That's it, isn't it? That's why they left Bryngolau. They have a dratted key!"

Robin didn't say a word. He silently took the waterskin back from Portia and began stowing the rest of their provisions in the backpack. Titania stared up at them in disbelief. "Why are you doing this? Why are you putting my people in danger?"

"We're not putting anyone in danger," Portia shot back. She got to her feet and shook her tired limbs. "All we want to do is save Rose."

That afternoon it stopped raining, and mist began to rise from the sodden ground. Portia ran a hand over her face—it was dripping wet, and when she ran her tongue over her lips, she tasted a hint of salt. From somewhere in the fog came a seagull's cry. They had reached the coast. Finally.

Portia quickened her pace. Maybe Ben and Gwil had already moved on. That would actually be a good sign, as it would mean they had found a way to help Rose. Still, Portia was hoping to catch up with Ben before he left for the Pale Tower. It worried her to think of him going there with only Gwil for support. Then again, if it came to a fight, she'd probably be no more help than the timid salamander.

At least we've got Robin on our side now, she told herself. Her new ally had shifted into his fox shape some time ago and was trotting lightly ahead of her along the narrow sandy path while Portia carried his backpack. Now and then bushes of yellow broom emerged from the fog, only to disappear again just as quickly.

It couldn't be far to World's End now. The air was thick with the smell of seaweed, and soon Portia could hear the boom of crashing waves. She followed the path up a hill, until it ended on a grassy cliff top. Robin was nowhere to be seen.

"Brilliant," she muttered. She considered risking a whistle, but decided against it. There was a light wind blowing up here, and the fog was getting a bit thinner. Portia followed the sound of the waves until she reached the cliff edge. It looked as if the land had broken off and fallen into the sea long ago, leaving behind a sharp drop to the jagged rocks below.

The cliff edge was strangely sickle-shaped, as if a giant sea monster had taken a bite out of it.

Portia brushed the curls from her face and took a step back from the brink. Fog billowed past her, and when she turned around, the path had already disappeared behind a gray wall.

She felt goose bumps prickling her arms. *It's just normal fog*, she told herself. *No need to panic.*

It was strange, though. Hadn't the wind been blowing

just a moment ago? Now it was perfectly still, and the sound of the waves below was oddly muted too. Portia gulped and walked back toward where she thought the path should be. Damn it! Where was Robin? She was just about to whistle when she saw something moving in the fog.

"Oh no," she whispered. Suddenly she was ice-cold. A few meters ahead of her, tendrils of thick fog emerged from the gray mist and began to grope along the ground like tentacles. Then they drew back, only to grow into a dense, seething brew of fog. And it was moving toward Portia.

Arawn's fog, she thought, aghast. *Oh, it's the fog that wipes memories!*

She stumbled backward, but it was too late. The swirling wall of fog was surging toward her. She just had time to fall to her knees and bury her face in her hands before it engulfed her.

I don't want to forget. Oh, please, no. Portia squeezed her eyes shut tight, waiting to feel the fog seep into her head, but nothing happened.

When Portia cautiously opened her eyes and looked around, she found herself in the middle of a gray cloud. Then she gasped with shock. She was not alone; barely an arm's length away stood a young woman. A woman . . . or a ghost? Everything about her was pale: her skin, her hair, her skirt, her blouse. She was staring off to her left into the fog, and didn't seem to notice Portia.

Portia was utterly bewildered and hardly dared to breathe. Suddenly a jolt went through the pale woman's body, and her eyes widened. Portia turned her head just in time to see an enormous figure in a black hooded cloak, taller than a full-grown man, come rushing out of the fog, brushing past her so close that Portia fell to the ground. The creature swooshed toward the woman, cloak blowing. The woman stumbled backward, but whatever it was had already grabbed hold of her.

"No!" Portia cried, scrambling to her feet. She didn't know what was going on, but the black-clad stranger was surely up to no good. He was holding the woman's face in both hands now, and suddenly glittering symbols began to glow on her cheeks. She squirmed and pulled at her attacker's wrists, but he wouldn't be shaken off.

Sympathy struck Portia like a bolt of lightning. She leapt toward the pair without a second thought and grabbed the attacker's sleeve, but to her surprise her fingers closed on thin air. With a gasp, she pulled her hand away.

The cloaked figure's arm dissolved into dark smoke, and wisps of fog began to rise from the fighters' bodies. Their silhouettes were already blurring when the black-clad figure finally let go of the young woman. No sooner had his spindly fingers loosed their grip than he collapsed like a puppet when its strings are cut. The woman still stood as stiff as a post, however—her eyes rolled upward, her mouth contorted in a silent scream. Her figure grew ever more transparent, but the symbols on her face burned as bright as white-hot iron. Portia stared at her, dumbfounded. Then she heard someone call her name, and in the same instant the two figures disappeared entirely. Their bodies vanished, leaving nothing but a cloud of swirling fog.

"Portia?" Robin grabbed her arm and anxiously looked her up and down.

Portia just shook her head, staring at the spot where the pale woman had just been.

"What was that?" she asked hoarsely.

"A memory." Robin's hand was still on her arm, and she was grateful for it. His grip was firm—at least that wouldn't dissolve into the fog.

"A memory?" she repeated.

"That must have been Arawn's enchanted fog," Robin explained. "That's how Mistwalkers are born. Arawn's fog steals your memories, but neither the memories nor the emotions they evoke disappear. Those memories leave the person, but then they become one with the fog." Robin let go of her arm and looked around, clearly worried. "The fog holds on to everything, and sometimes lost memories reappear as so-called chimera—moving images that others can see as well."

Portia tried to focus on his words, but her thoughts clung to his first sentence like a cat's claws. "You mean it really was Arawn's fog?" she asked, hugging herself.

"Only a wisp of it," Robin said. "Not enough to do us any harm." He fell silent and looked around them nervously once more.

She should have been relieved, but instead her head was filled with swirling questions. "If that was a memory we saw, whose was it?" she asked.

"It belonged to the woman."

Portia's hands fell to her side. "How do you know that?"

"I was there when it happened."

"You were *there*?"

Robin nodded. "The woman you saw—her name was Hermia. She was one of Rose's friends."

The group photograph from Bramble's shoebox flashed in her mind's eye. One man and five women. Which one had been Hermia?

"What you saw was a memory of the end of our final battle, when Rose and the others were trying to put the Gray King to sleep," Robin continued. "The black-cloaked figure—that was Arawn's hunting master. It is said Arawn forced him into his service long ago. Hermia was preparing our trap for the Gray King. I wanted to help, but the hunting master got to her before me. There was nothing I could have done. He put a spell on her and made her Arawn's huntress in his place, releasing him from his servitude." He faltered. "I've never told Rose. She's always believed that Hermia died in battle."

Portia's gaze wandered back to the fog. She still had a nervous feeling in the pit of her stomach. "I don't understand," she said. "When you told me about Arawn earlier, you said that the enchanted fog follows him wherever he goes. So what's it doing here? We locked Arawn in the Borderlands!"

"I'm asking myself the same thing," Robin muttered.

The fog was lifting now, and soon they could make out the cliff edge through the haze. Robin frowned, then turned suddenly pale.

"May the spirits be with us," he whispered. "If we can see Hermia's memories, then it means she must be weaving the fog."

"What?" Portia asked, confused.

"As Arawn's huntress, she has the ability to control the fog too. That's why he sends her ahead of his army, so she can dissolve as many foes as possible." He spun around. "Portia, did anyone follow you into Faerie?"

Portia was startled. "No. No, of course not. We closed the door, just like Rose told us to."

"Before any fog had made it through?"

Portia was about to say yes, but then she remembered the thin threads of fog that had floated through ahead of them. "There was some fog . . . ," she admitted. "It came through the Faerie Door with us." Panic fluttered in her throat. "But no one came through with it, I'm sure. We were alone, so . . ." She fell silent when she saw the fear on his face.

"As huntress, Hermia can take on the fog's form. She can dissolve and reform at will."

Robin ran his hand over his mouth and stared at the fog surrounding them. "We've let the huntress into Faerie."

"She wants the key." Titania's voice was low and bitter. Portia looked down at the jar on the backpack. "That's why she's come slinking into my realm. She wants to open the doors for Arawn."

Portia looked up at Robin. "Does that mean she's going after Ben? And Gwil?"

Robin didn't say a word, nor did the Fairy Queen. Why had she been silent for so long anyway?

"Robin!" Portia grabbed his arm. "We have to get to World's End! Right now!" What if it was already too late? Why had she let Ben head off without her in the first place?

"Tell her," Titania snapped.

Portia frowned. Tell her *what*?

Robin looked at her, and her hand slid off his arm. In the gloom of the fog, his face looked as forlorn and gray as the doomed Hermia's.

"We are at World's End."

"What . . . ?" Portia just stared at him. Then her gaze wandered back to the shreds of fog drifting above the empty cliff top, with the crescent-shaped bite taken out of its edge.

Once released, the fog will devour any trace of life it comes across, until all lands are empty and silent.

Rose's words echoed in her head like a muffled bell. Finally she understood. World's End, the great library of the Salamandrau, had disappeared. An icy cold crept into her heart. Where were Ben and Gwil?

Metamorphoses

◇ PORTIA ◇

Portia crouched on the deserted cliff top, her hands clasped so tightly in her lap that her knuckles were white. Robin was gone. He had shifted into his fox shape again and was searching the fog for a trail. Any tracks, any sign that might suggest Ben and Gwil were still alive.

Portia's thoughts were going round in circles. If she had been here, if she had gone along with Ben's plan from the beginning, could she have helped? Again and again in her mind's eye, she saw herself leaving her backpack by his bed as he slept. If only she had talked him into staying with her.

"We're wasting our time!" cried Titania suddenly. The jar was sitting next to Portia on the ground, but she refused to look at it. That didn't stop the queen from ranting, though.

"While we're sitting around doing nothing, that fog's spreading throughout my realm," she said. "And if those damned traitors really did have a second key, Arawn's fog witch will have it now. She'll open the doors! Don't you get it?"

"Ben and Gwil are alive," Portia retorted firmly. She

was drowning in guilt, but couldn't let Titania see that. She had to stay in control.

"Oh, wake up, you silly goose! Your human friend and the salamander are history!"

"No, they are not!" Portia grabbed the jar and leapt to her feet. So much for staying in control. Titania let out a startled scream.

Portia was about to hurl the jar to the ground when the fox emerged from the fog and shifted back to his human shape midtrot.

Portia ran to meet him. "And?" She felt sick with tension.

"They're alive."

Portia almost hugged him. "Where are they?"

He glanced at Titania. "On their way to the World Door in the Pale Tower."

Titania swore and slammed her hand against the glass.

Portia ignored her. "What about Hermia?"

"Following close behind."

That meant there was still a chance to save Ben and Gwil. A chance that was growing smaller by the minute.

Stay in control, she told herself, and squared her shoulders. "Then we have to hurry."

The fox trotted ahead, through wet grass and wild sprawling hedges. Portia ran behind him for mile after mile, her hands tightly clutching the straps of the backpack. She was doing her best to keep up with him, but no matter how hard she tried, her legs just wouldn't go any faster. On the contrary, in fact—her legs didn't want to run at all.

Her lungs were burning, and she had a nasty stitch as well.

Think of Ben. Think of Gwil.

Portia squeezed through a gap in a hawthorn hedge and slipped down a rocky slope on the other side, crashing down hard on her bottom. The jar in the backpack rattled, and a volley of curses rang out behind her. Portia tried to get back to her feet, but her right leg buckled beneath her and she sank back to the ground. For a moment she just sat there, eyes closed and panting.

Robin returned to her side in his human shape. "Are you all right?"

Portia nodded. She wiped her muddy hands on her trousers and winced. Robin took her hand in his and turned it upside down. She had grazed the skin on her palm.

He tutted. "Hand me the backpack, will you?"

Portia did as she was told, and Robin opened it. Titania was kneeling inside her jar, her whole body trembling. Portia couldn't tell whether it was from fear or anger, but then again she didn't really care.

Meanwhile, Robin rummaged about inside and pulled out a leather bag, which he opened and laid on the ground in front of him. A dozen vials were tucked in small loops attached to the inside of the bag, which also held two clay pots and several wax-paper sachets. Robin took out a pot.

"More magic potions?" Portia asked.

Robin pointed at the vials. "Those are, yes. The rest are just things that can come in handy on a long hike." He opened the pot. "This one is iodine salve."

Titania snorted dismissively. "Amateur."

Ignoring her, Robin applied the red salve to the scrape on Portia's hand. Portia winced again. Her hand stung, but the exhaustion that was weighing down the rest of her body was worse.

"You don't happen to have a magic potion to make me super-fast and super-strong, do you?" She meant it as a joke, but Robin raised an eyebrow. "Do you?" Portia asked again, suddenly hopeful.

Robin looked at her thoughtfully, then plucked a vial from the bag and held it up. A clear golden fluid sloshed inside the cut-glass container.

"A metamorphosis charm," he explained.

Portia's heart skipped a beat. "Metamorphosis," she said. "What . . . what would I be turning into?"

"Into your spirit animal. The one that matches your soul," Robin replied. Portia's mouth was suddenly bone dry.

"Great!" Titania snarled. "Then she'll turn into a tortoise, and what good will that do?"

"Would it last forever?" Portia asked.

Robin shook his head. "No, the effect wears off after a while." He looked her in the eye. "You don't have to do it. I can keep running on my own and try to close in on Hermia."

Portia thought about it for one, maybe two seconds. She could stay behind, yes. But would she be able to live with it if she gave up now? The answer was clear.

She set her jaw and took the vial from Robin. "Hopefully, my spirit animal is faster than I am. How much do I have to take?"

"One drop will do, for now," Robin said.

Titania pressed both hands against the glass jar. "She'll panic. She won't be able to handle it."

Portia pulled the cork from the vial and stared at the golden potion. *I'm not afraid*, she repeated. Then she raised the vial to her lips and trickled a drop onto her tongue.

The Pale Tower

The Pale Tower was a ruin of black stone rising from
the earth into the sky like a broken tooth. It stood in the
bend of a bay on an island that seemed to consist entirely of
craggy rocks. About a mile of sea separated the Gray King's
fortress from the shore.

Ben stood above the bay, looking down at the waves. "I'm
not a strong swimmer," he admitted.

Gwil pulled a piece of paper from his pocket and unfolded
it. "According to Tegid's map, there should be a causeway,"
he said. "Perhaps we can't see it right now because the tide
is high. Let's wait until it goes out; then we should be able
to walk over."

Ben glanced at Gwil. "The suspension of your spell ends
tonight, doesn't it?"

Gwil sighed and returned the map to his pocket. "Ah,
it won't be the first time I've been outside Fairy Hill past
curfew. It'll be fine."

Ben could feel doubt gripping his stomach like a cold
fist, but Gwil smiled.

"What do you say we find a sheltered spot and have a
bite to eat?" Gwil asked.

As dusk fell, they were sitting on the beach, protected from the wind by the surrounding slopes. Bramble and honeysuckle grew above their heads, while gray pebbles stretched down to the sea in front of them. The water came and went in soft waves over the flat stones.

Tegid had packed plenty of provisions, and eating was more than welcome. Ben chewed on a piece of dried apple and looked out toward the Pale Tower. The black castle stood out even more distinctly now against the pink evening sky.

"If there's a guard up there, he'll be able to see us, won't he?" he asked. The rune-carved broomstick was lying at Gwil's side, and the chair leg was sticking out of Ben's backpack. He still had a hard time believing that their "weapons" would be of any use.

"The castle in our world is deserted," answered Gwil. "Only once we open the World Door will we enter the Borderlands."

"So the castle on the other side of the door isn't deserted?"

"It wasn't as long as Arawn was sleeping there. But now he's awake. He has long since left the fortress behind to search for an open door." He put his half-eaten roll back into his food bag. "Are you full?"

Ben nodded. Gwil stowed what was left of their provisions in his backpack, then stretched himself out on the pebbles, stuffed his cap under his head like a pillow, and closed his eyes. After a few seconds, he placed his left hand over the mark on his right wrist.

As quietly as he could, Ben reached into Portia's backpack, checked that the ember pebbles were still in their place, and pulled out the travel diary and a pen. Then he leaned back against the slope, rested the diary on his thighs, and began sketching the Pale Tower. The reassuring weight of a pen in his hand was always comforting when he was afraid.

"You draw?"

Ben looked up in surprise. Gwil was still lying down, but his eyes were open and fixed on Ben.

Ben shrugged. "Sometimes."

Gwil sat up. "May I see?"

Ben hesitated for a moment, but then handed Gwil the notebook. The salamander looked at the sketch of the Pale Tower and nodded approvingly.

"This is very good," he said as he flicked through the pages.

Ben knew what Gwil was going to find, but he didn't dare ask him to give the diary back. He had drawn a few sketches while they were at World's End: a seagull in flight, Tegid carrying a stack of books, and the moon-moth fluttering between the shelves. . . .

Ben felt his face burning. He waited for Gwil to scold him for having spent his time doodling rather than poring over books.

Instead Gwil smiled. "You have a gift," he said.

Ben's cheeks burned all the more at these words, but he also felt as if a ray of sunlight had burst through the clouds to hit him in the chest. He plucked up his courage and said, "There's a drawing of you on the next page, actually."

Gwil turned the page, and his smile grew broader. "Very good indeed. Perhaps you should stay in this world and become my apprentice."

That made Ben smile in return. "My mum's waiting for me," he said. But just for a moment he imagined what it would be like to stay with Gwil in this world. A scribe's apprentice. What would he learn? How to make ink? How to write runes and make them come alive?

"Of course, you have to go back," Gwil said hurriedly. "No one should take a child away from their parents."

"It's just Mum. My dad died last year." Ben had no idea why he was telling Gwil this. Normally he avoided drawing attention to his dad. Or to the empty space where his dad had once been.

Gwil looked at Ben thoughtfully, then handed the diary back with a solemn nod. "I am very sorry to hear that."

To his surprise, Ben realized that Gwil's sympathy didn't bother him. And he was even more surprised by how good it felt to confide in him. He remembered the funeral, all those people in their black suits and dresses, asking him how he was holding up, the concern on their faces. . . . When he couldn't take it anymore, he had gone and sat at the top of the stairs, then watched from above as the mourners came and went from his home. And all the while, he had felt the closed bedroom door behind him. He was afraid to go in there, knowing that his dad would never sit on the edge of his bed and read to him again. He knew it, but a part of him just didn't want to believe it.

The truth was, he still didn't want to believe it.

Ben took the pen and looked out to sea at the castle again. A fortress that existed in two worlds at the same time. No, in three: Faerie, the Borderlands, and—if Tegid was right—the Underworld, Annwn. Ben drew the castle's broken tower and filled the outline with dark blue shadows. He thought of the *Book of Return*, and of Orpheus, who had tried to bring his wife back from the Underworld. *Don't think about it*, he told himself. But as he drew, he kept seeing the black door leading to the Underworld.

Tegid said he had never heard a story of anyone being successfully rescued from the Underworld. But did that really mean it was impossible to come back from Annwn?

The tide began to fall in the early morning, exposing the causeway. A walled walkway led from the beach to the island, where it ended at the foot of a flight of steps cut into the rock. From there it was just a short climb to the fortress wall.

Rain clouds were gathering overhead as Gwil and Ben entered the courtyard of the ruined fortress. The wall behind them was half-collapsed, and the ground was strewn with rubble from the collapsing turrets. Only the keep stood unscathed at the center of the castle.

Ben stared up at its dark walls. In the middle of the keep was a closed door. He could sense immediately that it was a World Door. Perhaps his senses were sharpened, now that he had crossed two world borders. Whatever the reason, the door had a magnetic pull on him.

Gwil stared long and hard at the door before setting down his backpack to find all that they would need for the key spell.

"Ready?" he asked when he had done so. Ben nodded.

They squatted down, and Gwil set a wooden bowl on the ground between them. It was carved all over with runes, as was the little knife that Gwil handed to Ben.

Ben, who had memorized Merron's instructions, took the knife, scraped a bit of soil from between the cobblestones at his feet, and dropped it into the bowl. Gwil took the knife back, shaved a few slivers of wood from the door, and dropped them on top of the soil. Then he cleaned the blade with some of Tegid's honey brandy before pricking his and Ben's thumbs, and finally letting a drop of blood from each fall into the bowl too.

Gwil whispered the rune spell, as if hoping that this way, no one in this world or any other would notice what they were up to. As he spoke, the runes on the inside of the bowl began to glow, and the mixture of soil, wood shavings, and blood started to spin and soon formed a vortex. The little whirlpool turned faster and faster, whispering like the sea wind blowing over a beach.

A faint tremor passed through the door, making the old wood groan and creak. A gust of wind ripped through the ruined castle. Gwil shuddered but carried on speaking the rune spell. Ben felt as if he could hear each of the elements in the bowl. There was another gust of wind—and then silence.

Ben leaned forward.

"It worked!" Gwil said, clearly stunned. He was right. At the bottom of the bowl lay a key, moist and glistening, as if it had been washed up by the sea. Ben's heart was thumping in his chest as he took the key, got to his feet, and with a trembling hand pushed it into the lock of the World Door. He held his breath as he turned the key—and then heard the lock click open.

The World Door swung open, and Ben was hit by a wave of musty air. He was about to pass through the doorway when Gwil grabbed his shoulder.

"I'll go first." Fear was written all over Gwil's face. Nevertheless, he clutched his broomstick and went ahead through the door. Ben clenched his fist around the key and took a firm grip on his chair leg before following Gwil across the border between the worlds.

In the Borderlands the castle was as much of a ruin as it was in Faerie. The entrance hall beyond the door was bare and deserted. The torch holders on the walls were empty, and the flagstone floor was riddled with cracks and potholes where the rainwater had been pooling for what must have been ages.

Three paths led out of the hall. A passageway was in the left corner of the room, while a staircase led upward from an archway opposite the World Door. The third way out was through a gaping hole in the floor, beneath which a flight of stairs descended into the darkness.

Gwil stood with his broomstick raised, as if expecting a horde of Gray Riders to storm into the hall at any moment.

Ben hurried to his side and waited, holding his breath in anticipation, but when a few seconds had passed without any attack, he let out a sigh of relief.

Gwil lowered the broomstick. "We'd better lock that door," he said.

Ben nodded and turned around before recoiling, aghast.

In the doorway stood a woman of night and shadow, her whole body wrapped from head to toe in a black veil, and a crown of spindly branches on her head. As if in slow motion, she lifted her head and sniffed, like a hound catching a scent.

Ben gave a stifled scream and stumbled backward into Gwil. The key slipped from his hand to the floor, and the woman *hissed*. It was the ugliest sound Ben had ever heard.

Gwil grabbed Ben's shoulder and pulled him back. Stepping in front of him, he raised his staff again, holding it diagonally at chest level. Ben raised his own weapon with a trembling hand. He tried to speak the spell to activate the runes on the chair leg, but the words caught in his throat. Gwil succeeded, but the runes on his staff glowed only dimly.

The woman in black stared at them. Clouds of fog billowed up from beneath the hem of her dress before collapsing once more. She held out her hands, and the fog curled up to swirl about her fingers. As Ben and Gwil watched, the swirls of smoke grew thicker and thicker before transforming into three pale dogs with pointy ears and long snouts. No sooner had they taken shape than they moved forward, silently baring their teeth.

Gwil's whole body was shaking, but he stood his ground. Ben ran a hand over his mouth, whispering the rune spell. *Please*, he begged. But the chair leg in his hand remained . . . a chair leg.

The dogs were moving closer.

They're trying to surround us, Ben realized with horror. Gwil took a step back and turned his staff so he was holding it like a spear. The dimly glowing runes were flickering now, but at least it seemed as if that was keeping the dogs from attacking.

Ben glanced down at the key, now a foot away from him. "Gwil."

"Down the stairs," Gwil commanded.

Ben looked over at the hole in the floor. It was the closest way out, and yet it seemed like it was miles away. "Gwil," he tried again. "The key!"

"The stairs!" Gwil spat.

The woman in black whispered something, and the dogs crouched and flattened their ears. Their eyes glowed menacingly.

"Now!" Gwil shouted, and as if on command, the dogs leapt forward. Gwil backed off, swinging his broomstick as he went. The runes lit up, burning bright white, and two of the dogs shied off to the side, but the third came straight on, and the next moment it was clutching the staff in its jaws.

"Run!" Gwil screamed. Then he dropped the staff, spun around—and fell.

"Gwil!" Ben's blood froze. A tendril of fog had caught

Gwil by the ankle and brought him down. Now three more tentacles had emerged from the haze to grope toward him. Without thinking, Ben grabbed his chair leg, leapt forward, fell onto his knees, and thrust the wooden staff into the tendril that was holding on to Gwil's leg. As he did so, he called out the rune spell. This time the runes on his chair leg glowed brightly, and the fog tentacle disappeared in a puff.

Ben was gripping his staff so tightly that he could hear the wood splintering. He spoke the runes once more, but now in the sequence that stood for *protection*, and struck the flagstones with his chair leg. A flash of light pulsed from the staff to the ground, and for a brief moment, a pale blue ring glowed around Ben and Gwil, pushing the fog back like a force field.

"Ben!" Gwil staggered to his feet and put his arm round Ben's shoulders. They looked on, dumbstruck, as the woman in black bent down and picked up the key. The dogs had returned to her side; two of them were looking up at her while the third watched Ben and Gwil with its gleaming eyes.

Ben's mouth was bone dry, and his heartbeat was pounding in his ears. "Why aren't they attacking us?"

"We don't matter anymore," said Gwil in a hollow voice.

More and more fog poured through the doorway. The ground disappeared beneath a white carpet, and shapes began to emerge from the murk—half-formed creatures and strange, ephemeral beasts, like demons in a steaming cauldron.

The woman stood in the midst of the maelstrom, drawing runes on the back of the World Door. The wood smoldered at the touch of her fingertips. Then she reached for the hunting horn at her hip. Gwil's fingers dug into Ben's shoulder.

"She's calling the Gray King!"

Ben was transfixed, but Gwil pulled at his arm.

"Ben," he urged. "Ben, to the staircase!"

Ben got to his feet. As soon as the chair leg left the ground, fog surged into the circle of protection.

Panic began to rise to his throat, but he let Gwil usher him through the hole in the floor. He turned around just in time to avoid falling down the steps. Gwil hobbled ahead, with Ben following him into the darkness. They had made it to the first landing when they heard the call of the horn above their heads. A long, high-pitched wailing sound.

"Sweet spirits!" That was as far as Gwil got before the castle was shaken by a thunderous crash.

The Dogs of Annwn

Robin hadn't lied, after all. The metamorphosis didn't hurt. Quite the opposite. The sweet, resinous taste of the potion was heavy on her tongue, but her body felt light. The world was a soft blur of colors that flowed around her like cool, velvety water. She could feel her body changing, but the transformation felt right, like a homecoming.

Portia opened her eyes and breathed through the nose of her spirit animal. For the first time, she saw the world with new eyes, and with a sharpness she had never before experienced. She could feel the earth beneath her four paws and taste the approaching evening on her tongue.

Meanwhile, Robin had removed everything he could from his backpack and fastened it to Portia's back like a saddlebag. Then he squatted down in front of her, took her head in his hands, and stroked her fur with his thumbs.

He grinned. "You've got quite the thick coat for a tortoise." Portia nudged him with her snout, and his smile grew even broader. He stood up, rubbing his hands. "Shall we?"

Portia put one paw in front of the other, digging her claws into the soft ground. She had control over every part of her new body, and it was unbelievably easy. She could feel her leg muscles brace, and how her whole being was anticipating the run. Portia shook her limbs, and heard an indignant scream coming from the backpack. She bared her teeth in a grin.

Robin gave a little bow in front of her, and then shape-shifted himself. The fox winked, turned tail, and dashed across the hillside. And the wolf that had once been Portia loped after him.

They ran all through the night, but the wolf didn't mind the dark. On the contrary—it was in its element. When a strip of lemon-yellow light lit up the horizon, the scent of the air began to change. Portia could taste sea mist, salt, and a bitter hint of algae. She licked her lips and kept on running.

She could keep up with Robin now, running full speed through grassy meadows, leaping over rocks she would have had to skirt as a human. She raced through fields of nettles without feeling a thing and tore through thick hedges without receiving a scratch. Her wolf body felt amazing. It moved in bouncy strides, wholly muscles and tendons, all working in unison, never growing tired, tearing across the land like an ice-gray wind.

The wolf's senses were sharper, too; Portia experienced the world more completely, and in more colors. She could hear the grass crackle beneath her paws, the rustling of a mouse in the undergrowth, and the fox panting ahead of her. She knew she could easily overtake Robin if she wanted to, and that certainty filled her with pride and excitement.

The only problem was the bundle on her back—without

that extra burden, this journey would have been perfect. Now and then Portia even forgot why they were running so fast, and what dangers awaited them at the end of this wild chase.

Eventually they arrived at their destination. Robin led her through a thicket of honeysuckle before coming to a halt at the top of a steep slope. Below them was a bay, and in the middle of the waves sat a craggy island. At first, all Portia could see on the island were black rocks, but after a while she made out the outline of a ruined castle.

When she looked around, the fox had disappeared. In its place stood Robin, in his human shape. Portia looked out to sea once more, feeling the wind blowing on her muzzle and caressing her fur. She could still smell the fox on Robin. It seemed the wild animal in him was never fully gone, not even when he was human.

Robin took the bag off Portia's back. "Well?" he asked. "Don't you want to shift back?"

Portia didn't know whether the potion had simply worn off, or whether Robin's question had triggered the change—but the wolf shape fell off her like a coat. One moment she was on four paws, and the next she was on two legs, standing at the cliff edge in her girl shape. Unlike her transformation from girl to wolf, turning back was actually unpleasant. Her stomach cramped painfully, and when she took her first breath as a human, her knees buckled beneath her. She missed being a wolf immediately. She breathed in deeply, but she could no longer notice all the subtle details of smell and scent.

247

Robin was still looking at her. "The first time is hard," he said. "But you'll get used to it."

Before Portia could reply, she was interrupted by Titania, whose angry tirade could be heard even from inside the backpack.

"Get me out of here, you maggot-spawn!"

Portia sighed and took the jar out. The Fairy Queen looked as if she had put her fingers into an electrical socket—her hair was standing on end, her wings were trembling, and her face had turned a bright red.

She glared at Portia and Robin, panting. "I will never ever forgive you for that."

"Cheer up, Your Majesty," Robin said. "We've arrived."

"As soon as I get out of here . . ."

". . . you'll skin me alive, I know, I know." He picked up the backpack and threw one strap over his right shoulder. "Portia, would you mind carrying the ego-in-a-jam-jar?"

"Sure thing." Portia picked it up. The memory of being a wolf was already fading. The regret remained. *I was free*, she thought. *I was the wind.* She wished she could have kept the experience somehow, like a smooth pebble you carry in the pocket of your coat.

Focus, she told herself. *This isn't about you.*

Robin had found a path leading down to the bay, and so they began their descent. Titania had seemingly exhausted her repertoire of insults and was now kicking and throwing herself against the side of the jar. At one point it almost slipped from Portia's hands, but she just managed to hold on to it and wedged it under her arm.

"You stop that now, or—" But that was as far as Portia got before she was interrupted by the piercing sound of a hunting horn.

A shiver went down her spine. She had heard that sound before. Between the doors, when the hunt had been after her and Ben.

Portia and Robin stood stock-still.

"We're too late," Titania said, her voice breaking on the last word. "The door is open."

Portia leapt off the path and onto a pebble beach. She was about to run straight to the causeway leading out to the island, but Robin grabbed her by the arm.

"Wait." He pointed out to sea. The causeway to the Pale Tower was clear, but fog was rising from the ruined walls to wreath the island in an ominous gray haze. Fear gripped Portia's heart.

Titania swore and shot Portia and Robin a venomous look. "Great," she said. "So what's your grand plan now?"

Portia looked at Robin, but he just shrugged.

"The causeway," he said. "We have no choice."

Titania snorted. "Oh, yes, what a fabulous idea! Just walk right into the enchanted fog. Then at least you'll get it over with quickly!"

"No one said it was going to be easy," Robin said. His voice sounded calm, but his face betrayed his anxiety. Portia's stomach churned.

"This is madness," Titania raged. "How do you think this will end? If you're very lucky, you might be able to take out one of Arawn's riders. Maybe two. And then what? He can call upon hundreds of riders in his army. Thousands, if he wishes. Not to mention his dogs. And you're about as much of a threat to them as a flea to a pack of wolves."

Robin spun around to face her. "That's true, *Your Majesty*," he hissed. "But we'd have a good chance if you'd only stop your temper tantrum."

Titania stared at him, wide-eyed. "Excuse me?!"

"Fight with us," he said. "You hate the idea of the Gray King overrunning everything as much as we do. So buck up and fight with us!"

But if he thought he could appeal to Titania's sense of honor, he was wrong. "You pathetic little creature," she hissed. "I've defended my world against hordes of enemies worse than anything you've seen in your worst nightmares. It's thanks to me that my home still exists! I will fight. I'll have to fight, now that Arawn is on the loose again. I'll defend my world with everything I have." An eerie glimmer flitted across her skin. "I will fight," she repeated. "But I won't waste my strength on a fight that's already lost."

Her passionate tirade left Portia speechless. Was Titania right? Were they wasting their time? What would happen to Meralyn and the other inhabitants of Fairy Hill if the Gray Army reached their home?

"Listen to me, Goodfellow," Titania urged. "I must return to Bryngolau. I must warn my people, no matter the cost. We must be ready when Arawn attacks. Unless it's already too late!"

"What if we can stop him here?" Portia asked.

Titania groaned. "Spirits, give me strength. How? Do you honestly think you can defeat him? While you're prattling nonsense, my people are *dying*." She swore again and rested her forehead against the glass wall of the jar.

Portia and Robin looked each other in the eye. Portia nodded, and Robin took the jar from her hands. "Your Majesty," he said. Titania didn't acknowledge him, but he continued regardless. "I'd like to propose a new deal. You lift the spell you put on Portia." At that, Titania did look up. Robin carried on, determined, "You lift the spell, and in return I'll set you free so you can return to Bryngolau."

Titania eyed him suspiciously. "You'll set me free?"

He nodded. "Lift the spell; then we'll be on our way, and—"

"Wait," Portia interrupted. Robin frowned, but she bent down to bring her face closer to the jar. "The deal will be as Robin says, but you must also promise that you won't punish Robin, Gwil, Ben, or me."

"Hah!" Titania scoffed. "As if any of you will make it out of this doomed place anyway."

But Portia carried on, ignoring the Fairy Queen's words. "And you must also release the salamanders from their servitude."

Titania fell silent. Robin looked at Portia in disbelief, but she stared down at Titania defiantly.

Eventually Titania spoke, in a clear, firm voice, "No."

"You said you wanted to protect your people at any price." Portia clenched her fists. "Well, this is the price." She had made so many terrible decisions since entering Faerie. She wanted to get something right at last.

Robin was subtly shaking his head, but Portia didn't give an inch. Of course he could have concluded the deal without her, since he had imprisoned Titania in the first place. But instead he waited.

"Very well," Titania said eventually. Portia was about to cheer out loud when she noticed Titania's smile. "I accept. But on one condition," the Fairy Queen went on. "If by some miracle you happen to survive this mess, you and the boy will return to the Human World, but you will give me your key."

"Agreed," Portia said, but Titania hadn't finished yet.

"Neither you nor any other human will ever be welcome in my world again," she declared. "And if anyone dares to cross the borders of my realm, I will imprison them in the split trunk of a dead tree for two lifetimes."

Portia felt goose bumps creeping up her spine. She was starting to wonder whether it had been such a great idea to make those extra demands—but it was too late now to take them back. Not if Titania was really willing to set the salamanders free. She thought of the black bands around Meralyn's and Gwil's wrists. She thought of how she had suffered when trapped in Fairy Hill herself—the feeling of suffocation, the frustration and anger. And she had only worn the mark for two days.

"Agreed," she said, half expecting to hear a thunderclap.

Titania raised her chin triumphantly. Then she turned to Robin. "And the same applies to you." Portia spun around just in time to see the look of shock on his face.

"If you survive, you too will be banished from my world,"

Titania said. "You will leave here with the humans, and this time you won't come back."

"We agreed you wouldn't punish Robin," Portia said, breaking in, but Titania cut her off.

"I'm already showing great leniency by letting him go," she said. "I can do no more. Take it or leave it."

Portia looked at Robin for support, but he just stared, stone-faced, at the jar in his hands. He would never agree to these terms! Portia could have kicked herself. Why had she gotten them into this mess?

"Agreed," Robin said.

"What?!" Titania looked as shocked as Portia felt. She was about to protest, but a look from Robin silenced her.

He raised the jar, so Titania was at his eye level. "Well?" he prompted.

Titania clenched her fists, but nodded in agreement. "We have a deal."

Robin didn't waste another second. He placed the jar on the ground and mumbled a few words. The invisible runes on the glass lit up briefly before it exploded with a loud bang. There was a flash of light, and then Titania stood before them in the midst of the shattered glass, back to her full size: a rumbling, sparking thunderstorm in fairy form.

Portia backed away with her heart in her mouth. Titania was *crackling*, as if she was about to send an angry pulse of electricity across the beach. There were no irises or pupils in her shining silver eyes. "I should skin you alive this moment," she growled.

"We have a deal," Robin reminded her calmly. Portia

admired him for that—she was fighting the urge to make a run for it. Titania would never keep to their deal! She'd rip them to pieces, turn them into earthworms, or maybe just incinerate them with thunderbolts.

"So be it," Titania said. She made a dismissive gesture with her right hand, and the tattooed band around Portia's wrist glowed like liquid silver. Pain bit into her bones, but then the silver pooled on her skin and hardened, before shattering and falling to the ground in a rain of ashes. All that remained was a pale line.

Portia gasped in surprise and relief. The latter was short-lived, as Titania stepped swiftly forward and grabbed her by the hair. "I hope the fog gets you," she hissed. "I hope it devours you both, bones and all."

No sooner had she spat out these words than she shifted into her dragonfly shape and shot off like an arrow, away from the coast and the mist that was spreading across the bay like a cloud of pestilence.

The wall of fog was already halfway across the causeway. The closer they got to it, the faster and shallower Portia's breathing became. She forced herself not to look back. One glance at the safety of the shore, and she would have turned tail and run. As the first threads of fog began to curl about her ankles, her whole body grew rigid. Robin was walking ahead of her. He didn't slow his pace, but Portia saw his shoulders tense as the fog enveloped him. She held her breath and followed him into the gray wall.

It was as if the fog had already dissolved the world

beyond the causeway. Apart from their steps ringing out on the stone walkway, all was completely silent. Portia was trying to focus on her feet when Robin suddenly stopped. She almost stumbled into him.

"We're not alone."

She stood at his side, her heart pounding. Now she heard it too. The scraping of claws on stone and sand. A growl. Slinking shadows in the fog.

"Run."

Portia was transfixed by the movement in the mist. It took a few moments for Robin's command to register.

"What?" She turned toward him, wide-eyed.

Robin let the backpack slide from his shoulder to the ground. "Run to the castle as fast as you can."

"No, I—" Portia began, but broke off when she heard a guttural growling right behind her. She spun around to see the skull-white head of a hunting dog emerge from the fog. Three more shadows were creeping along the causeway.

Portia backed away and stumbled over Robin's backpack. She winced, and caught a glimpse of red smoke in the corner of her eye. When she looked around for Robin, he was already shifting shape. His eyes were glowing gold, and a blood-red sheen rippled across his skin and clothes. His mouth was curled into a wild grimace, revealing sharp teeth.

"Run," he whispered. "Now!"

A chilling howl came from the depths of the fog, then the drumming of paws on wet sand and a chorus of wild snarling as the dog pack surged forward.

Portia grabbed the backpack and ran.

Mistwalkers

When they were deep in the belly of the Pale Tower, Gwil came to a halt. He was out of breath, and so was Ben. They leaned, panting, against a stone wall at the foot of the staircase. A few moon-moths fluttered about them, but otherwise there was nothing but pitch-black darkness above and below them. The passages underneath the castle must have been carved into the rock of the island.

Ben stared back up the staircase, his heart pounding, expecting at any moment to see a dog leap from the shadows. But nothing stirred.

"I think we got away," Ben croaked. "What do you reckon?"

When Gwil failed to reply, Ben took a good look at him for the first time. "Gwil?"

Gwil was bent double with his hands on his thighs. His whole body was trembling.

The spell. Amid all the chaos, Ben had completely forgotten that the time limit on the suspension of the spell had run out. Gwil sank to his knees, and Ben squatted next to him.

"It's bad, isn't it?" he asked anxiously.

Gwil briefly placed a hand on Ben's knee, only to remove it again right away. The skin around his mark was red and inflamed. "Ben, I'm so sorry. . . ."

Ben was already removing the pouch of ember pebbles from his backpack. Gwil tried to turn away, but Ben took Gwil's left wrist in his hands and looked him in the eye. "Please."

Gwil looked back and nodded.

What do you do when all your plans have failed? Ben had no idea, but he did know that he needed to get as far away from the woman in black as he could. So he continued his descent into the depths of the Pale Tower. Perhaps there was another staircase somewhere in this underground warren, leading back up to the courtyard. Then he could get out of the castle to . . . to where, actually? If he didn't get back to the World Door, he would be trapped in the Borderlands. He and Gwil, who was now sitting on Ben's shoulder in his salamander shape.

A dozen steps later, Ben lost any hope of finding an escape route. The staircase ended in a windowless cellar without a door. The stone walls were mottled with moon-moths, which gave off a pale greenish light. The damp chill settled onto Ben's skin. He ran a hand over his face and squinted into the darkness. Then he saw the door.

He knew immediately what was in front of him; the rough black wood and the ring-shaped knocker of tarnished green metal looked exactly like the door in the *Book of Return*. Ben could hear the sound of his own breathing in the stillness of the room, and everything else instantly lost its meaning. Nothing else mattered. He had found the door to Annwn.

A few moon-moths tumbled lazily through the air to land on the door knocker. The Door of the Dead stood in the middle of the room, beneath a chiseled stone archway. In just ten paces, Ben was standing in front of the portal to the Worlds of the Dead.

He stared at the moon-moths twinkling on the door ring, and for a moment he forgot all about the danger he was in. He had found it. His mind was filled with the question of what was behind the door. How big was Annwn? If you tried to find someone there, you'd probably be wandering around for days or weeks searching for them. . . . Or maybe not?

Gwil stirred anxiously on Ben's shoulder, but Ben barely noticed the salamander. He touched the lock with his fingertips, just to know what it felt like. An icy breeze blew through the keyhole, chilling his knuckles. Ben took hold of the door ring and was about to pull it when Gwil nipped his earlobe.

"Ouch!" Ben drew his hand back as if he had been burnt. All of a sudden he was back in the cellar again. He took Gwil off his shoulder and held him in the palm of his hand. "What is it?"

The salamander turned his head to point toward the staircase. Ben looked nervously over his shoulder. Fog was pouring down the stairs and rolling across the floor to wash over his feet.

Ben backed away until he came up against the Door

of the Dead. Someone was coming down the stairs, but it wasn't the woman in black or one of her dogs. The woman striding through the fog was slim with short, curly hair, wearing a poppy-patterned skirt and a blouse that must once have been red. Now everything about the woman was washed-out gray, as if the fog had sucked all the color out of her.

"Rose?" Ben asked in disbelief. The woman stepped from the staircase onto the floor of the cellar.

Ben's heart gave a little leap. It really was Rose. But even though she was looking directly at him, she didn't seem to recognize him. In fact she didn't seem to realize there was anybody other than herself in the cellar. Her eyes darted about the room, as if she was upset by what she saw. Or rather, what she didn't see. Ben placed Gwil back on his shoulder and approached her cautiously.

"Rose?" he called out. "It's me, Ben."

But Rose didn't hear him. A wave of fog broke about her legs, and she let out a deep sigh. She turned even paler, and her outline flickered as if she was in an old silent film.

Why was she down here? What was she looking for? Ben put his hand on her arm but drew it back right away. She felt cold, and too soft somehow—as if his fingers would go right through her if he squeezed any harder.

Suddenly Ben gulped and slapped a hand to his forehead. He had just remembered why he was in the castle in the first place. Ridik's feather! Gwil scuttled back and forth on Ben's shoulder while Ben frantically fumbled in his jacket pocket for the memento. When he found it, his hands were trembling so much that it almost slipped from his grasp. Then he looked up and gasped in shock. The specter that had once been Rose had turned around and was gliding back toward the stairs, carried by a pale wave of fog.

Oh no. Ben hurried after her, and bounded up the first two steps—but then he stopped short. He looked back over his shoulder at the door to Annwn. The dark gateway standing on an impossible border. Ben hesitated, until Gwil nipped his ear once more.

"I know," Ben whispered. Gripping the feather tightly, he set off after Rose.

No matter how fast Ben ran, Rose got further and further away, turning around corners and climbing ever higher into the tower. He had given up calling her name. Stopping was not an option, but he began to doubt he would ever be able to give her the feather.

It just has to work, he told himself defiantly. It just had to.

The stairwell Rose was rushing up was so narrow that Ben touched the walls on both sides as they went. Moon-moths followed him like tiny torchbearers, and whenever he left them too far behind, he was plunged into pitch darkness.

Ben gritted his teeth and kept climbing while Gwil clung to his shoulder with his tiny feet. The salamander gave Ben hope. He had to rescue Rose from the fog, and not just to save her, but also because it was their only chance of making it out of this castle alive. Rose would know how to deal with the woman in black.

Finally he had reached the end of the staircase and

found himself in a large hall, dimly lit by the light coming through two arched windows. Somehow he had ended up on one of the keep's upper floors. There was no sign of Rose anywhere, and to make matters worse there were two ways she could have gone. On the left of the hall was a flight of stairs leading down, while on the right a staircase climbed upward.

Ben took Gwil off his shoulder and held him up at eye level. "Any ideas?" he asked.

Gwil scurried back and forth on Ben's hand but seemed to be as stumped as Ben was.

Ben cursed himself. If only he hadn't been so distracted by the door down there in the cellar, he could have reacted faster when Rose showed up. Ben decided to try the stairs leading up first. He put Gwil back on his shoulder and set off toward them.

It seemed the hall had once been an audience chamber. There was a dais in the middle of the room, and on it stood a high-backed chair of worm-eaten wood. It was the first piece of furniture Ben had seen in the castle, and the sight of the empty chair—the *throne*, he corrected himself—made him shudder. He found himself tiptoeing past the dais.

The throne and dais were surrounded by a ring of standing stones. That was strange, Ben thought—as far as he knew, stone circles were usually found outdoors. He passed close to one stone on his way to the staircase and saw that its surface had been carved with a pattern of knots and snakes.

Ben put his foot on the first step and stopped. Gwil

crawled closer to Ben's neck, and Ben could feel the salamander's small body. The staircase above him was as black as the night, but Ben could hear a swishing sound in the darkness, and soon the shadows began to stir.

"Rose?" Ben called, even though he already suspected who was coming. He stumbled backward, but it was too late. The woman in black emerged from the shadows and strode down the stairs, heading straight for Ben. He didn't even notice Ridik's feather slipping from his fingers.

A Glimmer of Hope

Portia sat on the steps leading up to the Pale Tower, staring back at the beach. Below her, the fog still covered the causeway, but the sounds of the battle raging inside had faded. She had heard it all—the panting and barking of the dogs, the snarling of the fog. She had seen red lightning light up the fog like an Otherworldly thunderstorm, and the sight had frozen her feet to the ground.

But now it was completely silent. The fog was rolling like a stormy sea, and an ominous stillness had settled over the causeway and the bay.

Portia's head was spinning. She felt like she was stuck in a time loop. This was how she had lost Rose. Rose, who had gone into the fog alone to give them time to escape. Had that fog and the creatures that hunted in it now devoured Robin as well?

She hugged her knees to her chest. It was just too much! A strangled sob escaped from her throat. Portia wanted to pull herself together; she wanted to be strong. But no matter how hard she tried, things spiraled further and further out of control. She really was useless. Worse than useless! Other people had put themselves in danger because of her. And now? All she wanted was to curl up somewhere and not see or hear anything anymore.

Portia leaned forward and pressed her forehead against her knees. *Five more breaths,* she told herself. *Come on. Five more breaths, and then...* But that was as far as she got.

Something emerged from the fog and stepped onto the causeway. The red fur had lost some of its sheen, but for Portia it was as if the clouds had parted to reveal a clear blue sky. Relief flooded her heart—for exactly one second. Then the fox collapsed to the ground and lay still.

No! Portia ran to the causeway and fell to her knees at his side. Arawn's dogs had mauled him badly. The fur on his left flank was crusted with blood, and a nasty wound gaped on his right hind leg. He was breathing but didn't shift back into his human shape.

"Robin?" Portia whispered, gently stroking his head. The fox's eyes flickered open for a split second before closing again.

Portia looked down at the injured fox, and then along the causeway to the rough steps climbing to the castle and the fog king's home. Never in her life had she felt so helpless.

Because there was nothing else she could do, she carried the fox up to the Pale Tower. She stopped in the courtyard of the ruined castle and stared at what was left of the World Door. Broken wood hung from twisted hinges. The ground was strewn with charred splinters. The doorway itself stood open and unguarded.

She needed no explanation to understand what had happened. Someone had made sure the door would never be closed again. The Gray King could come and go freely now.

The fox stirred, and she shifted his weight in her arms. Portia knew they had to keep moving, but the sight of the destroyed door had drained all her remaining energy.

"That's the door to the Borderlands, isn't it?" she asked.

The fox glanced at the archway and twitched an ear. Portia could guess what he meant.

We're done for.

No one stopped them from passing through the doorway. Portia should have been relieved, but instead the same question kept going round and round in her head. Where were Ben and Gwil?

When she had carried Robin through the door to the Borderlands, he squirmed from her arms and finally shifted back to his human form. He leaned on Portia's shoulder, and together they limped to the end of the hall, where Robin slid to the ground and sat with his back against the wall.

He looked no less battered in his human shape. He had a bruise on his cheek, his waistcoat and shirt were torn open at the side, and one trouser leg hung in tatters.

"Spirits of the moonless night," he groaned.

Without a word, Portia pulled the backpack from her shoulders and handed him the leather satchel holding the potions and healing salves.

"Thank you." He took a clay pot from the satchel, unscrewed the lid, and rubbed some ointment onto the wound on his leg. As his fingers touched the cut, he hissed and grimaced in pain.

Portia sat down cross-legged in front of him. She could feel the sting of the wound almost as if it had been hers. She couldn't stop thinking of how Robin had fought for both of them. Her guilty conscience weighed down on her like a heavy blanket.

Meanwhile, Robin put the pot of ointment down and gingerly felt his ribs before quickly pulling his hand away. He leaned back against the wall with a sigh. His forehead was beaded with sweat, but when he closed his eyes, his features seemed to relax.

"What a mess."

Portia didn't say anything. She looked around the empty hall. Aside from the splintered door and a couple of sticks lying around on the floor, there was nothing to show what might have happened there.

"Do you think Ben and Gwil are okay?" she asked after a while.

Robin gave no reply but pointed to one of the sticks. "Fetch me one of those, will you?"

Portia frowned, but did as he asked. Robin took the piece of wood and turned it over in his hands. To Portia it looked like a broken broomstick. He brought it close to his face and whispered something. Blue runes glowed faintly on the wood.

"Attack and defense runes," he said. "You've got to hand it to the salamander—he was well prepared."

"Was?" Portia repeated, a lump in her throat.

"Let's not lose hope," Robin said, tapping the stick with his hand. "This doesn't mean anything. They could have been in a fight and managed to get away. If we could, why not those two?"

Guilt welled up inside Portia like brackish water. Her gaze wandered to the wound on Robin's leg before her eyes blurred with tears. She felt a lump in her throat and looked away hurriedly. "I should've helped you," she said. "I'm so sorry."

All of a sudden she felt his hand on her cheek. Startled, she spun around. There was a new, soft expression on his face.

"You're being too hard on yourself," he said. When she only gawked at him in response, a small smile tugged at the corners of his mouth. "Anyway, you don't have to worry about me," he said, his hand falling to his side. "Takes more than that to finish me off."

You're being too hard on yourself. Robin's words dripped like liquid sunlight onto the guilt and tension that was coiled so tightly around her heart.

You're being too hard on yourself. Portia was about to ask him what he meant by that when she saw something moving out of the corner of her eye. Just a few feet away from them was an archway in the wall, and out of it . . . Portia froze.

Robin sat bolt upright, alarmed. "What is it?"

Before she could reply, a finger of fog felt its way into the hall.

Robin leapt to his feet, brandishing the rune staff

two-handed, but his injured leg gave way beneath him. Portia sat, petrified, while the fog rolled ever more thickly through the archway. Then a figure stepped out of the murk.

"Portia," Robin warned. But she didn't listen. She stared, spellbound, at the woman emerging from the archway. Portia's heart gave a little jump, as if it were about to take wing. It was Rose! She came out of the fog with her head held high, and seemingly unharmed. Portia was about to run to her aunt when she realized that something was seriously wrong. Rose's steps were oddly sluggish, and her eyes darted about her as she walked. She seemed to be looking for something, and didn't notice Robin or Portia at all. Portia felt a chill in her blood.

Robin tried to get to his feet again, only to sink back to the floor with a cry of pain. Rose turned around at the sound, but her eyes slid over Robin as if he wasn't there. She hesitated for a moment and was turning back toward the archway when Robin reached out to touch the hem of her skirt. She stopped and looked straight at him this time, but still her gaze remained blank and empty.

Robin looked up at her intently. "Rose?" he pleaded.

For a split second it seemed as if Rose might be able to break through the veil of oblivion. A look of sorrow passed briefly across her face, but then she turned and went back through the archway, the fog trailing behind her like a veil.

Robin moaned softly and fumbled at his collar. Portia was so shaken by the encounter that she barely noticed him. "Was that"—Portia tried to recall the word—"a chimera? A memory, like at World's End?"

"No," Robin replied hoarsely. "That was Rose. It's not too late! The fog hasn't dissolved her yet." He pulled out a chain from underneath his shirt and yanked it so that the links broke. "Here. Take this," he said, holding the chain out to Portia. It had a silver locket dangling from it. Portia thought the locket looked familiar and then realized why—she had seen it in Robin's quarters back in Fairy Hill, next to a vase of yellow roses.

She raised her eyebrows. "What do you want me to . . . ?"

"Take it to Rose," Robin urged her. "If anything can free her from the power of the fog, it's this."

"How could your locket help her?"

"It's not mine. It belongs to Rose. It was a gift." He pressed the chain into Portia's hand. "Show it to her, and she'll remember who she is. Remember what . . . or rather who is important to her."

Seeing that she was still hesitating, Robin gave her a gentle push. "Come on now, go. Bring Rose back. It's our very last chance." He closed his eyes and leaned back against the wall again. "We'll need her help to get out of this mess."

Rosethorn and Brambleblossom

⌘ PORTIA ⌘

Portia climbed the staircase, higher and higher to the upper floors of the castle keep. She carried the rune staff in her hand. Rose could use it as weapon if Portia succeeded in bringing her back. *If.*

Portia set her jaw and climbed on. The locket was in her pocket, but she didn't really believe Robin's plan would work. Was the necklace a gift from Rose to Robin, or one he'd given to her? A gift that Rose had returned? The Adar had suggested that Robin had once been in love with Rose, but had she loved him? And would that emotion still be strong enough to bring her back to herself?

She followed the wisps of fog floating ahead of her up the staircase until she came to an attic room with a ceiling of dark wooden rafters. The only light filtered through a round window.

Rose sat on the windowsill, plumes of milky mist swirling around her and pouring down onto the floor.

Portia propped the staff against the wall, slid a hand into her pocket, and slowly began to walk toward Rose. When she reached the edge of the fog, everything in her screamed to turn back, but still she went on. It felt weird inside the fog—as if a creature with a dozen soft hands were caressing her.

With every step, she felt more and more strange. What was she doing here? How had she ever thought she could stand up to a king of the Underworld? She would be lost in the fog. She was lost already. Every memory of anyone who had ever meant anything to her would trickle away like sand between her fingers. She frowned. A guilty conscience was nothing new to her, and neither was fear, but this . . . this feeling was unfamiliar. It was as if an antenna in her heart were picking up radio waves from other people's emotional worlds. She felt deep grief and sorrow, and a yearning to see her loved ones again. Portia shook her head, but couldn't dispel those unfamiliar feelings. Instead she felt a wave of fear rising within her.

Bubbles of guilt rose to the surface of her consciousness. Her recklessness had not only put Rose and Ben in danger, but a whole world too. And her mother? What about her? Portia imagined her mum hearing that her daughter had gone missing in the Welsh mountains. In her mind's eye she saw the shadow of despair fall onto Gwen's face, and felt her mother's anguish as if it were her own.

You're being too hard on yourself. Robin's words were still fresh in her memory, and so was the warmth of his hand against her cheek. Portia took a deep breath and clenched her fists so tightly that her fingernails dug into her palms. *Keep walking*, she told herself.

"Aunt Rose," Portia said when she was finally standing

in front of her. The blank look on Rose's face made her want to run away. Instead Portia reached out and took her hand. She was afraid that Rose would dissolve at her touch, but although the hand was cold and damp, it was still solid and real.

"Rose, please, you have to remember!" Portia pressed Robin's locket into the palm of her hand. Nothing happened. Not even the slightest flicker of emotion showed on Rose's blank, doll-like face.

Tears pricked Portia's eyes. "Please," she pleaded. Desperately she fumbled at the locket until she found the clasp. She opened it, expecting to find a photograph inside. Instead she found a flower pressed under glass. Suddenly she remembered the box of odds and ends in Bramble's room. The locket she had seen there was almost identical—except that rather than a dog rose, this one held the white flower of a blackberry bush.

Portia also remembered the night Robin had tried to steal the key. Bramble had complained that the fox kept stealing things from the house. Of course! It was all so obvious now. The locket *had* been a gift. From Bramble to Rose.

The fog had filled the whole room now, and the tower's walls were disappearing behind the gray haze. Portia gulped and held the open locket out to Rose.

"Do you remember Bramble?" she asked. Rose's empty eyes seemed to look right through her, but Portia refused to give up.

Rose frowned. Then she leaned forward and looked at

the locket. Portia's heart was beating wildly. It was working! It had to work!

Rose placed a fingertip on the glass. Portia was watching Rose's face so closely that she didn't notice the voices at first. Only when she heard someone laugh did she startle and spin round. She saw nothing but fog and thought she must have been mistaken—until she saw a sudden movement in the murk. A light flickered and danced through the fog. The swirling vapors parted like a curtain to reveal a courtyard. Two young women were running across the cobblestones, laughing with their long black graduation gowns gathered in their hands. Portia backed away in alarm, but just as the women were about to reach her, the scene dissolved. The show wasn't finished, though. The women's images had barely faded away when another scene appeared in a different corner of the room. *Memories*, Portia thought. *These must be Rose's memories!*

This time, a living room appeared in the fog, with a fireplace, armchairs, and a sofa. A group of young people had made themselves comfortable in the room. One woman was slouched in a chair, puffing on a cigar, while another lay on the thick carpet, and two more were sitting on the sofa. In the armchairs on either side of the fireplace sat a man and a woman. This time, Portia recognized the group. They were Rose's friends from her student days. Portia didn't know the others' names, but the women sitting on the sofa had to be Rose and Bramble. The young woman with the cigar was telling a story, while the others laughed along heartily. Then the scene began to fade, but not before

Portia had noticed Rose reaching for Bramble's hand.

Behind Portia's back, another scene flickered into life. She turned around to see white rocks, the deep blue sea, and a small island emerging from the ocean like a turtle's shell. In this memory, Rose and Bramble were both older. They stood side by side, looking right at Portia and smiling. Then a gust of wind blew Rose's hat off.

Portia was spellbound. Something strange was happening to the fog. Where before disappointment and despair had lurked in it like cold spots in a deep lake, now Portia could feel relief, happiness, and a deep confidence that everything would be okay. She had no idea whether they were her own feelings or Rose's memories hanging in the fog like dewdrops and clinging to her skin, but she smiled anyway.

And then a very simple image appeared. It was Bramble, looking as she did now, with her gray hair and half-moon glasses. She was sitting in her armchair in Afallon, a book in her lap and Marlowe asleep at her feet.

The fog rippled, collapsed, and then surged quickly past Portia. She turned around once more. Rose had gotten to her feet and was standing in the center of the fog. It wasn't flowing past her now but back to her, or rather back *through* her, swirling around her, hugging close to her and seeping into her skin. Flickering images wandered over her arms and face, like a film projected onto a wall. And then the fog evaporated entirely, the walls of the room were visible again—and Rose was back. The real Rose, awake and alive, with her bright red poppy-patterned skirt and her curly, gray-streaked hair.

She took a deep breath.

"Rose?" Portia felt as if she had just stepped off a swaying deck and onto solid ground.

Without a word, Rose walked over, sank to her knees, and pulled Portia into a hug.

The New Hunting Master

∾ BEN ∾

When Ben came to, he was lying on a stone floor. He gingerly felt the back of his head and winced as his fingers touched a lump. Had he fallen? He sat up clumsily. The backpack's twisted straps cut into his shoulders. He freed himself of the extra weight and then started with fright. Gwil was gone!

Suddenly Ben was wide awake. Frantically he searched the floor around him. Where was the salamander? What had happened? A rumbling snort interrupted the panic-fueled swirl of thoughts in his head, and he froze. Bit by bit, his memories came back. The throne hall. Looking for Rose and instead finding . . . Ben shivered. He lifted his head and saw the stone circle, the throne, and behind it—the woman in black.

The sight of her hit him like a punch in the chest. She was looking toward the window, but the fog hound sitting by her side was staring directly at Ben.

Without taking his eyes off the woman, he lifted himself into a crouching position. He was just about to stand up when a second dog materialized so close to him that he fell backward in shock. Ben crawled away on his hands and knees until he bumped into one of the giant standing stones. The dog watched him with its strange eyes but did not attack.

The woman in black stood there, bolt upright, until a hunting horn called outside, somewhere in the distance. She lowered her head at the sound, and the tension seemed to leave her body. Her voice was like the rustling of dead leaves.

"He is coming."

Arawn! Arawn was coming! Ben felt the fear course through him like fire. He had to get away!

He slid up along the stone, but had barely gotten to his feet when one of the dogs bared its sharp teeth and he fell to the ground once more. He scrabbled backward and pushed his back against the stone. The dog came closer until it was right in front of Ben, so close that Ben could hear the growling deep in its throat. It snarled, and then dissolved in a swirl of fog. Ben gasped, and then saw the woman in black approaching, her veils streaming behind her. The next thing he knew she had grabbed him by the shoulder.

"No!" He tried to struggle free, but she pulled him to his feet and pinned him against the stone.

Ben squirmed and craned his head to avoid looking at her. Everything in him was screaming *No*, but he could no longer utter a sound. The woman leaned in ever closer, and he felt her breath on his skin, cold and biting, like the air on a white-frosted winter morning.

When she spoke, her voice was barely more than a whisper. "I'm tired." A sigh, a rustling of the veil. "So tired."

Ben sobbed and squeezed his eyes tight shut. Bony fingers dug into his shoulders. Rough fabric grazed his cheek, and then the woman in black blew gently on the standing stone at his back. The stone shook; then there was a grinding sound, and dust began to trickle to the floor. Ben's eyes snapped open when he felt something thick and rough coiling around his arms. The scream stuck in his throat.

The woman was standing so close that her forehead was almost touching his. Behind the veil, where her eyes should have been, there were only two black holes. Then she glided away from him, like a spider leaving the prey caught in its web.

Ben looked down and realized with horror that two thick gray stone snakes were now wrapped around his upper arms, and as hard as he tried, he couldn't get free. He could only watch as the woman removed her gloves. Her hands were thin, pale, and covered in a pattern of tiny runes. When she raised them in front of her, the pattern lit up, sending shimmering blue runes and knots swarming across her skin.

The sight sent Ben into a state of blind panic. He struggled desperately, throwing himself from side to side, but to no avail. The woman held her glowing hands out toward him. Ben wrenched his head away, but she seized his face in both hands and held it steady.

"Please," Ben sobbed. "Please don't!" His breath came in short, choppy gasps, and stopped entirely when he felt the runes touch his skin. It felt as if tiny maggots were crawling across his cheeks. He closed his eyes again and wished with every fiber of his being that either he or the ties that bound him would disappear. But there was no escaping that grip, or the runes taking possession of him.

The Gray King's Huntress

Portia hugged Rose tight, breathing in the scent of mint and lavender clinging to her clothes. After a while, Rose gently let go. She brushed the curls from her great-niece's face and smiled.

"Brave girl." She looked down at the locket in her hand and brushed the blackberry flower with her thumb before closing it and putting it into her skirt pocket. "Is Robin with you?" she asked.

"Yes," Portia replied. "I would never have gotten this far without him."

Rose nodded and got to her feet. Portia did the same and felt a wave of confidence surge through her. Everything would be all right now.

"Let's go and find him," Rose said. "You have to tell me everything."

"It's a long story."

Portia took the rune staff from where it stood propped against the wall and handed it to Rose, who raised an eyebrow.

"Combat runes?"

"Ben and Gwil must have used it," Portia explained. "At

least that's what we think, but ..." She paused and stared at the doorway. A small black-and-yellow salamander had just appeared at the top of the staircase.

"Oh no!" Portia hurried over and placed the salamander on the alm of her hand.

Rose rushed to her side. "What's the matter?"

"It's Gwil," Portia cried. "He's shape-shifted." She held him at eye level, but, of course, in his current shape, Gwil couldn't tell her what had happened. Portia looked expectantly down the staircase, willing Ben to appear. But no one came. Her face fell.

Rose put a hand on her shoulder. "Portia," she said gently. "Where's Ben?"

Portia ran down the staircase holding the salamander like a compass, with Ben's name ringing in her head like an alarm bell.

"Portia," Rose called after her, but she didn't listen. She jumped off the final step and charged into the hall. What she found there made her stop in her tracks. Ben! Ben with his back to a stone and Arawn's huntress looming over him.

"No!" Portia felt as if her insides were turning into water. Light flashed from the huntress's fingers and ran over Ben's face. It was exactly like the scene she had seen in the fog at World's End. The memory of when the former hunting master had forced Hermia to take his place!

"STOP!" The cry cut through the air above Portia's head like a whip. The next moment, Rose pushed Portia aside as she ran past.

The huntress spun around, just in time to evade Rose's attack. Ben collapsed, the glow on his face dimming. Portia was jolted out of her state of shock. She put Gwil on her shoulder and ran as fast as she could to Ben's side, skirting the fighting women.

The woman in black swirled toward the middle of the room with Rose hot on her heels, rune staff in hand. With every swing of the staff, the runes glowed and blue light shot from its tip like a sickle blade. Portia leapt between two of the standing stones and came skidding to a halt in front of Ben.

"Ben!" Then she saw the stone bands holding his arms. "Rats. What the heck are they?"

Ben opened his mouth to speak but couldn't utter a word. Fear squeezed Portia's heart like a fist. She looked into his eyes and saw they were dark with pain and shock. Then she put herself between him and the fighting women, clenching her fists. She had no idea how, but she was going to protect Ben, whatever it took.

The fight between Rose and the woman in black raged across the hall. Gray hounds joined the fray, but Rose quickly cut them into foggy swirls with movements so fast that Portia couldn't follow them. With each of Rose's blows, rune light flashed across the hall. Arawn's huntress whipped her many black veils through the air to parry the attacks. It looked as if she had grown half a dozen tentacles.

Rose dodged one of the lashing veils, taking cover behind

a standing stone. The huntress didn't hesitate for a second. She reached out her arms, sending the tentacles of her robes swishing around the stone. Rose dove headlong to the floor, then jumped to her feet and ran straight toward the huntress, sweeping the veils to one side and slamming her shoulder into her opponent's midriff.

Both fighters went down, and the woman in black let out a shrill scream. Her veils billowed about her, and she clawed at Rose's face with her fingers, but Rose broke free and pinned the huntress to the ground with her knees. The black fabric of her dress rose up in the air to form a giant claw, but before it could snap shut, Rose grabbed the rune staff in both hands, held it up like a dagger, and brought it down onto the veiled woman's chest. A deafening crash rang out in the hall, like a shattering wall of glass, accompanied by a blaze of blinding blue light.

When Portia dared to look again, the huntress and Rose remained frozen in the middle of the hall like statues. The black veils hung in the air for a moment and then fell to the floor. Once again, time stopped. Then at last Rose took a rattling breath.

"Thank goodness," Portia croaked.

Behind her, Ben moaned. Portia spun around to see the stone bands holding his arms crumble to dust. He slumped forward, and she leapt to catch him. Together they sank to the ground. She put her arm around him, and he rested his head on her shoulder. As soon as he did so, Gwil scuttled over to nuzzle his snout into the boy's cheek. Ben's smile was weak, but he was *smiling*.

"It's all right," Portia said. "It's all right, we're okay." She still couldn't really believe that it was true.

Ben tried to stand up, and Portia helped him to his feet. Her relief was so immense that she felt like planting a kiss on his cheek. Ben seemed to be about to ask her something, but before he could even open his mouth to speak, a piercing scream rang out.

Portia spun around. At the other end of the hall, Rose was kneeling next to the fallen huntress. She held the black veil in one hand while the other was pressed to her mouth.

"Oh no," Rose groaned. She hadn't realized who she had been fighting. Until now.

"What . . . ," Ben began, but Portia was already on her way over to Rose.

"I'll explain later," Portia called over her shoulder. In just a few steps, she was by Rose's side. Rose had already removed the crown of branches from Hermia's head, and pulled the veils aside from her face. The woman underneath the black fabric was old. Very old. She had dark circles around her eyes, her cheeks were sunken, her lips bloodless and chapped, and her skin was almost completely covered in a web of runes. She blinked once, staring up at Rose with dull eyes.

Rose stared back, stunned. "Hermia," she whispered.

"Who?" Ben asked in a weak voice. Portia hadn't realized he had followed her.

She touched his hand. "Later," she promised.

Rose's eyes filled with tears, and she pressed a hand to her mouth once more. She shook her head, as if refusing to accept what was happening. Hermia sighed heavily and raised a hand. Ben stiffened, but she only gently touched Rose's wrist and slowly shook her head with great effort. Rose grimaced in pain and grief and took her friend's hand.

Hermia squeezed her fingers in return, and then closed her eyes. "Tired." The word was barely a whisper. Then the former huntress's hand went limp. It was over. Rose sobbed and stroked Hermia's ruined face.

Portia took a step toward the two women. What could she do to comfort Rose? Every word, every gesture seemed ridiculous and inadequate.

A thin, colorless strand of hair had settled on Hermia's face. Rose tenderly brushed it aside and kissed her forehead. "*Swirne saff*," she murmured.

"She's got the key," said Ben. Rose looked up at him in surprise. "Gwil and I made a second World Key," he explained. "And she took it from us."

Rose's gaze drifted back to her fallen friend's body, but she made no attempt to search her dress. Instead Gwil scuttled down Ben's arm and between the folds of the garment, before reappearing with the key in his mouth. Ben took it and put it safely in his pocket.

Rose looked him in the eye. "Are you okay, Ben?" she asked in a hoarse voice.

Ben nodded, but his gaze was still fixed on Hermia's face, and the runes running over it like chains.

"Oh, what have we done," Rose groaned. Then she took the hunting horn that Hermia had carried on a strap at her hip, touched her friend's face one last time, and got to her feet. She took the black veil with her.

Companions in Arms

⁓ BEN ⁓

A narrow gate led out from the rear of the Pale Tower, to where a semicircular courtyard had been carved out of the rock. It was bordered by a parapet of black stone from which a steep flight of steps led down to the sea below. Ben and his companions watched as a bank of fog rolled toward them from the horizon.

"Is that him?" Portia asked.

"Oh, yes," Rose replied. "That's Arawn. The Gray King."

"How long will it take him to get here?"

"Not long," Robin said, and glanced at Rose. "I suppose you have a plan?"

By way of an answer, Rose held up Hermia's black veil. She whispered into the fabric, and runes unfurled on it like lightning-blue flowers.

"A charm cloth?" Robin asked.

"It worked before," Rose said curtly.

Robin sighed. "So you still want to take on Arawn. You realize we came all this way to save you from him?"

Rose eyed him coolly. "I'd have come here a long time ago if I'd known we'd left a friend behind."

Robin winced and bobbed his head as if to admit his guilt. "I know."

There was a story behind their words of which Ben knew nothing. The woman in black must have played a role in it, but her attack was still too fresh in his mind and he didn't want to hear about her yet. Just thinking of the runes crawling on her flesh made him queasy.

"Someone has to stop Arawn," Rose said eventually. "Especially now that we can't close the door to Faerie. Titania won't be able to gather her army fast enough to push him back at the doorway."

She turned to Robin. "Could you take the children back to Bryngolau?"

"No way!" cried Ben and Portia at the same time.

Rose frowned, but before she could argue, Robin cut in. "I think it's better if we stay together." He shrugged. "They'd catch us before we got there anyway."

"Sweet spirits," Rose whispered, pressing her fingers to her forehead.

Portia gently put a hand on her arm. "So what's the plan?"

"Arawn doesn't know yet that his huntress is dead." Rose closed her eyes briefly before placing her hand on the hunting horn slung over her shoulder. "We'll lure him up these steps with the horn. If we can distract his pack and catch him on his own, I can use the charm cloth to put a sleeping spell on him."

"I'll do the distracting," Robin said immediately. "I'll hide among the rocks by the steps and watch out for them from there."

"Will you be able to manage that with your injured leg?" Portia asked.

The corners of Robin's mouth twitched into a smile. "I told you before . . ."

". . . it takes more than that to finish you off." Portia finished his sentence and grinned back.

The three of them were totally focused on each other—they reminded Ben of a band of heroes from one of his books. Meanwhile he felt like he was in the audience, watching them perform, but that was all right with him. He reached for Gwil, who was still sitting on his shoulder, and stroked his head with a finger.

Robin handed the rune staff to Rose with an exaggerated bow. She shook her head in mild exasperation but gave him a tired smile as well.

"The four of us against the Gray King and his horde," Robin said, and grinned. "What could possibly go wrong?"

"Oh, I could give you a long list of things if you'd like," said a voice behind them. "But we're running out of time, aren't we?"

The companions spun around as one. Titania stood in the gateway to the Pale Tower. The last time Ben had seen the Fairy Queen, she had been dressed to the nines in royal finery. Her current appearance could not have been more different. She was wearing a dirty, crumpled nightgown, and her hair stuck up crazily, like a bird's nest. Ben wasn't the only one left speechless at the sight.

"I thought you didn't fight unwinnable battles?" Robin said eventually.

"Oh, shut your mouth," Titania hissed as she stepped into the courtyard.

Rose bowed. "Your Majesty."

Titania looked her up and down. "So, they did bring you back, then."

"I was lucky," Rose said.

"Luckier than you deserve," Titania snapped. She strode past Rose and gazed icily toward the horizon. They could hear the ominous drumming of hooves now. Titania turned back to the companions and crossed her arms. Ben saw that her fingertips were blackened with soot.

"So you plan to send Arawn back to sleep?" she asked.

Rose seemed surprised for a moment but recovered quickly. "Yes."

"And how do you plan to do that?"

Robin opened his mouth to reply, but Rose nudged him with her elbow before he could do so. "We were going to use a charm cloth," she said. "But now that you're here—charm stones would increase the cloth's power."

Titania snorted derisively, but went over to the top of the flight of steps leading down to the sea. There she crouched down and placed her hands on the rocks on either side of the path. The ground beneath their feet began to shake, sending Ben stumbling against the stone parapet. A deafening rumbling and grinding of stone filled the air, and dust began to trickle down into the courtyard from the surrounding rocks.

"This can't be real," Portia gasped.

The tumult grew louder still as rock teeth sprouted from the ground around them. Shards of stone crashed down onto the steps, and the whole island rumbled as if a dragon were stirring deep inside it. In a few seconds, it was all over. Standing stones as tall as people now ran along either side of the steps like battlements. Ben stared up at them in awe.

Titania rose to her feet and spoke over her shoulder.

"Rune speaker. Your turn."

Rose went over to the standing stone closest to her, placed both hands on its surface, and began to whisper spells into the rock. Ben's heart began to beat faster. He knew what was coming, and yet the sight of it was amazing. Runes began to blossom all over the stone, before trickling down it into the island's rocky core, only to re-emerge at the base of the stone opposite. Ribbons of runes twined along the battlements like ivy tendrils. Ben could sense the air crackling with magic. It was very different from the woman in black's creeping, eerie enchantment. Rose's rune spell was bright and positive. Ben was tempted to touch one of the charm stones just to feel it.

Rose stepped back and spoke a final word, at which the runes faded.

"I see you're disguising the power of your runes." Titania smiled grudgingly. "Arawn won't notice how strong they are until he and his pack are standing between the charm stones. Not bad, Human. Perhaps we do stand a chance after all."

"So we have permission to fight by your side now?" Robin asked. "What an honor."

"As if you have any idea what *honor* means." Titania snapped her fingers and pointed at the veil that was tucked under Rose's arm. "Give the charm cloth to Goodfellow. You're a better fighter than he is."

Robin narrowed his eyes, but Rose shrugged and handed over the veil.

"What about us?" Portia asked.

Rose hesitated for a moment, before reluctantly unslinging the hunting horn from her shoulder. "Someone has to blow the horn to lure Arawn up the steps. Can you do it?"

Portia took the horn. She was very pale, apart from two deep-red blotches on her cheeks—but her voice was steady.

"Yes," she said.

Ben admired her for that.

"And what do we do if Arawn makes it all the way up here?" she asked.

"Then we die," Titania sneered.

Rose shot her an irritated glare before turning back to Portia. "If it looks as if we're going to fail, you must hide in the fortress. Wait until Arawn and his hunt have passed through to Faerie; then travel across the Borderlands by foot until you reach the door to the Human World."

Portia opened her mouth to object, but Titania beat her to it. "Excuse me?"

Rose ignored her. "Arawn will think only of the open World Door in this tower. If you hurry, you can get home before he has razed Faerie and his thoughts turn to our own world." She laid a hand on Portia's shoulder. "Remember to close the door behind you. Go to Afallon, and tell Bramble—"

"Over my dead body!" Titania cut in. She marched toward Rose, who whirled around, and raised the rune staff.

"You would give up my world to the fog?" Titania hissed angrily.

"I'll do everything I can to stop him from getting through the doorway," Rose shot back. "But the children belong in their world. That's not up for negotiation."

Ben admired her determination but wondered why Titania would be willing to negotiate in the first place. Just then, Titania turned her gaze on him like a spotlight.

"You," she said. "You and the salamander. You have a key."

His hand darted automatically to the key in his pocket—he couldn't help it. Titania's silvery eyes flashed hungrily, but Rose stepped in between the Fairy Queen and Ben with the rune staff raised.

"There's no time to argue," she said. "So stop puffing yourself up like a blowfish, and let's get this done."

The insult seemed to knock Titania off balance. Ben blinked in surprise, while Robin turned away to hide his grin.

"You're pushing your luck, Rosethorn," Titania said slowly. "We shall see how much of it remains. After the battle."

"If the children are to travel to the door of the Human World, they'll need someone to guide them," Robin said with a nod toward Gwil. "Would you be so kind, Your Majesty?" he asked.

Titania stared at him. Ben was sure she would have loved to crush him to dust. Instead a thin and entirely malicious smile appeared on her face. "Your list of debts is getting longer and longer," she said. Then she swept over to Ben and plucked Gwil from his shoulder.

"No!" Ben cried in shock, but Titania was already speaking the words of a spell. A puddle appeared out of nowhere on the cobblestone floor, and Titania dropped the salamander into the water. There was a bang and a cloud of steam; then Gwil was lying on the ground in his human shape, crumpled and pale.

Titania dusted off her hands, as if she had just touched something dirty. "Happy now?"

The call of the hunting horn echoed across the bay like a drawn-out scream. Ben's blood ran cold. Next to him, Portia lowered the horn and watched the fog wall rolling across the mudflats toward them like a waterless flood. She stiffened when an answering call came from a horn deep within the fog.

Titania stood at the parapet, her long hair blowing in the wind. "So it begins," she said.

Rose turned to Portia. "You know what you have to do?" she asked for the umpteenth time.

"Keep trying to lure the Gray King up here, then wait and see if we need to hide in the fortress," she repeated.

"And then?" Rose prompted her.

"If all else fails, get to the door to the Human World as fast as we can."

"You'd better be fast," Titania sneered. "Once Arawn gets wind of that key of yours, he'll hunt you down without mercy. Who knows, he might even leave my world alone."

Ben fingered the key in his pocket once more and glanced over at Gwil. Titania had lifted the spell on his mark, but while he said he was no longer in pain, he looked pretty worn out.

"Are you sure you're feeling okay?" Ben asked quietly.

Gwil gave him a wan smile. "Better than before."

Meanwhile, Robin folded the charm cloth into a square and went over to Portia.

"Here," he said, handing her a small glass vial. "Just in case."

"Are we ready to go now?" Titania demanded.

"But of course, Your Highness." Robin curtsied, clenched the cloth between his teeth, and shape-shifted in a cloud of red smoke. The fox ran down the steps with the charm cloth in its mouth. Rose went after him, but Titania turned to look Ben up and down one last time, as if trying to pin him in her memory like a butterfly. *Later,* she mouthed silently, then went down toward the battlements.

"Sweet spirits," Gwil muttered.

"She'll snatch the key the first chance she gets," Portia predicted.

"That's if we survive this," Gwil replied miserably. Seeing Portia's distraught expression, he hurried to correct himself. "Which of course we will!"

Portia shook her head, smiling. "I've missed your optimism, Gwil."

A dog howled in the advancing fog, and Gwil and Portia ran over to the parapet. Somewhere down below, a merciless enemy was drawing closer and closer. A decisive battle was approaching, and Ben should have been totally focused on it—and yet he was distracted. Even if the battle did go well, what then? They would return to Bryngolau, or go straight across the Borderlands to the Human Door and go home from there. Ben's hand went back to the key in his pocket. If Titania really took the key, all the World Doors would be closed. Including the door to Annwn.

Ben looked back toward the castle. He remembered the smell of the Door of the Dead, and the cold air blowing through the keyhole. His hand clenched around the key. He looked over at Gwil and Portia. They both seemed grimly focused on the coming battle. Ben's guilty conscience gnawed at him, but this was his last chance.

Ben was just an invisible boy after all. Someone people forgot about quickly. He wouldn't make any difference to the battle anyway. He took a deep breath and turned back toward the Pale Tower.

The Door of the Dead

The fog had settled around the island like a thick blanket of snow. It was dead silent. There was no clatter of hooves now, or any other sound. It was impossible to tell whether Arawn and his pack were already climbing the steps.

Portia forced herself to blow Hermia's hunting horn once again. Its screeching drone made her feel sick, like the sound of someone scraping their fingernails down a blackboard. As she took the horn from her lips, she caught Gwil looking at the scar on her wrist. His face darkened.

"Titania," he said curtly.

Portia shrugged. "You were right. You can't trust her."

Gwil clenched his fists. "Curse her."

For a second Portia thought of telling Gwil about her deal with Titania, but then she decided against it. What if Titania died before she could free the salamanders? Or what if the Fairy Queen somehow tricked her way out of the agreement? Portia just didn't want to give Gwil false hope.

Below them the fog was crawling up the steps, smothering the rocky hillside as it went. Somewhere down there, Rose, Titania, and Robin were hiding. Portia knew she wouldn't be much help in the battle but still felt as if she should be doing something more useful. She would never get used to the idea of standing around waiting while others risked their lives.

"Agreed," she said after a while. "I'm just glad that you and Ben are okay. Your plan was the better one after all."

Gwil gave a hollow laugh. "I'm not so sure about that," he said. "We should've realized we were out of our depth when we were trying to turn a chair leg into a weapon! Right, Ben?"

He turned around, and with a twinge of guilt Portia did likewise. Ben was usually so quiet that it was easy to forget to include him in a conversation. She expected to find him standing somewhere behind them, but he was nowhere to be seen. Portia looked around but the court-yard was empty.

Gwil frowned. "Ben?" he called.

"Ben!" Portia shouted. No answer.

Portia swallowed against the unease clenching her chest. *Don't worry*, she told herself. *He must be somewhere nearby.* But a part of her knew that wasn't true, and the worry growing inside her made her pulse flutter.

"Where is he?" she asked.

"I have no idea," Gwil said, still frowning.

Feeling queasy, Portia looked down at the steps leading to the sea. Had Ben gone after Rose? But that made no sense! She was walking over to the top of the stairs to get a better look when the silence was broken by an angry cry. A sound like fizzing and crackling electricity came from somewhere inside the mist, followed by a deafening bang. A shock wave rippled through the fog, chasing clouds of vapor before it like a herd of fleeing deer. A shrill screech tore through the air, and the next moment the fog drew back out to sea—before rushing forward to break against the island like a giant tidal wave. Portia lost her feet as the rock beneath her cracked and shook with the impact. She fell onto her back but picked herself up immediately. Tendrils of fog came snaking up the stairs, and the runes on the standing stones began to glow.

Another furious roar came from down below. Portia clapped her hands to her ears and backed away, bumping into Gwil. He grabbed her shoulder and spun her around.

"Ben still has the key, doesn't he?" he asked.

"Yes, but . . ."

Gwil's grip on her shoulder tightened as a look of horror spread across his face. "I'm afraid I know where he is!"

☙ BEN ❧

The Door of the Dead creaked like the hull of a ship on a stormy sea as Ben pulled it open. For a moment, he thought about leaving the key in the lock. But what if one of Arawn's servants found it? No, better to keep it safe. He thrust it into his pocket, before crossing the edge of the world and closing the door behind him.

The fog on the other side was thicker than any he had seen so far. He couldn't make out even a meter ahead of him. Thick white clouds of fog engulfed him, caressing his skin.

The air he breathed was cool and fresh, as if there were a lake or river nearby. Were there even such things as hills, valleys, and rivers in this place? As Ben walked on, he found himself more and more fascinated by the shapeless, drifting world surrounding him. He knew that somewhere back there Portia was in the courtyard with the horn, and that his friends were locked in battle with the master of the Underworld. And yet the thought drifted away from him like a boat setting out to sea in hazy dawn light. The further it went, the easier it was for him to focus on his goal.

Ben had no idea where he was going or where to begin looking for his father. But the painful longing lodged in his chest like a fishing hook tugged him onward, deeper and deeper into the Underworld.

Ben waved his arm through the murk and watched as thin tendrils of fog twined about his forearm. For a moment it looked as if the fog was rising from his skin—it had to be some kind of optical illusion, he thought. Ben brushed the fog off and went on his way. After a while, the clouds parted to reveal a cluster of slate houses ahead of him. He recognized it immediately. Trefriw!

Ben was standing on the bridge over the River Crafnant. It was the middle of the night, and a starry sky stretched over the rooftops of the town. An eerie silence reigned.

With a queasy feeling in his stomach, Ben set off once more, now walking up the high street. Lights were burning in some of the windows, but there were no other signs of life in any of the houses. Ben wondered if it was past midnight already, then remembered that this wasn't the real Trefriw. He walked on, as somewhere deep in his mind an alarm bell began to ring.

Ben knew the town so well that every step he took felt like coming home. He turned a corner and went uphill, past the cemetery, until finally he was standing in front of his house. The walls glowed dimly in the moonlight, but the blue door and windows looked black. One light was on upstairs, in Ben's window.

Ben screwed up his courage and entered the house. As he stepped through the front door, it felt as if something had fallen into place. Like when a piece of a jigsaw fits neatly in its intended spot.

I'm home, he thought. *I'm home, and Dad is already here. He got off work early today and came back with a dog-eared paperback someone had left on the bus.* Tom could never bear to leave forgotten books behind.

Ben pulled the front door shut with a clunk. The house was warm and smelled of the detergent his mum used for the curtains. Ben walked across the soft carpet to the stairs and began to climb them. He was so filled with hope and fear that he could hardly breathe. He wanted so, so much for his dad to be waiting for him upstairs. He hoped—no, he believed—it would come true, but at the same time the fear of walking into an empty bedroom was overwhelming.

His breathing grew shakier with every step until he was

at the top of the stairs. His bedroom door was standing ajar, a thin sliver of light spilling out onto the landing.

Ben could hear two voices coming from the room. First, a child's voice, high and hesitant, and then, the deep, warm voice of a man.

"'In a hole in the ground there lived a hobbit. Not a nasty, dirty, wet hole, filled with the ends of worms and an oozy smell, nor yet a dry, bare, sandy hole with nothing in it to sit down on or to eat: it was a hobbit-hole, and that means comfort.'"

Tears burned in Ben's eyes. *I'd forgotten the sound of his voice*, he thought. *I'd almost forgotten.*

He pushed the door open.

A World of Fog

Portia hurried after Gwil, running down the staircase that wound deep into the guts of the castle. "Why would Ben want to go to the Underworld?" she asked, leaping over a crumbling step.

"I think he wants to look for his father," Gwil answered.

"What?" Portia felt a stab of pain in her heart.

"He told me his father had passed away," Gwil said. They could see a faint light at the bottom of the stairs now, and Gwil quickened his pace. "And he was asking Tegid all sorts of questions about the Underworld. I think he wanted to know whether it's possible to bring someone back from there. And . . . oh no."

Gwil came up short at the bottom of the stairs. Portia pushed past him and into the cellar, desperately hoping to find Ben. But the room was empty, apart from the old, blackened door at the center.

They were too late. Portia saw her backpack leaning against the doorframe, confirming her worst fears.

"Oh, Ben," Portia groaned.

"He was so fascinated by the Door of the Dead," Gwil said ruefully. "When we came down here the first time, he wanted to open it—I could feel it." He pressed a hand to his mouth, shaking his head. "I should've known he would try again," he lamented. "Who wouldn't want to go through a door if they knew a lost loved one was waiting on the other side?"

"Could he actually do it?" Portia asked. "Bring back his dad, I mean?"

Her heart ached in sympathy with Ben as she imagined the weight of the sorrow that had driven him through the door.

Gwil shook his head. "No. When the soul moves on, it doesn't just go to a different place; it also takes a different form. Some transformations cannot be reversed."

"So what will happen to Ben?" Portia pressed on. "When he finds his father, what then?"

"I don't know," admitted Gwil, wringing his hands. "Perhaps he'll find his way back, or perhaps he'll get lost. Or perhaps he won't even want to come back. The fogs of Annwn bring consolation, freeing the soul of all grief and regret. But they also make you forget that there's another world, and why you might want to return there."

Portia could feel icy cold trickling into her veins. "He'd become a Mistwalker," she said in a calm voice that was at odds with her feelings. "Like Rose."

Gwil nodded. He touched the lock with his fingertips. "I should've warned him."

Portia doubted that it would have made any difference at all. She understood why Ben had crossed over into the Underworld. And she didn't blame him for it, either. Gwil was right. Who wouldn't take that opportunity? At the same time, she couldn't just leave Ben. She wasn't going to let someone go into the fog alone again.

She gave the iron door ring a cautious tug, and to her surprise it moved. The door was ajar. She drew her hand back, hesitating for a moment. Out on the island, Rose and the others were fighting Arawn and his army. She had no idea how the battle was going. Had they defeated him, or had he managed to break through them to the World Door? She imagined returning to the Human World alone, knowing that Ben would be forever wandering the Underworld. She came to a decision.

"I'm going after him."

"What?" Gwil stared at her.

Portia handed him the hunting horn. "Go back and explain to Rose what happened. But only . . . only once the battle is over, all right?" She reached for the door ring again. "I'm going to get Ben. I just have to."

"But it won't work," Gwil protested. "The fog—"

"I know what I'm getting myself into," she said, cutting him off. She knew if Gwil continued, she would lose her nerve. "I won't let the fog drain me. Anyway, we don't have a choice. We can't let Ben down."

She looked Gwil straight in the eye, and he returned her gaze. Then he raised his hand, as if to hold her back, but let it fall to his side.

Portia gritted her teeth and pulled the door open. Fear burned in her chest. She had no idea what was happening outside, whether the fog had surged across the courtyard and into the fortress. Perhaps the Pale Tower had already sunk into oblivion, and this grim door in front of her was all that was left. She had to help Ben. But what if she ended up lost on the other side? Portia closed her eyes.

"Good luck," Gwil said, and with that Portia stepped through the doorway.

Portia pulled the Door of the Dead shut behind her, looked up, and stumbled back against the closed door. Ahead of her lay a thick bank of fog, and it was coming closer, pale and hideous, a blind, groping mass. Everything in her shied away from touching it. There was something hungry about the white murk, which swelled and contracted like a grasping hand.

The fog will suffocate you. You will drown. You will never find your way home.

"Pull yourself together," Portia muttered to herself. Then she peeled away from the door, held her head up, and walked straight into the maelstrom.

Portia took shallow breaths. The less fog made it into her lungs the better. She couldn't see her feet, but felt the soles of her boots touching water, and heard the splish-splash noise of her steps as she walked. The fog swirled all around her, clinging to her skin like damp cobwebs.

Just as it had earlier back in the castle, it felt like the fog was feeling and sensing her, its every touch sending shivers through her body. Her pulse fluttered with fear, her limbs grew heavier with every step, and she felt a knot of grief form in her stomach. Gwil had said that the fogs of

Annwn relieved wandering souls of their misery. But for some reason, it was different for Portia. All the feelings of sorrow and distress that had ever been absorbed by the fog poured into her, filling her head and seeping through her skin. She felt like a sponge soaking up fear and grief. She took one step, and another, and then stopped short. Portia bent double, resting her hands on her knees, trying to make herself as small as she could, to protect herself. But she could feel her consciousness getting swept away in a torrent of strange feelings.

I don't want to leave yet. Please, I don't want to leave. I wanted to tell her ... I wish I had just one more ...

When Portia came to her senses again, she was cowering on the ground, curled up in a ball. It was just too much. Feelings of longing, regret, guilt . . . They all rushed through her. She didn't want to take another step; she wanted to disappear, to dissolve. If her whole self was blown away like dandelion seeds on the wind, then at least all the pain would be over.

With her eyes tightly shut, she fumbled for her pocket and pulled out Robin's glass vial. When it was lying in her hand, she opened her eyes. What was left of the metamorphosis potion glowed like liquid amber inside.

Emotions hammered against the last of the walls protecting Portia's consciousness as she plucked the cork from the vial. She brought it to her mouth and let a drop of the smooth syrup-like substance fall onto her tongue. The taste of honey and resin exploded on her taste buds, and warmth spread through her body as if she was soaking in sunlight. It filled her completely, dissolving all her pain, every anxious thought, and turning it all into light. Her whole consciousness was focusing on this one sensation.

When Portia opened her eyes yet again, she saw the fog through the wolf's eyes. The strangers' emotions had receded and no longer plagued her. She shook her wolf body, and little droplets of fog flew from her coat. She sniffed the air, sorting through the smells of fog and water, until she identified a specific scent that she had already followed all the way from the mountains to the coast: *ink, human*. Ben. The satisfaction of having found the trail filled her whole being. She picked up the vial with her teeth and loped onward. The fog had no power over her now.

Where the Wild Things Are

When the fog finally cleared, Portia found herself in a place that was an exact replica of Trefriw. It was the middle of the night, and an unearthly stillness lay over the town.

Portia trotted up the middle of the high street. Ben's trace was so clear that it could have been a luminous thread stretching ahead of her. It led her up a hill to where a narrow house stood at a bend in the road. A light was on in an upstairs window.

The wolf was leaving Portia as she reached the steps leading up to the front door. She could feel it going, and for a heartbeat she clung to her animal soul like a child to its mother's hand. The next moment, she was standing in front of the door as a girl, and the memory of the torrent of emotions she had experienced in the fog was churning inside her like a flash flood. She screwed her eyes shut, leaned her forehead against the door, expecting to be overrun with feelings at any moment—but nothing happened. It seemed she had left the fog behind, at least for now.

Portia took a deep breath and glanced over her shoulder. The street, cemetery, and church lay in darkness. For a brief moment it seemed a completely normal scene, until she spotted the first tendrils of fog creeping over the cemetery wall.

Portia reached instinctively for the little vial, but realized that only a few drops of potion were left at the bottom. Would it be enough to let her find Ben and get back to the door? She slid the bottle back into her jacket pocket. She would save the wolf's protection for the very last minute. She forced herself to turn her back on the fog and opened the door.

She entered a dimly lit hall, from which a flight of stairs led to the floor above. A clock hung on the wall, its hands frozen in time. Slowly she climbed the stairs. The house gave her goose bumps. It seemed as if the walls might dissolve into smoke at the slightest touch. Was this just another memory? If so, it felt pretty convincing. Convincing enough to be mistaken for reality.

At the top of the stairs, she found herself facing a closed door. A strip of light was leaking out from underneath it. Portia could hear muted voices inside—a man saying something she couldn't make out, and a child laughing. Portia braced herself, and then pushed the door open a crack. Ben was right there. He was sitting on the floor with his back to the wall. Portia's heart almost stopped. He was as pale as a ghost, and the colors of his clothes were washed-out and dull. He was staring straight ahead of him.

Portia pushed the door all the way open with a trembling hand. Her mind was racing, trying to come up with a way to wake Ben from his stupor, when she noticed the other people in the room.

A bed stood against the left wall, with a man and a boy sitting on it. They were leaning against the wall too, and the man had his arm wrapped around the boy's shoulders as he read from a book in his lap.

Portia didn't need an explanation to understand what she was looking at. The man had to be Ben's father. And the little boy with the messy hair? That was Ben. A younger version of him, an illusion, a memory that had come to life. Except *life* wasn't quite the right word.

With a heavy heart, Portia stepped into the room and went over to where Ben was slumped on the floor. Without a word, she sat down next to him, close enough for their shoulders to touch.

The man and boy on the bed didn't seem to notice them at all. For each of them, only the other existed—as well as the story they were reading. A reading lamp on a shelf above the bed lit up a section of the wallpaper. Wait, no, it wasn't wallpaper. A whole forest sprawled across the bedroom wall, with its slender tree trunks running behind the bed, and its branches and palm leaves reaching all the way up to the ceiling. Here and there, Portia could make out shadowy figures between trees. Were they wolves? No, these creatures were too tall and broad to be wolves. They had furry coats and pointy ears. They crept through the forest, peeking out from behind tree trunks and blinking their big lantern-like eyes.

The man pushed the book over to the boy, and the young Ben read aloud from it in a high but firm voice.

"'All that the unsuspecting Bilbo saw that morning was an old man with a staff.'"

It was from *The Hobbit*, Portia realized, and couldn't help but smile.

"That was my dad's favorite book," said the Ben next to her.

His voice was so much more troubled than that of the little boy on the bed. He still wasn't looking at her. Portia took his hand in hers and hissed in shock when she saw the thin wisps of fog rising from his skin and through her fingers. He was disappearing, and she had nothing, no keepsake, to bring him back!

"Ben?" Her voice sounded much too thin. For one strange moment, she saw her mother, sitting on the windowsill with the same empty look in her eyes as Ben's. A cold blast of paralyzing fear made her feel small and helpless.

For a moment, all she wanted to do was run away. Anything would be easier than facing Ben's blank face. But she couldn't do that. She couldn't leave him behind. Her heart would break and she would never be able to put it back together again.

She shifted around so she was crouching right in front of Ben. She took both of his hands in hers this time, and he flinched. It was only a weak reaction, but it was something, and it gave her hope. He wasn't completely gone yet.

"Ben?" she repeated.

"He can't hear me," Ben said. He blinked, and the deep sorrow in his eyes made Portia's heart ache. "Is that really my dad?"

Portia would have given anything to say yes. Instead, unable to speak a word, she just shook her head.

Ben lowered his gaze, and then the rest of him seemed

to sink down too. Something that must have kept him going for a long time had finally snapped. Portia opened her mouth to comfort him, but in the end she simply leaned forward and gently pressed her forehead against Ben's. His hands were still in hers. She could sense Ben's inward struggle—how part of him wanted to disappear, but the rest of him didn't want to leave.

She risked a glance down and saw that color was returning to Ben's skin and clothes—slowly, though, like a sunrise in winter. When the first sob came, she squeezed his hands, and finally—finally!—Ben responded, squeezing her fingers in return.

Ben cried silently, his whole body trembling. "He's not coming back," he sobbed, his voice breaking. Portia hugged him and held him tight.

A Wolf's Heart

Ben followed Portia down the stairs on wobbly legs, away from the room with the forest on the wall, away from the rustling of book pages. He wouldn't have been able to do it alone, but with Portia at his side, he felt just strong enough. When he got to the bottom, he turned around—and realized that his dad hadn't followed him. A strip of light was still shining out under the door. It was strange, but somehow Ben took comfort in that sight. His dad would always be somewhere, and always be with Ben, or a part of him—even if the two people on the bed had been no more than an echo.

He wiped the tears from his face. How strange—he was exhausted, as if he had been running for miles and miles. At the same time, he felt lighter, as if a burden had been lifted. Why? He hadn't achieved what he'd set out to do. He wasn't going to bring his father back. He knew that now. But perhaps it was the knowledge that he had tried everything that helped him finally to let go.

Ben took a deep breath, then he turned his back to the stairs and walked to the door. Portia opened it, and Ben heard her gasp just as he reached her side.

Trefriw had been swallowed by fog. Or rather, it had disappeared as if it had never existed. Ben stared at the white-gray nothingness outside and steadied himself on the doorframe. It was impossible to say whether there was solid ground waiting for them at the bottom of the stairs leading down from his front door—or an abyss.

"Do you know how to get back?" he asked weakly.

Portia pulled a small glass vial from her jacket pocket and clenched it in her fist. "I hope so." She looked at Ben and smiled, but he could see she was tense and tired. Probably exhausted from everything she had done for him. Ben hunched his shoulders. He wanted to apologize, wanted to tell her that he had never meant to put her in danger—but Portia was already pulling the cork from the vial. A golden liquid glittered at the bottom.

"Ready?" Portia asked.

Ben could only nod.

Portia brought the vial to her mouth and emptied it in one gulp. Her eyes flashed with the same color as the liquid in the vial, and in the next moment, she disappeared in a puff of golden-yellow smoke. When the smoke cleared, a wolf with an ice-gray coat and black-tipped ears stood in Portia's place.

Ben stared in amazement, but the wolf didn't waste any time. It nudged Ben with its snout and then started down the steps, before stopping and turning to look at him expectantly. Ben shuddered, picked up the empty vial, and followed the wolf that had once been Portia into the fog.

~

Ben kept his hand firmly on the wolf's back for the entire journey. All around them, the fog swirled and danced, twisting itself into bizarre shapes, but the wolf loped determinedly onward. Ben wished he could be as calm. On his way to the Trefriw in the fog, he had been fixated on finding his dad—but now, there was nothing to distract him from his surroundings.

The fog was as thick as ever, but now there were shadows moving in it—tall, slender silhouettes that seemed to approach before disappearing at the last minute. Ben felt as if he was being watched, but told himself it was just his imagination. That was until he noticed the face. It was floating just a few paces to his left, like a mask without a body. Startled, he stumbled into the wolf, which simply lowered its head and kept going. Ben dug his fingers into the wolf's fur and stared into the fog. The face stayed where it was, its dark, hollow eyes following him. With a great deal of effort, Ben managed to look away and fix his gaze on the fog ahead of them. Then he almost cried out. Another face emerged from the fog ahead of him, and then another behind it. Soon more and more of the shadowy figures could be seen. They were human, or at least humanlike creatures, and they formed what looked like an honor guard on both sides of the pair. Their silhouettes were barely visible in the fog, and yet their long, pale faces were following Ben.

He was ice-cold. Who or what were these figures? What were they waiting for? He moved closer to the wolf and felt that it was shivering. Alarmed, Ben looked down at his companion. The wolf took one more faltering step before coming to a stop and lowering its head to the ground. Ben quickly knelt at its side and put a hand on its head. The wolf gazed up at him with golden eyes, and then convulsed as if in great pain. Golden lightning flashed through its fur. Startled, Ben pulled his hand away. The wolf *glowed*, then dissolved into glittering smoke and transformed back into Portia.

No sooner had she returned to her human body than she sank to her knees. Ben caught hold of her just as the fog spirits fell onto her like a swarm of furies. Portia let out a hoarse cry and curled up into a ball. Ben wrapped his arms around her protectively. The nightmare creatures glided around and over them like living shadows.

Ben thought his heart would stop from fear. He could feel Portia shaking like a leaf as she whimpered in his arms. Desperately, he looked around. There, between the wafting fog ghosts—a black shadow. *Please, let that be the door!*

More and more fog spirits surged toward them, eager to touch them. Ben gritted his teeth and got to his feet, pulling Portia up with him.

"Go away!" he yelled at the fog ghosts. They flew off, only to turn and fall on Portia again a moment later. With all her weight on his shoulder, Ben dragged them both toward where he thought the Door of the Dead should be. He forced himself to keep staring straight ahead. He could hear Portia moaning softly at his side, and that kept him going until at last he found what he was looking for. It *was* the door! Only a few steps stood between them and the way out now, and Ben almost believed that they were going to make it when one of the spirits burst out of the fog ahead and surged toward them. There was no time for caution now. Ben picked up Portia bodily and ran headlong toward the spirit. Just before they collided, he wrapped his free arm protectively about Portia's face—and jumped.

They crashed through the fog spirit like a fist through a wall of liquid cold. Ben slammed into the door with his shoulder, bursting it open, and together they tumbled through.

The Gray King

Portia and Ben landed on the floor of the cellar in a tangle of arms and legs. Portia felt a stabbing pain in her wrist as Ben fell on it, but he quickly jumped to his feet, slammed the door shut, and turned the key in the lock.

Portia stayed lying on the floor, weak and exhausted, her clothes sticking to her sweat-soaked body. When she closed her eyes, she could still feel it all—the touch of the fog, the strange emotions assaulting her mind . . . She buried her face in her hands.

"Portia?" She heard Ben asking in a timid voice, "Are you okay?"

All she could do was nod. *It's over*, she told herself. *It's all over.* She lowered her hands and looked at Ben. His hair was sticking up like a scarecrow's, and his face was still red and gleaming with sweat. Portia forced herself to get to her feet. "Never again," she croaked. "Never again will you catch me going anywhere near that fog."

Ben smiled sheepishly, then reached out to put a hand on her arm. "Thank you," he said. "Thank you for coming to get me."

In spite of everything, Portia smiled. "Don't worry about it."

That was as far as she got. From somewhere nearby came the sound of a stifled scream, before Gwil came rushing into the room and fell to his knees in front of them. He patted their heads and faces anxiously with his trembling hands, as if to make sure everything was in its right place; then he drew both of them into a tight hug.

"Ben!" he sobbed. Then he finally relaxed his grip, and beamed down at them with his arms about their shoulders.

"Mission accomplished," Portia joked in a weak voice. Gwil smoothed her curls. "You brave, brave girl," he said, squeezing her shoulder and glancing back toward the staircase leading up to the keep.

Portia frowned. "Gwil? What's going on?" She felt a cold hand grip her heart. "What's happening up there?"

"Arawn, he . . ." Gwil wiped his forehead. "He made it into the tower. The rune stones didn't stop him. He was too strong."

"What about Rose? And Robin and Titania?" Ben asked anxiously.

"Alive," Gwil replied. "They're defending the door. Or at least they were when I left them. It doesn't look good."

Portia's mouth was as dry as dust. She glanced at Ben, and saw he looked almost as pale as he had in Annwn.

Gwil grimaced. "Rose told me to come down here and hide. But if the Gray King makes it into Faerie, then . . . then . . ." He clapped a hand to his mouth.

Ben grabbed Gwil's sleeve. "But we have to help them!" He twisted his fingers into Gwil's robe. "We could carve new runes—you've still got your knife, after all!"

Carve them into what? Portia thought. She desperately racked her brains for another plan. Then her gaze fell on the key, still in the lock of the Door of the Dead. She remembered something that Rose had said—that Arawn was obsessed with conquering one world after another. If he took over Faerie, what next? Wouldn't he want to move on to the next world, the Human World? But for that, he would need a key.

Portia wet her lips. *Once Arawn gets wind of that key of yours, he'll hunt you down without mercy.* That was what Titania had said. What was more important to Arawn? To seize a single open door? Or a key that could open the way to all the worlds?

"We're just not powerful enough, Ben," Gwil was saying. "If even Titania can't stop him, our runes would be as much use as throwing a handful of flower petals."

"But we've got to do something," Ben exclaimed desperately.

"I've got an idea." Portia turned around to face both of them. "Ben, do you still have the vial of metamorphosis potion?"

With a frown, he pulled it out from his jacket pocket. "But it's empty."

"I know." She took the vial from him and explained her plan.

Gwil climbed the stairs so quickly that Portia struggled to keep up. Moon-moths glowed on the walls like veins of quartz in granite.

"When Meralyn finds out I let you take a risk this big, she'll have my guts for garters," Gwil predicted. Portia remembered the combative gleam in Meralyn's eyes, though. She doubted the seamstress would object to their plan. Ben had given her the key, and she had it clutched in her fist now. Robin's vial was in her jacket pocket. Her plan was as simple as it was crazy.

They had nearly reached the top of the staircase when a tremor shook the whole castle. The walls groaned, and dust trickled from the ceiling. Ben and Portia cowered, and Gwil's arms shot up to protect his head.

"Sweet spirits," he gasped.

Portia's heart hammered in her chest, but she urged the salamander on. "Keep going, Gwil!"

Gwil shook his head but kept on climbing. As they walked, the sounds of battle grew louder—the clash of weapons, the crackling of rune magic, the growling and howling of a whole pack of hounds. Up above, the staircase flickered with blue light. Portia was so nervous, she could hardly breathe. She could feel the teeth of the key biting into her sweaty hand.

"Oh," Gwil muttered under his breath as he raced up the last few steps. Portia followed close behind, and together they burst out into the entrance hall of the keep.

It was utter chaos. The hall was filled with thick, roiling clouds of fog that surged and broke against the walls and ceiling.

Rose stood amid the storm, assailed from all sides. There were fog hounds among her attackers, of course, but other, more monstrous creatures too—fog serpents with horned dragon heads, demonic birds with cruel beaks gaping wide. . . . Rose's rune staff cut through them like a blade through soft butter, but no sooner had she fought off one foe than the next fell on her. Portia scoured the battlefield for Rose's companions and saw Titania, conjuring a hedge of stone thorns from the ground with one hand while she wielded a crackling, sparking sword of light and air with the other. Fog warriors in tattered cloaks tried desperately to get past the thorn hedge to the World Door, but the Fairy Queen held them off—until one of them ducked underneath her slashing blade and thrust his curved knife into her side.

No!

Gwil cried out, and Portia spun around to see what looked like a tiny bolt of red lightning flashing low through the fog to launch itself at Rose's attackers, its teeth bared.

Robin! Portia's heart almost stopped. The fox ripped one of the fog hounds in two, but then a clawed hand shot out of the fog to grab him by the throat.

"No!" Portia screamed, and then she recoiled as a creature from a nightmare stepped out of the fog. It was Arawn himself. A bare stag's skull gleamed under the hood of his long gray cloak. The prongs of his antlers glowed with ghostly light. He was tall—taller than a normal human man—and his tattered garments formed a halo of smoke and shadows around his figure. He lifted the fox's body up in the air as if it were weightless. Robin squirmed and kicked, but Arawn only tightened his grip around his neck.

"HEY!" Portia was shocked by the sound of her own

voice. Panic churned in her stomach, but somehow she managed to take a step forward, holding the key in her fingertips.

Don't drop it, she told herself. *Don't drop it.*

"ARAWN!"

The Gray King turned around to face her. Red lights glowed in the dark empty sockets of the stag's skull.

Portia had no idea where she found the courage to keep going. "Arawn!" she cried. She was sick with fear, but still she managed to raise her arm and hold the key up high. "Is this what you're looking for?"

"Portia . . ." She heard Gwil whisper close to her ear. Arawn was staring straight at her, his eyes glowing. He relaxed his grip and let the fox fall to the ground. Then Arawn launched himself at Portia.

Never in her life had Portia run so fast. She hurtled down the stairs to the cellar, sure she was going to trip at any moment. *Don't think, don't think*, she urged herself. If only she could have shifted to her wolf form!

Arawn was breathing down her neck. She could sense his presence like a blast of freezing air on her back. Finally—the last steps! Portia leapt down and came skidding to a halt on the stone floor of the cellar. Something soft curled around her ankle, but she tore herself away, sprinted across the room to the Door of the Dead, put the key into the lock, and looked anxiously over her shoulder.

Fog came surging down the stairs and flooded across the cellar floor. Arawn wasn't far behind. As he came down the steps, it looked for a moment as if his white skull were floating in the darkness. Then he stepped into the cellar, his cloak billowing around him like steel-gray wings. Portia spun around, pulled the door open, took the key from its lock, and stepped underneath the arch of the door. Her breath was coming in short, panicky gasps. She had never wanted to be this close to Annwn ever again. But she had to follow through now.

She pulled the vial from her jacket pocket, and held it in her hand next to the key, clenching her fist around both, so that only the key's silver teeth were visible above her thumb. The metal shimmered like crystal in the rippling light of the moon-moths.

Please, don't let me mess up now.

She drew her arm back, but at the same moment she felt something slap painfully against her ankle, and a tendril of fog coiled around her foot like the end of a whip. The fog lasso yanked Portia's leg backward, but she gritted her teeth and managed to stay on her feet. Then she let the key slip back into her fist. She held it tight and hurled the vial through the doorway, into the dark realm of the dead. The glass bottle glinted silver in the light of the moon-moths before it disappeared into the fog. Portia had barely let go of the fake key when another tendril lashed around her ankle and pulled her off her feet. She fell headlong to the cellar floor, her chin jarring on the stone, and lifted her head to see fog streaming out of the Door of the Dead, groping toward her like a giant hand. She knew what it wanted—to drag her back through the doorway to Annwn, back to that

323

quagmire of sorrow and despair. Portia curled up with her arms over her head as the two fog whips tightened their grip on her legs and dragged her across the floor. Arawn strode past her, his cloak billowing, and through the doorway into Annwn. Two more fog tendrils curled around Portia's wrists, pinning her down as white clouds poured through the doorway and surged toward her, but she could still see Arawn. His dark cloaked form cut through the fog of his own world as he hurried after the key he so desired. Any second now he would find out what she had really thrown through the doorway. Portia opened her mouth, even though it meant breathing in the fog surrounding her.

"Now!" she yelled, and the Door of the Dead slammed shut behind Arawn with a bang. Ben leapt out from his hiding place behind the stone archway and leaned against the wood with both hands.

"The key!" he called. Portia threw it toward him, sending it skittering across the floor. For one terrible moment, she thought it was going to bounce past Ben, but he stuck out a foot just in time and trapped the key under it. Then, as quick as a flash, he picked it up, shoved it into the lock, and turned it. The fog that had surged through the door only moments before now drew back, rushing down the wood and disappearing into the floor in an instant. The tendrils holding Portia's legs writhed and struggled, before breaking apart and evaporating.

Portia picked herself up and rushed over to Ben.

"Lock it again," she urged him. Ben turned the key once more just as something slammed against the other side of the door with the force of a battering ram. Ben and Portia leapt back, startled. The cellar was filled with the sound of splintering wood and groaning metal, and the key . . . the key was still in the lock!

Portia cried out in alarm, but Ben jumped forward and snatched the key from the keyhole. He had hardly done so when the door shuddered under the impact of another mighty blow. The moon-moths on the cellar walls took flight and fluttered about in alarm. Portia took Ben's hand, and together they backed slowly away. Another bang. The door was shaking in its hinges, but it was holding firm. It was holding firm! Just as Portia was letting out a sigh of relief, they heard a bloodcurdling scream coming from the other side of the door. All the hair on her arms stood on end as Arawn raged against the closing of the border of his world.

"Let's get out of here," Ben croaked, but still they stood rooted to the spot, spellbound by Arawn's wordless screams. Fingers scratched and tore at the unyielding wood; then two fists pounded angrily against it. Arawn screamed and screamed. Not in anger but despair. Portia felt a lump in her throat, and was overcome by the feeling that they had done something terrible. The fog of Annwn that had almost buried her beneath the emotions of thousands upon thousands of souls—Arawn had no escape from it now.

He's feeling all of it, Portia thought, horrified. *Just like I did*. Had that been why he'd left his world in the first place?

Another blow slammed against the door, hard enough to send tremors through the archway and the floor. Dust and mortar trickled from the walls. For one wild moment, Portia felt an urge to set Arawn free. This time, it was Ben who grabbed Portia's hand, and pulled her toward the stairs. They didn't turn their backs on the door until they reached the bottom step. Arawn's wailing followed them far up the gloomy stairwell.

✍ BEN ✍

"Damn it, damn it, damn it," Portia muttered under her breath as they climbed the stairs. Ben knew how she felt. He would have added a couple of "damn its" of his own if he hadn't been so out of breath. The sound of Arawn's desperate pounding on the door pursued them as they went, making the walls shake, and chilling Ben to the marrow. When another piercing scream echoed up the stairs, Portia pressed her hands to her ears, but kept scrambling upward. On the next landing they came across Rose rushing in the opposite direction, surrounded by a cloud of moon-moths, with her rune staff in hand. She cleared the final two steps in a single bound and grabbed Portia by the shoulders. "Where the hell have you two been?"

"I'll tell you later!" Portia pleaded, just as another scream hit their ears. Rose's eyes widened; then she nodded.

"Very well. Hurry up, then," she said, waving Portia and Ben past her up the stairs.

The entrance hall was a mess. Chunks of rock had been ripped from the castle walls and lay broken on the floor. The floor itself had been torn open too, pulled up into rock splinters that loomed overhead like the walls of a stockade.

Rose's companions in arms were gathered at the back of the hall. Gwil was leaning over Robin, who was crouched on the floor in his human shape. Titania stood further off, holding a hand to her side and staring up at something. Ben followed her gaze and saw the last remnants of fog swirl along the ceiling and disappear between the ancient wooden boards. Arawn's magic had been broken.

Gwil noticed them at last, and let out a cry of joy before running to meet them.

"Did you manage to lock him in?" he asked. "Did it really work?"

"It did," Ben answered. When he saw the happiness spreading over Gwil's face, he felt prouder than he ever had before.

Rose stared at them in amazement, but before she could ask any more questions, Robin came hobbling over. He looked at Portia as if he had no doubt that the trap for Arawn had been her idea. "Crazy human girl," he said, but his voice was warm and full of affection. "Are you okay?"

"Yes," she replied, her voice hoarse. "But please let's get out of here now."

"With pleasure," Robin said. There was a gash running across his forehead. "Rose?"

Gwil put an arm around Ben's shoulder and nodded toward the border between the worlds.

"Shall we?"

Sunlight was streaming through the doorway. The blue skies of Faerie awaited them on the other side. Portia went over to Ben's side and nudged him gently with her elbow. They exchanged a look, and Ben felt the bond that their shared adventure had forged between them.

"Let's get out of here," he said, and smiled.

Farewell to Faerie

The fairies' feast of celebration lasted into the small hours. That was no surprise—there was a lot to celebrate after all. Titania's glorious triumph over the Gray King for a start. (She conveniently neglected to mention the part the humans played in their victory.) The Fairy Queen had returned appearing every inch the heroic, benevolent ruler, battered but undefeated, and so touched by the courage of her salamander subjects that she had graciously decided to lift the spell on their people.

Titania's talent for self-promotion was truly impressive.

The last guests had just dragged themselves off to a quiet spot to get some rest when the first rays of sunlight lit up the horizon. A soft blue dawn stole across Moon Lake, where the celebrations had once again been held. Portia sat at the end of the jetty sticking out into the lake, her legs dangling over the edge. The wooden boards around her were strewn with burned-out lanterns, and white flower petals floated on the surface of the water below.

There were probably still a few salamanders stumbling merrily about in the woods above, but down here the hollow of the lake was dead quiet. *Not long till*

Peaseblossom or Cobweb shows up to take us to the Human Door, Portia thought. The Queen had taken the key from Ben a long while ago.

Portia felt someone walking on the jetty and turned around to see Ben coming toward her with a steaming mug in each hand. He sat down next to her and offered her one. "Tea?"

"Thank you." She took the mug, breathing in the scent of summer herbs and lemon balm.

"We're going home today," she said, surprised by the lack of excitement in her voice.

"Yes," Ben said. "Have you talked to Robin?"

"No," she replied. Robin had disappeared the night before, shortly after Titania had lifted the spell on the salamanders. The celebrations must have been hard to take—the salamanders' joy rubbing salt in the wound of his own banishment. Portia had hoped their victory might convince Titania to change her mind. She should have known better. Titania had already kept her part of the bargain and released the salamanders from their servitude despite her misgivings. Now she was adamant that Robin must keep his pledge too, and submit to being banished forever from Faerie. It was a small but spiteful consolation for the concession Portia had wrenched from her.

"Look!" Ben held up a slim package made of colorful fabric. "A gift from Meralyn." He opened it to reveal a page of parchment inside.

Portia raised an eyebrow. "Is that what I think it is?"

"Oh, yes."

Portia smiled. Now that Meralyn was free, it seemed she no longer cared a jot about Titania's orders.

"Gwil's leaving today too," Ben said after a while.

"Leaving? Where's he going?" Portia asked, surprised.

"World's End. He wants to look for Tegid. He thinks that if we could bring Rose back, then there must be a chance for Tegid, too."

Portia had never met Tegid, but she could tell that Ben had been deeply affected by the loss of the librarian to the fog. "I'll keep my fingers crossed for him."

"Me too," whispered Ben.

The sky above was brightening as the sun rose over the valleys in the east. The leaves of the oak trees rustled in the gentle breeze. This was how Portia wanted to remember Moon Lake—still and peaceful.

Once they crossed the border, there would be no coming back. The thought filled Portia with a strange sadness. The sensible part of her was anxious to get back to their world as soon as possible. She was worried—about Bramble and her mother. And yet, somewhere deep inside, Portia couldn't help but wonder what there was left to discover in Faerie. That part of her wanted to choose a different path, wanted to return to the mountains beyond Bryngolau, or venture deeper into the woods of the birds' realm, wanted to explore the other regions of this world, and find new borders to cross. She could do it all standing on her own two feet. Or her own four paws.

Portia blew on the tea before taking a cautious sip.

"It feels weird, doesn't it?" Ben said. "To be leaving, I mean."

"Yep," Portia replied as she took another sip. Ben set his mug down on the jetty, took off his boots, and dangled his feet in the water. They sat side by side and looked out across the lake as flower petals bobbed about their ankles.

"'It's a dangerous business, going out of your door,'" muttered Ben under his breath.

Portia couldn't help but smile. Perhaps she wasn't the only one in two minds about their farewell to Faerie.

"'You step into the road,'" she said, continuing the quotation from *The Lord of the Rings*, "'and if you don't keep your feet, there is no knowing where you might be swept off to.'"

Ben grinned. They clinked mugs and waited for the dawn to break.

⁀ BEN ⁀

It was already afternoon when they reached the Human Door: Ben, Portia, Rose, and Robin, escorted by Peaseblossom and Cobweb. The latter had been entrusted with the key, and flashed glares of warning at anyone who dared look at it for too long. When she opened the door, Peaseblossom immediately rushed to her side and craned her neck to peer through to the other world. Cobweb sighed and yanked the other fairy back by her dress, then impatiently ushered Rose and the others through. "Come along now. Chop, chop!"

"You always did have such charm," said Robin drily as he passed.

"Enjoy your banishment," Cobweb shot back.

They were barely through the doorway before it slammed shut behind them with a bang. If a period could make a noise, that is what it would sound like.

Ben sighed with relief. On the other side of the forest, just a few miles away, was the real Trefriw. It was hard to believe.

"Well, that's that," Robin said calmly.

Rose shot him a sorrowful look. "I'm so sorry, Robin."

He shrugged, but still couldn't seem to stop staring at the door. Neither could Portia, who reached out her hand to rest it on the door handle once more.

"What will you do now?" she asked.

"Get a drink somewhere. Find an empty house to sleep in. It's not like I'm a total stranger in this world."

Ben tapped Portia on the shoulder. When she turned around, he pulled Meralyn's package from his pocket and raised a questioning eyebrow. Portia smiled and gave him a quick nod in return.

"Titania doesn't go around banishing just anybody. I'll simply take it as an honor," Robin said.

"Oh, don't be so dramatic," Portia said.

Robin spun around with a look of irritation on his face, and Rose seemed taken aback too, until Ben unwrapped the package and produced the sheet of parchment.

"Is that . . . ," Rose began.

"It tells you how to make a key," Ben confirmed. "A present from Meralyn. She copied the instructions."

Rose's eyes widened, but Robin looked down blankly at the parchment.

Ben offered him the sheet. "If you like, we can make another key right away. Then you can go back to your world. Titania doesn't have to know."

Robin thought for a moment, then shook his head. "Thank you, but I think this door is closed to me forever."

"Robin . . . ," Rose began, but he only shrugged dismissively.

"Bryngolau didn't feel like home anymore anyway," he said. "Even Oberon has left. Perhaps it was time for me to move on."

"But where will you go?" Portia asked. "You don't like the Human World, after all."

For the first time since they had returned from the Pale Tower, a smile crept over Robin's face. "There are other worlds."

"Then you'll still need the instructions," Rose said, giving Ben a pointed look. He understood and handed Robin the parchment.

Robin frowned. "Shouldn't we make another copy?"

Rose shook her head. "I'd rather not."

"Too great a temptation for your beloved?" Robin asked.

"For both of us," Rose replied.

He grinned, folded up the parchment, and thrust it into his pocket.

"I think that may be wise," he said. "You were never quite right for this magic-less world either."

Rose clasped her hand in his, but Robin lifted her hand and planted a light kiss on its back. Then he pulled a glass vial from his waistcoat pocket. Portia's ears pricked up.

"Valerian, lavender, twilight herb, and a few other bits and pieces," Robin said.

"Oblivion powder?" Rose asked.

He nodded. "It won't work as well here as it would work in my . . . in Faerie. But it should be enough to make people forget the days you were gone."

"Good idea," Portia said. But had she been hoping there would be a different potion in the vial?

Robin shrugged. "It'll make life easier." He turned to Rose again, and this time, his smile seemed almost mischievous. "You might want to consider giving Bramble a dose."

Rose snorted and pocketed the vial. "Take care of yourself, you old troublemaker."

"Likewise." He turned to Portia. They looked straight into each other's eyes, and a small crease appeared between his eyebrows. He stepped closer, cocked his head thoughtfully, and smiled. "It's been a pleasure."

"You could say that," Portia answered with a laugh, but Ben thought he could hear a hint of sadness in her laughter. Then Robin gave a quick bow, and Portia, her eyes sparkling with mirth, replied by performing an exaggerated but very elegant curtsy.

Robin nodded to Ben and touched two fingers to his forehead in a farewell salute. Then he put the parchment between his teeth and walked away without another word. For a moment Ben was dazzled by a ray of sunshine breaking through the trees that made him blink. When he opened his eyes again, Robin had gone. In his place there was a fox, trotting swiftly away from them. For a moment, his coat flickered like a guttering flame between the trees; then he slipped behind a rock and was gone.

The Nissan was still waiting at the end of the track where they had left it. Rose hurriedly swept the fallen leaves from the windshield before leaping into the driver's seat and driving them all back to Afallon. No sooner had she pulled up next to the garden wall than Rose jumped out, leaving the keys in the ignition. She pushed open the gate and ran toward the house, with Ben and Portia close behind. The door was unlocked, and by the time Ben had stepped into the hall, Rose was already at the bottom of the stairs.

"Bramble!" she called. No answer. She went to the kitchen while Portia checked the living room.

"Bramble?"

Ben walked down the hall, a terrible suspicion forming in his mind. What if this wasn't the real Afallon? What if they had crossed the wrong border and were now in Annwn? The Worlds of the Dead had been deserted and still too, just like this. He imagined going home to find his mother gone, as if the earth had swallowed her up. *Rubbish*, he told himself, but still the thought gave him goose bumps.

Rose and Portia came back into the hall at the same time. "She's not here!" Portia said, clearly worried. Ben buried his face in his hands, but Rose laid a comforting hand on his shoulder. She looked toward the living-room door.

"I know where she is."

༄

Rose strode ahead of them, across the garden, past the hydrangea bushes, and into the orchard. Beyond the apple trees they could see the white wall of the writing shed gleaming in the sunlight. Ben dearly hoped that Rose had guessed right.

The door was open, and as they drew closer, they were able to see inside. Bramble was sitting at Rose's desk, resting her head in her hands.

Rose cupped her hands round her mouth like a megaphone and shouted again. "Bramble!"

Bramble started and leapt to her feet, knocking a vase off the table that tumbled to the floor and smashed to pieces. Rose rushed toward her, but Ben didn't see her leaping up the steps and into the shed, because a bolt of dog-shaped lightning hit him in the side.

Marlowe barked joyfully and jumped up at Portia before excitedly circling the two children with his tail wagging.

"Hello there, boy," said Portia, squatting down to greet the dog, who licked her face all over in welcome.

"Gross!" Ben exclaimed, but Portia just laughed and wrapped her arms around Marlowe.

"Good boy," she said, ruffling his fur.

We're back, Ben thought, still numb with disbelief. *We really made it back!*

He turned around. Inside the writing shed, Rose and Bramble were hugging each other tightly, and Ben was pretty sure that they wouldn't be letting go anytime soon.

London

✦ PORTIA ✦

Portia's autumn school break began with a rain shower, but as night fell over London, the clouds cleared, leaving only the scent of wet leaves in the air. A black starry sky arched above the little park across the street from her house, and the dim yellow light from the lampposts shone in circles on the sidewalk.

The fairy lights she had hung on her bedroom wall twinkled, surrounding maps of the world and Middle-earth. Piles of books sat on a sideboard below, next to a little rubber plant with drooping leaves.

Portia put a striped sweater into her suitcase. She had been packing and repacking since after dinner. There was always something missing or just too much. *Just make sure you don't forget your train ticket*, she told herself for the umpteenth time, and felt a tingle of excitement in her stomach.

Tomorrow. Tomorrow she was taking the train back to Afallon to celebrate Halloween with Ben, Rose, and Bramble. She pictured the glowing pumpkin lantern that would be sitting on the garden wall to welcome her, and smiled. Then she shut the suitcase and put it on the floor.

Her red travel diary was lying open on her desk. Ben had given it to her shortly before her departure from Wales, without telling her what was inside. She had waited until she'd gotten back home before opening it and finding Ben's drawings inside. Moon-moths in flight, Gwil's face, the bookshelves in World's End, a toad with dragonfly wings, and many more. All the Otherworld was hidden between the pages of a tatty old notebook.

Portia picked up the diary and went over to the window. By the glow of a streetlight she flipped to the final page, from which the face of a wolf looked up at her with golden eyes. She traced the lines of the drawing with the tip of her finger.

Their adventure in the Otherworld had lasted twelve days. In the Human World only five days had passed, but that was enough for them to have been reported missing, and for their families and friends to have been thrown into turmoil. Luckily, Robin's oblivion powder had allowed the memories of the drama to fade and everyday life to return. At least for those who hadn't crossed over to Faerie.

Portia closed the notebook and smoothed out a wrinkle in the cover. Why was she so excited? She was only going to Wales, after all. The door to the Otherworld was now closed. But that shouldn't matter. It would be enough to sit in the conservatory at Afallon, drinking milky tea and making up stories for Ben to draw. The blank sketchbook she had bought for him was waiting in her suitcase.

Portia was just about to turn away from the window and put the notebook in her backpack when she noticed something moving in the park outside.

There! She leaned her forehead against the glass. There was some rustling in a bush, and then a fox slid between the iron railings and onto the sidewalk. Portia clutched the diary tight to her chest. The fox trotted along by the railings with its head held low, until it reached a pool of light under the lamppost. Then it stopped and lifted its head. Portia held her breath. There were lots of foxes in London. Thousands of them. You saw them all the time once it got dark.

Portia couldn't be sure whether the shadow cast by the streetlight was that of a fox, or a man. *It can't be him*, she told herself. *You just wish it was.*

Down in the street below, the fox's ears twitched. Then he glanced up at Portia's window, and ran off into the night.

WELSH WORDS AND PHRASES

Yr Adar	The Birds
Ap	Son of
Caethiwa!	Lock them up!
Croeso	Welcome
Crwydriadgoch	Wretched red fleabag [approximately]
Damio	Damn
Ferch	Daughter of
Mwyalchod	Blackbird
Salamandrau	Salamanders
Swirne saff	Safe travels